A STRANGE COUNTRY

Muriel Barbery

A STRANGE COUNTRY

*Translated from the French
by Alison Anderson*

Europa
editions

Europa Editions
214 West 29th Street
New York, N.Y. 10001
www.europaeditions.com
info@europaeditions.com

Copyright © Editions Gallimard, Paris, 2019
First Publication 2020 by Europa Editions

Translation by Alison Anderson
Original title: *Un étrange pays*
Translation copyright 2020 by Europa Editions

Library of Congress Cataloging in Publication Data is available
ISBN 978-1-60945-585-9

Barbery, Muriel
A Strange Country

Book design by Emanuele Ragnisco
www.mekkanografici.com

Cover image: iStock

Prepress by Grafica Punto Print – Rome

Printed in the USA

CONTENTS

For Sébastien
For Gérard, my father

A STRANGE COUNTRY

BOOKS

戦争

WAR

There was a time when a great war, the grandest strategic game ever played, consumed two fraternal worlds.

I would like to tell you the story in the proper way, because it cannot be written in one single book. In fact, mankind and the elves would be more at peace with one another if they knew the four Books.

The four Books came from the four Sources, but they are customarily united in two motifs: murder, on the one hand; and poetry, on the other.

Book I—Those who have never prayed at night shall be denied the understanding of the price of desire—

Book II—Those who mistake force for courage shall be denied the privilege of striding through the realm of fear in peace—

Book III—Those whose eyes have never been burned by beauty shall be denied the right to die in the sun—

Book IV—But those who set conditions on love shall be granted the right to know the boundlessness of misfortune—

Who has time to think about the great Books when war is raging and the living are dying? And yet, their pages blend with the song of the earth and the sky, and can be heard in the very heart of battle.

同盟

ALLIANCE

In these tragic times, a company of elves and humans could hear the winds of dreams and believe in the rebirth of the four Books.

Among them were two young women, a priest, a painter, and a most remarkable elf, although the memory of centuries would not have retained his name—given his minor ancestry—had he not, during this long war, been the constant catalyst of encounters.

What follows is the story of the last alliance between humans and elves.

物語

TALE

However, before we begin, let it be known: we who live under the land of Spain are only responsible for the tale of the West. I know that in the East our people do not reside in the depths of the earth, but on the crest of a mountain, in the North on the shores of a frozen sea, and in the South on a plain inhabited by wild animals.

Who can hear us? We have neither heralds, nor tribunes, nor a face, and we listen to the dead telling us the story we murmur into the ears of the living.

ALLIANCES
1938

A t the beginning of this tale, the human world had been at war for six years.

The war was started by a coalition, the Confederation, led by the Italy of Raffaele Santangelo, and which also included, in particular, France and Germany. The rumors of war that had been circulating for several months were swept aside by a large-scale invasion, which flooded the members of the League: Spain, Great Britain, and the countries of northern Europe.

Spain was an unusual case: the king was the League's natural ally, but part of his army, which had long been preparing this betrayal, broke away and allied themselves with the Confederation. At the beginning of the war, the regular Spanish troops loyal to the Crown and the League found themselves surrounded by the renegade generals, and Spain was cut off from her allies.

A remarkable event occurred in 1932, during the first year of the conflict, when an independent civilian resistance was organized in the countries belonging to the Confederation.

Santangelo's intentions were clear right from the start. In reaction to the League's refusal to renegotiate the treaties from the previous war, he set out to redraw Europe's borders by force. In the name of Italian pride and racial purity, he implemented a policy of mass displacement of the peninsula's inhabitants. In 1932, he passed laws on ethnic exclusion that would soon be enshrined in the Italian constitution; by 1938, there were camps all over the Europe of the Confederation.

Alejandro de Yepes was born in the land he was now defending in the snow. Others were fighting for the outcome of the war, but General de Yepes waged war for the tombs and acres of his ancestors, and hardly cared whether the League eventually triumphed or not. He was the native son of a region so poor that its noblemen looked flea-ridden to the rest of Spain; and indeed his father, in his life-time, had been both thoroughly noble and thoroughly poor. People were starving as, from the promontory of the castillo, they admired the most sublime view in all Extremadura and Castile and León combined, because the fortress was situated on the border between the two provinces and with a single ges-ture one could release one's eagles toward Salamanca and Cáceres. Good fortune saw to it that Alejandro would return there after six years of fighting far from home, at a time when Extremadura was becoming pivotal to the major offensive which, it was hoped, would bring an end to the war. What's more, that same good fortune had enabled the young general to come home a hero, for he had displayed a strategic acumen that defied the understanding of his superiors.

Superiors who were very worthy. These men knew how to lead and how to fight and they found it easy to hate an enemy who was even more abject than the ones they had fought in the past. They claimed to serve the League as much as they served Spain, divided as she was by treachery, and they had waged both battles at the same time with the bravery that comes with the conviction of the heart. Surprisingly, most of the officers hailed from rural parts of the country, while the cities had sided primarily with the enemy. It was an army made of men accustomed to handling rifles since childhood, and the harshness of their land had made them rugged and wily in action. They chose to side with the League because they shared an allegiance with their ancestors and with the king, and had no qualms about fighting their turncoat brothers. The fact that they were outnumbered ten to one did not worry them; as such, temerity had been their first mistake: a sense of panache inherited from their fathers had compelled the officers to fight in the front line, until voices—including Alejandro's—insisted they could not send soldiers into battle without leaders. And since those leaders had amply demonstrated their courage, they did without the serenade of honor from then on. No one doubted, anyway, that true honor consists in paying respects to the earth and sky, and that to honor one's dead, one must live.

The Franco-Italian confederation had taken Europe by surprise, putting an unprepared Spain to fire and sword by releasing cartloads of men carelessly sent to die. The generals committed to the League knew that while the best officers had remained loyal to the king, their strength overall was a farce and they would not find salvation in numbers, but through a volley of miracles. However, during the weeks it took the allied forces to regroup, Lieutenant de Yepes accomplished a miracle. When his soldiers joined forces with the friendly troops, they discovered that the subordinate who was the most poorly equipped in men and arms in the entire army was the one who had lost the fewest men and inflicted the greatest losses on the traitors. In those days, there was a remarkable general by the name of Miguel Ybáñez, now deceased, who was serving as army chief of staff. He deliberately promoted valorous young officers at the same time as he disgraced those who did not manifest any tactical gifts and who, moreover, lacked all strategic sense. Proper tactics are the backbone of an officer, strategy is both his lungs and his heart. And since no one, when outnumbered ten to one, can afford to lack either spirit or ardor, Ybáñez wanted strategists, above all.

In Alejandro, he found one of high quality.

During the early days of the conflict, Lieutenant de Yepes was cut off from his command. His hands were free and his line was simple: he had to save on men, time, ammunition, and supplies. The regular troops were more spread out than they were and communication by land was impossible. They were about to run out of supplies and everyone was imagining imminent disaster: pulverized like rats, the isolated units would perish, surrounded by troops that were largely superior in number. Without communications, knowledge of the terrain is an army's only chance of survival. With a heavy heart, Alejandro sent valiant men out as scouts—more than he would have liked—and lost far more than he would have wanted. But enough men came back to give him a clear picture of the theater of operations, something to which the enemy, confident of their strength in numbers, paid only moderate attention. In constant retreat, Alejandro infiltrated wherever he could, like water trickling down a slope among roots and rocks. He sought out the best locations for provisioning and resistance, and harassed his adversary with lightning actions that made it seem he was everywhere at once. In combat, he held back his artillery, and his men came under fire when they were saving their own resources—to such a degree that one day in December, he immobilized the gunners for nearly half an hour. The enemy shells fell like rain and Alejandro's men prayed to the Madre, but when the enemy general, convinced all he had to do now was wipe up a handful of ghosts, launched his infantry on them, the same men who not that long ago had been praying now blessed their lieutenant for saving their fine ammunition from being too hastily deployed. They were spread through the valley in loosely-knit groups, and not as many men perished as the concentrated enemy fire would have liked. In the end, retreating once again to a place where they could withstand a long siege, they inflicted heavy losses on the other side. As day fell, the stunned adversary could not understand why they had not prevailed, and they realized that they had neither won nor lost the battle.

At the request of Alejandro—now promoted to major—Ybáñez appointed a man from the ranks as lieutenant, who would later become a major himself when Alejandro was made general. His name was Jesús Rocamora and, by his own admission, he hailed from the asshole of Spain, a little town in Extremadura lost between two deserted expanses of earth to the southwest of Cáceres. A large lake was the only source of subsistence for the poor wretches in the region, who were fishermen and went to sell their catch on the Portuguese border, which meant that their lives were spent between fishing and an equally exhausting walk beneath the evil summer sun and the biblical cold of winter. There was a priest there who made a similarly meager living, and a mayor who fished all day long. The curse of the times, for a decade now the lake had been shrinking. Prayers and processions did no good: the waters were evaporating and, whether it was the wrath of God or of Mother Nature, the subsequent generations would be reduced to leaving or to perishing. And now, through that irony of fate that transforms suffering into desire, those who once cursed their village came to feel a wrenching attachment to it, and although there was not much to like about their life, they had chosen to die there with the last fish.

"Most men prefer death to change," said Jesús to Alejandro one evening when they were bivouacked on a shady little plateau, musing that they themselves would probably be dead by the next day.

"But you left," said Alejandro.

"It wasn't because I was afraid to die," said Jesús.

"What other reason did you have?"

"It is my fate to know nakedness and to suffer for mankind. It started in the village, and so it must go on in the outside world."

Alejandro de Yepes kept Jesús Rocamora by his side throughout the entire war. This son of hell's fishing grounds was one of the few men to whom he would have entrusted his life without flinching. The other was General Miguel Ybáñez. Chief of staff of the king's army, a little man so bow-legged that people said he'd been born on horseback, he was reputed to be the best horseman in the realm, a rider who leapt rather than climbed into the saddle. From his perch, he would stare down at you with his shining eyes and nothing could matter more than pleasing him. From what fabric is the skill for command cut? Yet in his gaze there was weariness and sadness. Most of the time he listened attentively, made few remarks, and gave his orders as if complimenting a friend, his voice devoid of all military sharpness—in response to which his men went out ready to die for him or for Spain, it was all the same, because the specter of fear had vanished, for a time.

One must imagine what it means to inhabit the province of life and death. It is a strange country and its only strategists are those who speak the language. They are called on to address the living and the dead as if they were all one, and Alejandro was well versed in that idiom. As a child, no matter the path he took, he was irresistibly drawn to the walls of the cemetery at

Yepes. There, among the stones and crosses, he felt he was once again among his people. He did not know how to speak to them, but the peacefulness of the place rustled with words for him. What's more, even when it meant nothing, the music of the dead reached him in a place in his chest that understood, irrespective of words. In these moments of great fulfillment, he saw an intense sparkling in the periphery of his vision, and he knew he was seeing the manifestation of an unknown and powerful spirit.

Ybáñez was also an initiate, and drew the strength therefrom that made him such a singular leader of men. In the month of November of the third year of the war, he came to Yepes to meet Alejandro. The young major had left the North and gone to the castillo not knowing why he had been summoned. A few snow flurries were falling, Ybáñez seemed gloomy, and the conversation was unusual.

"Do you remember what you said the first time we met?" asked Ybáñez. "That the war would last a long time and we would have to track it down behind its successive masks? Everyone who failed to understand this is dead now."

"Others died who were aware of what was at stake," said Alejandro.

"Who will win?" retorted Ybáñez, as if he had been asked. "I've been endlessly harassed, both about the war and about victory. But no one ever asks the right question."

He raised his glass in silence. Despite its wretchedness, the castillo boasted a cellar of perfectly aged wines, vintages once offered to Alejandro's father Juan de Yepes, as well as to his grandfather, his great-grandfather, and so on up the line to the dawn of time. This is what happened. One morning, somewhere in Europe, a man would wake up and know that he had to set out for a certain castle in Extremadura, a place he had never heard of until now. It did not occur to him that this notion was either fantastical or impractical, and not for a moment did the voyager hesitate or doubt when he came to a crossroads. These men were prosperous winemakers whose cellars contained the fruit of their talent, and now they selected wonderful bottles that they would once have reserved for their sons' weddings. They arrived at the gate of the castillo, handed the bottle to the father, the grandfather, or one of Alejandro's ancestors; they were given something to eat and a glass of sherry; then without further ado, after standing for a moment at the top of the tower, they went away again. Back in their own land, every morning they would think of the glass of sherry, the generous bread, the violet ham; the day went on and their servants could see how greatly they were changed. What had happened at the castillo? As far as the counts of Yepes were concerned, nothing differed in any way from the usual customs of their rank, and they were unaware of the strange ballet by which others were lured by their castle. No one was surprised, the event occurred and was forgotten, and Alejandro was the first ever to concern himself with it. But when he inquired, no one knew what to reply, and he spent his childhood feeling like an anomaly within the anomaly of the castillo. When the feeling grew so strong that it caused a pain in his chest, he went to the cemetery and engaged once again in his commerce with the dead.

One must be grateful for this inclination for tombstones, for twenty years earlier, he was in the cemetery on the November day when his entire family perished. Men had attacked the castillo and killed everyone they found. No one knew how many of them there were, how they had come, or how they left. No lookouts—by which we mean the eyes of old women and shepherds—had seen them coming; it was as if they had come out of nowhere and returned there in the same way. Alejandro left the cemetery that day because the strange light tasted of blood, but as he headed back up to the castillo the only traces he saw in the snow were the pawprints of hares and deer. Yet before he even went through the gate into the fortress, he knew. His body urged him to fall to his knees, but he continued on his way, down his path of suffering.

He was ten years old and the only surviving descendant of his clan.

The funerals were remarkable. It was as if all of Extremadura had gathered in Yepes, their numbers swollen by travelers from the past who had managed to reach the village in time. It made for a strange crowd and, anyway, everything was strange that day—the mass, the procession, the burial, and the homily given by a priest cloaked in a wind-ravaged cassock. The wind had begun to blow when the coffins left the castillo, and stopped abruptly with the last word of the funeral oration. And then silence fell all around, until the bells tolled the angelus, and there was a feeling of departing an unknown land—this is what had quietly filled people's hearts all day long, this inner crossing, this aimless wandering along unfamiliar paths, undisturbed by the priest's Latin gibberish or the ridiculous sight of a procession of toothless old folk. Now they awoke as from a long meditation and watched Alejandro walking back up the steep slope to the fortress. Only one man was with him, and the village council was praised for its decision to entrust the child to his wise hands. Everyone knew he would take care of the castillo and treat the orphan well; they were glad that he would initiate him into certain higher things and, above all, they were relieved that they would not have to take charge of the matter themselves.

Luis Álvarez must have been in his fifties and, whether from the stubbornness or the negligence of the gods, was altogether a little man, somewhat bent and very thin. But when he removed his shirt for the hardest tasks, it was to reveal taut and astonishingly vigorous muscles flexing beneath his skin. Similarly, he had an ordinary, unexpressive face, shining with deep blue eyes, and the contrast between the anonymity of his face and the splendor of his gaze summed up everything there was to know about the man. His position was that of steward: he supervised the upkeep of the domain, collected the rent from the tenant farmers, bought and sold wood and kept the ledgers. His soul, on the other hand, made him the guardian of the stars of the castillo. In the evening when they dined in the kitchen of the deserted fortress, Luis spoke with his pupil at length, for this man who was dedicated to serving the powerful and dealing with trivial commerce was in fact a great intellectual and a masterful poet. He had read everything, then reread it, and he wrote the sort of lyrical poetry that only a fervent soul can produce—a poetry of incantations to the sun and murmurs of stars, love, and crosses; of prayers in the night and silent quests. It was in his poetry, during the hours when he wrote it, that he perceived at the edge of his vision the same light Alejandro received from his dead, and he alone, more than anyone, would have been able to answer the boy's questions about pilgrimage. However, he kept his peace.

And so, for eight years, every day at noon, you could see him come down from the fortress in the company of the adolescent and sit at his table at the inn, wearing the same white shirt with an officer's collar and the same light-colored suit, the same worn leather boots and the same wide-brimmed hat—straw in summer and felt when the first frosts arrived, in winter adding one of those long overcoats that shepherds on horseback are known to wear. They would serve him a glass of sherry, and he would stay for an hour while everyone stopped by, asking about his latest poem or the estimated price of cattle. When he was seated he seemed tall because he held himself straight, one leg over the other, one hand on his thigh, elbow propped on the table. He would take a sip intermittently, then wipe his lips with the white napkin folded next to his glass. He seemed enveloped in silence, although he spoke a great deal during these meetings that passed for banal conversation. His elegance was not intimidating; it was elevating, comforting. Next to him, Alejandro sat quietly, and learned the life of poor men.

A lesser-ranked man can hold an entire country together. Blessed are the lands which know the comfort of such a being, without whom they are doomed to languish and die. In fact, everything can be read in two opposite ways; one has only to see grandeur in the place of wretchedness, or ignore the glory that shines through decline. Poverty had not made the place indigent: it evoked a calming fragrance of splendor and dreams, made all the more remarkable by deprivation; and as long as Luis Álvarez was managing the fortress, it was considered a place to be proud of, despite the knowledge that its land was no longer fertile and its walls were crumbling. And so, after the murder of the Yepes family, the steward naturally took over the tasks they had once performed. He presided over the first village council meeting after the tragedy, and later, when people looked back, it appeared to them as a moment of great dignity; in our collapsing world, such memories are almost more precious than life itself. He opened the meeting, then said a few words to honor the dead, and there can be little doubt that these words kept Alejandro from the madness of sorrow and made him a sane man—in particular the final words, which were addressed to him, although Luis refrained from looking in his direction: *the living must tend to the dead.* The child was sitting to the right of his steward, his gaze was feverish, but stiller than a stone. However, after he had heard these words, the feverishness of his eyes flickered out and he wiggled on his chair like any boy his age. Then the steward called the votes in the manner of the ancestors, naming the families and striking with his hammer at each decision. When everything had been examined and voted on, he adjourned the meeting and asked the priest to say the prayer for the dead. As the old priest was stumbling over his words, he continued for him, and at the end the entire council voiced the responses— nevertheless, one should not suppose that Luis Álvarez reigned over the land solely because he respected the organization of its rites: if the steward of the castillo had a natural authority, it was because he had created bonds with everyone, bonds that were rooted in a soil so spiritual that anyone who knew its poetry was born to govern the land. In the end, just after the last *amen*, the women began singing an old song from Extremadura. A song that no one knows anymore today, in a language that no one can translate anymore, but by God, was the music beautiful! It mattered little that no one understood it; it carried a message from stormy skies and a fertile land where the joy of the harvests mingled with the struggle to survive.

It was Luis Álvarez, in the end, who shaped Alejandro's vocation for war. On the eve of his sixteenth year, they were sitting by the fire, and the adolescent was drinking his first wine. Since Juan's death, there had been no visitors to the fortress, but the cellar held a collection of bottles that would last for centuries. Alejandro was finishing his second glass of petrus when Luis recited the poem he had composed that morning.

"I find some of them in my heart," he said. "But this one came from another world."

> To the earth and the sky
> Live for your dead
> And stand vulnerable
> Before mankind

That in the final hour
Your noblesse will oblige us

"What determines noblesse?" asked Alejandro, after a moment's silence.

"Courage," replied Luis.

"And what makes courage?" asked Alejandro again.

"Confronting one's fear. For most of us, it is the fear of dying."

"I'm not afraid of dying," said Alejandro. "I'm afraid of being responsible for men and failing them because the devil in me will have triumphed over the guardian."

"Then you must go wherever you can wage that battle."

Two years later, Alejandro left for the military academy. He had neither money nor savoir-faire, which is why he was a mere lieutenant at the beginning of the war; nor did he have a talent for career intrigue. All he wanted was to learn. After the academy, he set about joining units whose leaders had their men's respect—and so he learned, and the day the war broke out, he considered himself ready.

Naturally, he was mistaken.

He learned his lesson from circumstance, then from a simple soldier, during one of the first battles. Alejandro had already noticed this man from the ranks who'd proved to be very efficient at carrying out orders. Something told him that the soldier was from a poor background, but nothing in Jesús Rocamora's behavior invited familiarity or condescension: he was an aristocrat of the sort who are not born in castles, but where noblesse oblige is written in the heart. He was handsome, too, with an open face and sharply-drawn features, shining blue eyes, and lips crafted by a lacemaker's needle. Like Alejandro, he was not tall, but he had a fine bearing, black hair, broad shoulders, and hands that were not like any fisherman's. In addition, he liked to embellish his speech with expressions that would make a hussar blush, then return to the absolute gravity that is the custodian of noble causes.

On the fifth day of the war, Alejandro's troops were caught in a pincer movement; the lieutenant from Yepes was witnessing the moment when his men no longer understood him and, in panic, began to do everything back to front. And then, thanks to one of history's false miracles, Jesús Rocamora was suddenly at his side, begging for an order, gazing at him like a dog at its master.

"We've got to wheel the artillery round on the north flank," cried Alejandro, for whom the appearance of a man ready to listen was a godsend.

Then he looked at him and suddenly realized that Jesús should have been with the third unit, six kilometers from there.

"And retreat through the southern pass?" shouted Jesús in turn.

Alejandro had given those precise instructions earlier, and several times over, but no one had wanted or known how to follow them. Jesús Rocamora, however, saw to it that followed they were. Better still, he did not leave his lieutenant for a second—no sooner had he set things in motion than he came back, the way a dog returns to his master, to wait for the next order, which he already knew. After two hours of this, they found themselves on the summit of an ineffable ridge, where an angel's fart would suffice to either precipitate them into the abyss or show them the pathway down the mountain. Alejandro shouted to Jesús: Go, go, stop asking for orders! Jesús looked at him blankly and Alejandro said again, Go, away with you! So the other man cleared off like a nasty cur and showered his men with orders, no longer even taking the time to return to his superior.

They survived. Then they talked. Every evening they would speak and their acquaintance grew in a brotherly mood that precluded any sense of hierarchy. Then at dawn, lieutenant and soldier would put on their insignia and fight side by side with respect for their ranks. When Alejandro ventured to admit that he would have liked a more enviable status for Jesús, the soldier said: Fishing is the only hell I will ever know on this planet.

It was also Jesús who taught Alejandro his greatest lesson about war, and turned him from a mere tactician into a strategist.

"It'll be a long war," he told his lieutenant, the evening they were bivouacking on the shady little plateau.

"So you don't think we'll end up surrendering fairly soon?" asked Alejandro.

"We are the lords of these lands, we won't lose them as soon as all that. But winning is another matter. It will take time for our leaders to comprehend that while the forms of war may have changed, the essence has remained the same. Once the fronts are stable—vast fronts, sir, the likes of which we've never seen—and the generals see that no one will carry the day any time soon, it will become obvious that everything has been staked upon tactics—outdated tactics at that—but that war is still just what it has always been."

"A duel," said Alejandro.

"A duel to the death," said Jesús. "Tactics can be adapted, but in the end the winner will be whoever is the best strategist."

"And what makes for the best strategist?" asked Alejandro.

"Ideas always triumph over weapons," said Jesús. "Who would entrust an engineer with the keys to paradise? It is the divine part in us that determines our fate. The best strategist is the one who looks death in the eye and reads there that he must not be afraid of losing. And with every war this changes."

"The real lords are the fishermen," said Alejandro with a smile.

And then Jesús told him the story of his moment of revelation.

"I'm the son of a fisherman, but from the moment I set eyes on the lake, at an age when I couldn't even walk or talk yet, I knew I wouldn't become one. After that, I forgot what I knew. When I was a boy, I followed in my father's footsteps. I knew how to set the nets and bring them in, how to mend them, and all the things you need to know for the job. My first fourteen years were spent between ropes and walking, and I didn't want to remember that first sight of the lake. But on the morning of my fifteenth birthday, I went down to the lake. It was a misty dawn, and someone had gone over the landscape with ink; the water was black while the mist created incredible images. That landscape . . . that landscape went straight to the heart. I had a vision of the lake—dried up—and of a great battle, and of the face of a child instantly erased by the face of an old man. Finally, everything disappeared, the mist rose to the sky, and I fell to my knees in tears, because I knew I was going to betray my father and go away. I wept for a long time, until my body was drier than the lake I had seen in my vision, then I stood up and looked one last time at the dark water. In that moment, I felt I had just been entrusted with a burden, but also that this cross to bear would free me from my shame. With the priest, I learned to read and write, and two years later I enlisted."

Surrounded since childhood by the kindness of his elders and the affection of his peers, Alejandro had never known the brotherly friendship of men who have lived through the same conflagration. At the age of eighteen he had seen the army as a place to fulfill his desire for courage, and he experienced solidarity with his fellow soldiers of the sort that comes with the imminence of combat. But he had never yet met anyone whose heart was in tune with his own. When he went back to Yepes during the last year of the war to set up his headquarters in the castillo, he walked up the main street through the village, happy to see people coming up to shake his hand, the old folk embracing him. Outside the fortress, the priest came to meet him with the mayor at his side, leaning on a cane. They were dressed in black, as awkward and gloomy as scarecrows, but their faces lit up, for once, with their pride in the fact that their young lord was one of the great generals of the day. Alejandro felt his heart racing with gratitude and cheer, to be acknowledged and celebrated in this way. Next to him, Major Rocamora was smiling, and the people of Yepes appreciated both his open gaze and his devotion to their general—if, on top of it, Alejandro had known that they rejoiced in his friendship with Jesús because it meant a lord was indebted to a fisherman, his emotion, no doubt, would have increased tenfold.

There they stood, the young general and his young major, at the top of the tower in the castillo, now that the war had been raging for six years, bringing with it all the plagues that every war always brings. They stood expectant at the top of the great tower, like the world holding its breath on the eve of battle, on the summit where the roll of a single pebble will determine victory or surrender.

"It's going to snow," said Jesús.

Alejandro had seen only two Novembers with snow: the one when his family was murdered, twenty years earlier, and the one when Miguel Ybáñez had come to see him in Yepes, three years earlier, in the days when the conflict was spreading farther than anyone would have predicted. After their conversation about the long war, Miguel Ybáñez had asked Alejandro to take him to the cemetery. The two men stood by the graves in silence, and after a moment, Alejandro saw the sparkling that was always there. Thick snowflakes began to fall and before long the cemetery was covered in a light powder that glistened in the late afternoon light. When they went away again, Ybáñez seemed lost in luminous, grave thoughts. The next morning, just before his departure, in a dawn of cruel frost, he told Alejandro he was appointing him major general and entrusting him with the leadership of the first army.

Three months later, the general from Yepes learned of the generalissimo's death, and he knew his life would be repeatedly marked by the murder of those who were dearest to him. For Alejandro, the death of Miguel Ybáñez was a personal tragedy, but it was also tragic for the soldier in him: the staff needed men of Ybáñez's fiber, and Alejandro had never met anyone else like him. His thoughts echoed with the words the general had uttered as he passed through the gate to the fortress.

"Meditate as often as you can."

Although he was from Madrid, Ybáñez had told him that he used to spend his childhood summers at his mother's family home, on the slope of a mountain overlooking Granada.

"Through meditation I learned the power of ideas," he said. "What else can you do when you see the sun rising over eternal snows and suddenly the Alhambra is there before you? Someday it will be destroyed, because that is the fate of works of human genius, but the idea behind it will never die. It will be born again elsewhere, in another form of beauty and power, because we receive the idea of it from the dead speaking to us from the sanctuary of their graves."

Pensively gazing into his glass, he added:

"That is why I conceive of the art of war as a meditation in the company of my dead."

Then he fell silent. After a moment, he said one last thing.

"Because ideas alone are not enough, one must also have a mandate. That is the question that no one ever asks me: who do we get it from and to what kingdom does it consign us?"

"We get it from our ancestors," said Alejandro.

"You are thinking about mandates and forgetting the kingdom," replied Miguel. "And yet tomorrow our kingdom will be covered with camps where people will be burned."

I have tried to describe Alejandro de Yepes through the three major figures of his youth, who shared the same aspirations in life. Why are some born to take responsibility for others, so that their lives become nothing but a succession of battles through which they learn to accept their burden? From that moment on, these battles, this burden, make them into guides whom their troops or brothers will follow to the gates of hell. However, this responsibility for other souls does not stop at the threshold to the cemetery, because the dead belong to the people entrusted to these singular men, and the terrible weight of the kingdom of the dead, the burning obligation to respond to the call, is what we refer to as the life of the dead: a silent, incandescent life, more intense and magnificent than any other, and a few individuals among the living have agreed to be its messengers.

Sons! To the earth and the sky!
Sons! Live for your dead!
Brothers! Stand vulnerable before us!
Brothers! Your noblesse will oblige us.

Book of Battles

戦

BATTLE

How did this war differ from the previous ones?

There was the fact that the Western world no longer knew its dead: either because it had grown old and was approaching an end it did not want to see, or because it had reached the limits of its dream and had to construct another one. In any case, it lacked the whispering of the dead, without which none can live honorably—who can call an existence decent if it has not received a mandate?

As for me, right from the start it seemed as if the battle would have to be resolved by radically rewriting the dream of history. Never had murder come closer to triumphing over poetry.

殺人

MURDER

The life of Alejandro de Yepes had begun with the murder of his family and continued with that of his protector, and he sensed, correctly, that he would endure other crimes. What he did not know, however, was that long before he came into the world, the source of his own story lay in a distant murder whose protagonists were strangers to him.

Given the fact that it had been committed neither for gain nor for power, but because the murderer had an obscure premonition that his victim had been sent by the devil, this murder occupied an unusual spot in the sequence of major murders, a spot that yielded up the hope of something beneficial.

Can one ever escape from the fatality of murder? Hope and horror—this shall all be told below. There is only fiction, there are only stories. It doesn't matter to me whether I know them in advance.

Now two hours have gone by and Alejandro de Yepes, from the tower of his castillo, is watching the snow fall in the night. He has just been woken, and he's not sure he understands what's happening.

"How long has the snow been falling?" he asked.

"For two hours," Jesús replied. "In two hours, six feet of snow have fallen."

"Six feet," said Alejandro. "And you say these men arrived without leaving footprints?"

"Our watchmen are positioned so close together that even an ant could not get through. And besides, what sort of man can make his way through this snow? I don't know how they got here but it was not by road."

"From the sky?"

"I don't know. Suddenly there they were in front of us, in the grand hall, and one of the redheads asked to speak to General de Yepes, adding that he was sorry about the snow."

He wiped his hand across his brow.

"I know, sir, when I tell it like this, it all seems so strange. But I would stake my life on it that they are not enemies."

"Where are they now?" asked Alejandro.

"In the cellar. It's what the redhead requested. He seems very well informed, I must say."

They looked at each other for a moment.

"Should I have them brought up?" asked Jesús.

"No," said Alejandro, "I'll go down."

And turning in a circle on himself:

"There's something about this snow."

"It's not falling the way it usually does," said Jesús.

The cellar extended beneath the entire area of the castillo. It was a gigantic place, lit by torches which the steward, back in his day, would hold aloft as he walked up and down the rows of bottles. On the floor of sand and hard dirt, Luis would trace figures with a rake, in keeping with his mood of the moment. When he walked on them the next day, they remained intact, and this was not, by a long shot, the only marvel in the place. You did not have to be an architect to realize that an entire castillo cannot stand on such a huge open space devoid of any pillars. You could walk along rows bordered by old copper chests that had been there for who knows how long, and the arrangement of the various wines was mysterious, too. Luis would lay the bottle he'd been given in a certain place, and the next day he would find it somewhere else. The only bottles that could be easily removed from their alcove were at the end of the last row at the very end of the cellar, where he had received the delivery of petrus for Alejandro's sixteenth birthday. Finally, on certain occasions, the door to the place was kept closed, and when it was opened again everything had changed, although the beauty of it never disappointed. No matter which torch Luis lit, it would project an iridescent glow that glistened on the copper racks, and perpetuated its sparkle from one end of the cellar to the other; moving lines of luminous pearls traced a perfect, translucent architecture in the space; rows of earth and sand were interwoven, creating a feeling of peace. Luis had to show visitors the way out, otherwise they would have stayed there for the rest of their days.

That night, the cellar was even more resplendent than

usual. In the tilted bottles, the wine shimmered with flashes of pale gold, and a strange glow cloaked the floor with dull silver. In one gloomy corner, they found the three men grunting like pigs beneath their dark hooded capes. The one who was laughing loudest had a few flamboyant locks of hair; the second one, who had brown hair, was so massive in appearance that the others looked like imps in comparison.

Motionless, arms crossed, six feet from the threesome, Alejandro cleared his throat. They paid no attention. The intruders had found a barrel somewhere, on which they had placed their glasses and an impressive row of fine vintages. Of course, all three were completely drunk, something Jesús summed up by exclaiming, "Oh, the bastards!"

Alejandro cleared his throat again, with no more success than the first time, while the third thief caressed a bottle of rare champagne, saying:

"What we need now is a bubble."

At the same time, his hat slipped back to reveal a similarly flamboyant head of hair; a bright reflection from one of the racks lit up his fine, squirrel-like features; then everything went dark again. The only light came from the crystal glasses where they had poured champagne while Alejandro and Jesús looked on in silence. There was something wrong, but devil take them if they could say what it was, other than that it had to do with the liquid itself, which the second redhead was pouring cautiously. The two other men, very focused, kept an eye on the operation. Finally, they all relaxed, and Jesús and Alejandro saw that the bubbles were hastening toward the bottom of the champagne glasses, where they dissolved in a tiny hissing maelstrom.

"*Santa Madre*," murmured Jesús.

A singular irony: while exclamations and throat clearing had not sufficed to distract the drinkers, this faint murmur caused all three to turn around at once. The first redhead stood up straight, somewhat painfully, and reached for a torch. His head was wobbling, he was squinting slightly, and intermittently let out strange noises. However, he seemed to be the leader, for the others looked at him and waited for him to make the first move.

"Well, well," he muttered.

Then he turned to his companions with an apologetic look. The tallest one pointed a finger toward his pocket and the redhead's face lit up as he repeated, *Ah, well, well!* And the three men flung their heads back to drink from flasks they pulled out from underneath their cloaks. Judging by the faces they were making, the liquid must have had a bitter taste, but the most remarkable thing was that they instantaneously sobered up, and stood solidly on their feet as if they had not just consumed half the cellar—all things which caused Alejandro and Jesús to raise an interested eyebrow, for they too were not averse to drinking.

They all looked at one another again in silence.

The leader of the group was a paunchy little man with a round face and round eyes, fair skin and countless freckles; accompanied by a fine double chin and an abundant mane of hair, sagging shoulders and an upturned nose; in a word, he was not particularly becoming. But no soldier can fail to discern the danger concealed by artless attire, and Alejandro and Jesús saw that the man's gaze belied his bearing, that however inoffensive and good-natured he might seem, it would be dangerous to underestimate him, and that anyone who had made that mistake had probably not lived to brood over it; in short, they saw that this amiable inebriate was one of their own kind.

"I owe you an explanation," said the man.

The tall, dark-haired man stepped forward, bowed briefly and said, "Marcus, at your service."

The other redhead did likewise and said, "Paulus."

To which their leader added, also bowing:

"Petrus, your humble servant."

Then, somewhat brazenly:

"May I tempt you with a little upside-down champagne?"

A moment passed. Alejandro was still standing with his arms crossed, a stern expression on his face, rigid and silent as he confronted the strangers. Jesús . . . well, Jesús could not help but want to taste the champagne. There always comes a time when a man of reason discovers a penchant for extravagance, particularly when he has witnessed lakes evaporating without warning and mist writing sibylline messages on the sky. Moreover, in spite of the fantastical nature of the circumstances, he trusted these men.

Alejandro, his face inscrutable, took a step forward.

Another moment passed.

He took another step, and smiled.

"Alejandro de Yepes," he said, holding his hand out to Petrus. "You are acquainted with my tutor, I believe? He just went by, behind you."

"Oh, we met earlier," replied Petrus, shaking his hand. "I am glad he appears to you as well."

"Didn't you see him?" Alejandro asked Jesús.

"No, sir," he replied. "You saw the steward's ghost?"

"Just behind that gentleman," murmured Alejandro, "just behind him."

He gestured invitingly at the barrel.

"If you would do us the honor of pouring some *upside-down* champagne."

Should we be surprised by such composure? Alejandro had been hearing the voices of the dead for so long that it didn't strike him as incongruous in the least that it was also possible to see them. Luis's apparition, strolling along the rows of bottles, had had its effect, and now it was with a certain interest that Alejandro awaited what might come next.

They sat down around the makeshift table.

"You just have to focus," said Petrus, slowly pouring champagne into two clean glasses.

"A nice little vintage," Jesús pointed out, "it would be a mistake to deprive ourselves."

"You haven't seen anything yet," said Paulus. "Once you've tasted champagne upside down, you can't possibly go back to right side up."

"Is that what you are doing with the snow, too?" asked Alejandro.

Petrus seemed astonished.

"It's falling the right way, I believe."

"He's referring to Maria," said Paulus.

"Ah," said Petrus, "of course. Yes, yes, there is someone who makes the snow fall for us, hence its appearance which is, shall we say, rather personal, more meditative, blurring the perception of the enemy."

"Airplane radar can penetrate snow," Jesús pointed out.

"I'm not talking about that enemy," said Petrus. "You will have observed that the climate has been somewhat changeable in recent years—storms, frost, floods."

"Is that your Maria, too?" asked Jesús.

"No, no" said Petrus. "Maria only orders snow, the enemy alone is distorting the climate."

Setting the bottle back down, he added:

"Champagne and ghosts, on the other hand—that only happens in this cellar."

Alejandro raised his glass and studied the pale liquid. The descending bubbles tickled his nose pleasantly, and he could imagine that it would cause a sort of little explosion on the tongue.

He was wrong.

There was even such a lack of explosion on the first sip, the taste was so flat, and the bubbles so devoid of any impact that Alejandro and Jesús, disappointed, looked at each other from under their brows.

"Just wait a moment," said Paulus, with the indulgence of the initiated for the erring ways of the layman.

And indeed, the marvel began to work its magic, for the two men were overcome by a sensation of lying in the grass, their eyes riveted on the heavens on one of those days when fate is affable. The earthy taste in their mouth harmonized with the celestial lightness of the champagne until it released a euphoria whose substance they would have found difficult to describe.

"This is the beneficial effect of the alliance between earth and sky," said Petrus. "As the bubbles head toward the bottom they preserve the celestial value of the wine but multiply its earthy value."

After smiling at his glass, all tenderness, he added:

"Although there is not much you can do if the substance you start with is mediocre."

When the first glass was empty, Alejandro and Petrus smiled at each other, and Jesús noticed the redhead's beautiful, thoughtful gray eyes.

"How did you get here?" he asked.

"Over the bridge," replied Petrus. "The bridge that joins our world to yours."

Then, after a moment's silence:

"To you, it's invisible."

"Are you dead?" asked Jesús. "Are you ghosts?"

Petrus looked at him, surprised.

"I don't think ghosts drink champagne," he said.

"If you haven't come from the other life, where have you come from?" asked Jesús.

"There is only one life, and it encompasses the living and

the dead," answered Petrus. "But there are several worlds, and our worlds have been communicating for a long time. In reality, the first crossing of the bridge took place here in Yepes, although we only found that out yesterday."

Picking up the champagne bottle, he added:

"I have a long story to tell you, so it deserves another little drop."

"Can you tell us the name of your country?" asked Alejandro.

"We call it the world of mists," answered Petrus. "The world of mists, where the elves live."

There was a silence.

"Elves?" said Jesús. "You come from the world of elves?"

He began to laugh.

"Or maybe you yourselves are elves?" asked Alejandro without irony.

Jesús looked at his general as if he were a hen wearing a wig.

"That doesn't strike me as any more surprising than all the rest of it," said Alejandro in response to his gaze.

"We are elves," Petrus confirmed, "yes, we are." And to Jesús, tactfully: "I see you are somewhat surprised, so allow me to pour you another glass."

He filled his glass and, with a slight tilt of his chin, motioned to Paulus to fetch another bottle.

"Another bubble?" asked Paulus.

"Allow me to offer you one of my favorite vintages," said Alejandro pleasantly, as if the previous bottles had come from some unknown reserve.

He headed toward the back of the cellar.

"I thought elves lived in the far north," said Jesús. "The far north of sagas and legends."

He looked at the glasses lined up in front of him and added:

"And that they didn't drink."

"You also believe that God the father lives in heaven and that he doesn't drink," answered Petrus.

On seeing Jesús's horrified expression, he added:

"I'm not saying he drinks, I'm not saying he drinks. Simply, we all know that the spirit of the world doesn't have a beard and isn't ensconced on a throne on a huge pink cloud."

Jesús looked just as horrified, but Alejandro, coming back from the depths of the cellar, distracted them.

"Interesting," he murmured, setting a bottle on the barrel.

Petrus leaned over to read the label and smiled.

"Amarone," he said. "The wine of stories."

Marcus frowned.

"We've run out of tea," he said.

"Such improvidence," said Petrus, still smiling.

He looked up and seemed to be addressing someone invisible:

"You will bring us some, won't you?"

"Was that tea in your little flask?" asked Alejandro.

"Yes," Marcos replied, "very concentrated gray tea."

"The tea of our world," added Paulus. "It has . . . uh . . . special properties."

He fell silent and looked questioningly at Petrus.

But Petrus didn't care and was smiling gratefully at the amarone.

"Elves," said Jesús. "Do you have wine up there, too?"

"No, alas," reply Petrus, with a sorrowful face.

He dismissed the distressing confession with the back of his hand.

"Which is why bridges are so important," he said. "And please bear in mind that it is not *up there*. Elves do not live in the sky. It's crowded enough up there as it is."

"Do you mean with angels?" said Jesús. "Have you ever seen any?"

Petrus smiled, amused.

"The only traffic jams in the sky are those of the sky's own fictions," he said.

He took a swallow of amarone and let out a long sigh.

"This is the best I've ever drunk," he said, "And under these favorable auspices, I will begin at the beginning."

Jesús laughed.

"Now that I know there are no angels in the heavens," he said, "you can begin wherever you like."

"Ah, but there are angels on this earth," said Petrus.

He caressed his glass lovingly.

"The bridge that connects the world of mists to the world of humans leaves from a sacred place on our earth we call the Pavilion of the Mists. By order of the guardian of the pavilion, the bridge makes it possible to reach any point on the earth of humankind. Its arch is shrouded in thick mist, in which the traveler immerses himself, the guardian fulfills his task, and the voyager finds himself where he wanted to be. Elves can come and go as they see fit, but this has always been impossible for humans. However, a few days ago, four of them crossed over for the first time."

He poured another round of amarone.

"There is a war on now. You know all about it: the fronts are endless, the battles, too, and no one seems able to carry the day. The Confederation, who were on the verge of victory two years ago, have now become bogged down in absurd tactics. As for the League, they have been worn down by the length of the conflict and the deadly violence of the cataclysms."

"Tell us about these cataclysms," said Alejandro.

"Elves cannot fight in your world," said Petrus. "Rather, to be more precise, they lose most of their own powers there, and it becomes impossible for them to kill. But we know how to make use of natural elements, although ordinarily we do not allow ourselves to go against nature. Unfortunately, there is a very powerful elf in our world, the one who started the war, who doesn't care about that prohibition and has been causing the climate to go off kilter, using it as a weapon."

"The war was started to by an elf?" said Jesús. "I thought it was Raffaele Santangelo's intrigues."

"The president of the Italian Council is an elf," said Petrus. Jesús's chin dropped.

"But Santangelo is just a lackey," continued Petrus, "who came into the world of humans to support the aims of his master, the cataclysmic elf who stayed behind in the mists. I'm sorry to sound so melodramatic, but that is more or less the true story."

Probably to cure himself of melodrama, he poured a third glass of amarone.

"Does he have a name?" asked Alessandro.

"We call him Aelius," said Petrus.

"Is ancient Rome in fashion where you live?" asked Jesús.

"Unlike humans, elves are not in the habit of using names handed down through their lineage. As it happens, one of us, a very powerful elf allied with the League, lives in Rome, so that is where we went for inspiration."

He gave a big grin.

"As for me, I made a point of combining Roman empire and French vineyard."

He simultaneously reassumed his air of gravity and took a long sip of wine.

"Don't you think it's strange that Santangelo hasn't won?" he asked.

"Everyone thinks it's strange," said Alejandro. "No one can figure out his strategy."

"You're a strategist and a member of the high command of the League," said Petrus.

Alejandro looked at him, thoughtful.

"I think Santangelo doesn't want to win," he said, "he doesn't want a victorious side busy dressing its wounds. He wants men to die, all men, no matter which side they're on. I've said this many times, but no one wants to believe that after the last conflict there could still be people who want total war. In spite of this, I'm convinced that is Santangelo's intention. Why? I have no idea."

"There is dark smoke over parts of occupied Europe," Petrus said. "Your aircraft detected it. What do you think it is?"

"Massive fires," said Alejandro. "But what are they burning, there?"

Petrus fell silent, his expression and gloomy.

"So that's it," said Alejandro.

"Never before has the human race been so passionate about exterminating its fellows," said Paulus, "and never before have the elves fought such bloody battles. Even the mists are at war, and our kind are dying by the millions."

"In the beginning Aelius only wanted humans to die," Petrus said, "but those who want the death of one end up wanting the death of all. They end up wanting death as a crown so that a chosen few can reign over the scorched earth."

"Why did he want humans to die?" Jesús asked.

"Because our mist is declining, and he is holding you responsible for this plague," replied the elf.

"The mist on the bridge?" Jesús asked.

"The mists of our world," Petrus answered. "We are a world of mists. Without it, we cannot survive."

"It is your oxygen?" Jesús asked.

Petrus looked at him, puzzled.

"Our oxygen? No, no. We breathe the same air as you. But we are elves. We are a community of mists."

He wiped his hand across his brow.

"This is the part I always have trouble explaining. I forget every time that you separate everything."

"Could he be right?" Alejandro asked. "Are we responsible for the decline of your mists?"

Petrus, Paulus, and Marcus glanced at one another.

"That is something we have wondered, too," said Petrus at last. "But even if you were, it would not warrant war. And I am convinced that is not the true cause."

"So what is the true cause?"

He smiled.

"The decline of poetry?"

It was Alejandro's turn to smile. The fact that Petrus had invoked poetry made him a brother to Luis Álvarez. Time fell away and he could see his tutor sipping wine by the fireside.

"The older I get, the more I look for fervor," Luis had said to him, "and the more I find it in places where previously I saw only beauty. You are young and enthusiastic, your mind is fresh and excited, but fervor is the opposite of that. When it deserts us, we turn agitated and feverish, when it takes possession of us we are transformed into a calm, tenebrous lake, darker than the night, more motionless than stone. In this condition, we can pray without lying."

"I never pray," Alejandro had said.

"Oh, you pray," smiled Luis, "you pray every day when you go to the cemetery. Humans never pray more than when they are listening for their dead. But you will have to pray even more if you want to pay your respects to the earth and sky, and you will have to instill the compassion of poetry into your prayers. That's where passion is found—and in its wake, comes beauty."

In the half darkness of the cellar, the amarone coated the glasses with a dark lacquer that reminded Alejandro of Luis's tenebrous lake, and he suddenly remembered what he'd dreamt that night. He was standing in the middle of a wooden veranda, facing a forested valley. The valley was shrouded in a mist penetrated with organic breathing, an inspiration infused with elusive, vibrant life. Alejandro stood for a long time looking out at the extraordinary landscape, and yet a veil of anxiety was gradually changing it. Just when fear supplanted the joy of being there, he turned around, and in the darkness of a wooden pavilion with windows that had neither panes nor frames, he saw a woman. He could not make out her features, but he knew that she was young, and he thought she was smiling at him. Then he woke up. He'd been dreaming about that woman for several years now, ever since leaving Yepes to become a soldier, and this time, just after he woke up, he had seen her face, her pallor and her arctic eyes. He couldn't have said now whether she was beautiful or ugly, he could have said nothing about her beyond her youth, her fairness, and the gravity of her eyes. He'd thought she was smiling at him, but in fact she was looking at him gravely, and his entire childhood was in that look, along with the valleys of Extremadura, its stones, its parched landscapes, the slopes of the bluff where he lived, the harsh winters, and the violet dawns.

"More prosaically," Petrus resumed, "I believe our mists are dying because things in general are dying. The only hope of saving it is to accept that it will be reborn in another form. That is what we are striving for, those of us who believe in the eternity of poems. There is no other way out. When everything is used up, it will mean the end of our known world."

"That is very moving," Jesús said, "but you still have not told us the reason why you have come."

"I'm getting there," said Petrus, in no way offended, "I'm getting there."

He drained his glass and looked dejectedly at the empty bottle. Alejandro stood up, went once again to the far end of the cellar, and came back muttering *interesting*, like the first time.

Petrus read the label and seemed moved.

Jesús leaned closer in turn.

"Nuits-Saint-Georges," he read, "vin de Bourgogne."

"I've been there often," said Petrus. "The first time I was quite young."

The memory pleased him and he smiled to himself.

"And I went back there exactly twenty years ago, right after my visit to the castillo in Yepes."

He was no longer smiling.

"We chose your fortress as a safe place for our protégée, Maria, whom you heard us speak of just now, the young woman who commands the snow. But when I arrived, your family had just been murdered, and I decided to hide Maria in Burgundy."

"Do you know who killed them?" Alejandro asked.

"Not yet," said Petrus, "but everything is linked. If we chose your fortress to accommodate Maria, it was because of a series of corroborating factors. Among other disturbing events, a few days ago we came to discover that the first elf who ever ventured into the world of humans probably came to Yepes. Moreover, the castillo has the same motto as our mists."

"*Mantendré siempre*,"[1] said Alejandro.

"Which is also the motto of our council," Petrus said.

"And Maria, what role does she play?" asked Jesús.

"Maria?" echoed Petrus, surprised by the question. "She unites our forces."

"She's an elf?" Jesús insisted.

Petrus hesitated for a brief moment.

"We're not sure what she is," he replied.

Jesús seemed to be on the verge of asking another question, but the elf raised his hand.

"Now, if you will, the time has come for me to tell you what we hope to gain from our meeting."

He glanced at his glass.

"Apart from these wonders," he added. "Of course, it is

---

[1] I shall always maintain.

rather difficult to sum up a war in a few words. But it so happens that the final battle will be fought tomorrow."

Jesús burst out laughing.

"Wars like that no longer exist," he said. "This is not Alexander at Gaugamela or even Napoleon at Wagram. There is no final battle."

"I'm afraid there is," said Petrus, "and it will be fought tomorrow, and you will be called on to play a part in it—if we manage to get you across the bridge."

He laughed quietly to himself. He suddenly seemed old, but his gaze was even more beautiful than at the beginning of the story; his eyes a flinty gray, glinting with silver.

"It is time for us to greet our lady and entrust the rest of the story to her," he said.

He stood up, along with the other two elves, and all three turned to one side and bowed deeply.

In the darkness before them stood the young girl whom the general from Yepes had already seen in his dreams.

Darker than the night
More motionless than stone
The lake where we pray

Book of Prayers

WINE

My people live beneath the enchanted earth of Yepes, and there is no more pleasant place for our purpose than the cellar of the castillo, for wine lays in the memory of centuries, stones, and ancient roots.

It should come as no surprise that elves are not familiar with the vine. For those who are together, reality suffices; these are not people of fiction and drunkenness. But the wine of humans is the brother of friendship and fables. It confers upon the whispering of the deceased the turn of phrase that will carry their words a great distance. Through wine, the bitterness of solitude turns sweet, in that exquisite relaxation that causes so much to blossom. It joins the nobility of the land with the chronicles of the heavens, the deep roots of vine stock with the clusters of grapes reaching for the sun—there is nothing better suited to telling the saga of the cosmos.

Still, there was one remarkable exception to the mists' indifference to the vine: Petrus was an accomplished elf and a master of wines. He could taste the poetry of his world, but he loved the stories of humans above all else, and he would gladly listen to them with a glass in his hand. Thus, he incarnated a bridge between the two worlds, as did all the other providential players in this war.

POETRY

I f there is one intoxication shared by humans and elves, it is poetry.

On a day of drizzle or a night of pale moon, welcome the winds from the moor and write verses in honor of the old poets. The breath of the world will pass through you and vanish, but trapped in your feelings, it will have acquired a singular form—the birth of poems.

Is She Beautiful?

Blonde, pale, and gracious, she studied them gravely and Alejandro's life tipped on its end.

For a long time, he'd been hoping the war would forge him, grant him the humanity he dreamt of. From Luis, he learned that a man must look to the stars for guidance; from Miguel, that kingdoms are born from ideas; and from Jesús, that the heart lives off bareness. He'd entrusted war with the care of turning this instruction into a sparkling in a cemetery, so that he would know how to honor his duty to his dead. Now that six years had gone by, there was something he could still not grasp, and he hoped the elves would supply the missing element to the fulfillment of his destiny, through the new, more beautiful and terrifying guise of a women's gaze. No one understands what happens in the fleeting instant of an encounter—eternity contracts into a divine vertigo, then takes a lifetime to unfold again on a human time scale. How long have we got? wondered Alejandro.

The young woman stepped into the circle of torchlight and smiled at him.

Alejandro's whole life rushed headlong into that smile. He was submerged by visions and, as in his dream, he was gazing out at vast expanses where the hours of his childhood could again be found. The key is in the landscape, he thought, and on his palm, he felt the brief touch of an illumination, but when his fingers seemed to have curled around it, he laughed at the thought that he could have grasped the flow of dreams. The slopes of Extremadura were those of a land where tiny villages were swallowed by lofty summits and deep valleys. Above the mountains was a sky of hastening clouds; on the edge of his vision, the sparkling light he'd always known; perched on an outcrop was a church where a piano waited. How do I know all this? he wondered, as he flew on an invisible eagle's back over the valley of the promontory, unending fertile plains, then finally the outskirts of an unfamiliar city.

"Rome," said the young woman.

Alejandro remained silent and she said:

"I dreamt of you when I was in the Pavilion, and our memories are mingling."

Alejandro still said nothing, and she seemed troubled. The wavering torchlight blurred her features, but when she'd said *mingling*, she'd taken another step forward. How old was she? he wondered, terrified. He studied her face, her blond hair, her light eyes. Could someone so young have such a gaze? he wondered again, then he found out she was a pianist. Is she beautiful? he thought, and although he could see every detail and every one of her features, he understood, intoxicated, that he did not know. He also saw that her forehead was too large and her neck too thin, and to him she looked like a swan adrift in improbable tropics. What an absurd idea, he thought; ever more lost and intoxicated with his own state of being lost, he laughed. He wondered how much time had gone by since she had appeared. Someone behind him cleared his throat and he shuddered. He stepped forward and bowed in turn.

"You are Maria," he said.

There was a faint sound and Petrus appeared next to him, unsteady, his nose red and his eyes hazy.

"No, no," he said, "Maria is in Nanzen."

Gripping the edge of his cape in vain, he almost collapsed

onto the young woman. With surprising agility, he caught himself just in time and, looking at her, he muttered, "My child, be good to Uncle Petrus."

Against her thighs she was holding a woven basket, and from it she removed three gray flasks which she handed out to the elves. They sobered up as quickly as the first time and Petrus, friskier than a filly, turned and continued to speak to Alejandro.

"Maria stayed behind at the Pavilion of the Mists."

"My name is Clara," said the young woman, and again she seemed troubled.

Petrus looked at her, then at Alejandro.

"I missed something," he muttered.

Jesús came in turn to bow to Clara.

"Are you Maria's sister? Are you elves?" he asked.

Petrus observed Clara with tenderness and pride.

"Exactly twenty years ago, less one day, two extraordinary children were born," he said. "The first one is standing here before you. Her father is the guardian of our pavilion, her mother is a remarkable woman, but according to all logic, Clara should never have been born, because unions between elves and humans have always been sterile. The other child, Maria, is waiting for us in Nanzen. She was born to the head of our Council and his elfin companion but, unlike us, and like Clara, her appearance is strictly human."

"You look perfectly human to me," said Jesús, surprised.

"Not in our mists," said Petrus. "There, you will see how different we are from you. We only adopt a single appearance when we are here. Only Maria and Clara, despite their elfin blood, keep the same physiognomy in both worlds."

"What do you look like when you are up there? Do you grow wings?" asked Jesús, obstinately situating mist and winged creatures in the sky.

"Nothing grows on us at all," said Petrus, taken aback. "Simply, we are multiple."

"Among elves, do you speak Spanish?" asked Jesús, ever pragmatic, now that he'd got going.

"Anyone who has stayed at the pavilion can speak every language on earth," answered Petrus.

"What is the role of Maria and Clara?" Alejandro asked.

"Well, to save the world," said Petrus.

"Is that all!" commented Jesús.

"The question," continued Petrus, ignoring him, "is how. Six years of war and we were still blind—until, four days ago, when we obtained possession of a gray notebook dating from the sixteenth century. It belonged to an elf who also crossed over the bridge. He was an extremely talented painter, and we still have one of his paintings, which you will soon see. But the most astonishing thing—and, for us, the most interesting—is that he was the first elf who stayed in your world for good and chose to live a human life."

Petrus scratched his head.

"It's a long story, and I cannot begin to tell it now. Let's just say that the notebook contains vital information, both for the outcome of the war, and for the future of our mists, and now we are in a position to determine our next move. Not the one that we would have dreamed of, to be honest—what we have learned forces us to make a radical decision. But we have come so far that we must risk everything or face certain death."

"Who, in your mists, makes such decisions?" Alejandro asked. "Is it you?" he added, turning to Clara.

She laughed.

"Decisions are made by the Council of Mists."

"Presided over by Maria's father, if I got it right," Jesús said. "So he is your king?"

"The head of the Council is at the service of the mists," said Clara.

"Is your mist alive?" Jesús asked, still determined to understand.

"Come, we have to go now," said Petrus. "Anything you don't know yet, you will find out once you cross the bridge."

"Cross the bridge?" echoed Jesús.

"We will try to cross with you," continued Petrus, "and that is why Clara is here with us, for humans can only cross in her company."

"I think there's something you've failed to take into consideration," said Jesús. "General de Yepes commands the first army. He cannot leave his post in the middle of an offensive to go off and sip tea in a celestial pavilion."

There was a moment's silence.

Then Petrus scratched his nose and said:

"Yet that is precisely the plan."

And to Alejandro:

"It will not constitute desertion."

He broke off. Alejandro was staring at him without seeing him, scrutinizing the darkness beyond. Petrus looked in the same direction.

"Ah, so there are the dead," murmured the elf.

Alejandro found it hard to breathe.

Before him stood all his dead.

They appeared to him just as they had looked in days gone by, and had he not known that they were dead, Alejandro would have sworn on his honor that they were not ghosts. His family, Luis, Miguel, the men who'd fallen under his command, villagers he'd long forgotten: all of them had come through the gates of death to join the battalion of the living.

"Why?" he asked, out loud, and the congregation of the deceased vanished, with the exception of Miguel and Luis.

It was the same sensation as eighteen years earlier, when his family was being buried, and the funeral proceedings were enveloped in the torpor of a dream. He conversed with Luis and Miguel, back from the dead in the form of images they shared with him; he saw his tutor, thirty years younger, leading a group of men, marching through a baking hot day. The white-hot earth buzzed with insects, and the men moved forward, a holy spark in their gaze. He studied the poet's face and his clear eyes, his aristocratic brow, his puny body, and he thought: the power of such a man! A new image appeared. A boy was slicing his way through the grasses down a gentle slope. The long stalks yielded to his hips then rose again with the smooth grace of swans. He made his way slowly through the wild grasses while time fell away, and all that remained was this walking through the fields. All I want is this ecstasy, thought Alejandro and, at last, Luis spoke to him. Once again it was the older man sitting at his councilor's table; by his elbow the glass of sherry shone brightly like a splash of blood, and the young general heard the words his tutor was saying, smiling, so handsome, so poor, and so worthy in his laughable stronghold.

"*Everything shall be empty and full of wonder,*" murmured Alejandro.

He awoke from his dream and saw that Jesús was looking at him.

"We're leaving now," he said. "We're crossing the bridge with them."

There was a silence.

"You didn't see them?" he asked Jesús.

"More ghosts?" Jesús asked.

Again a silence. Jesús sighed.

"I hope you know what you're doing," he said to Petrus.

"We haven't the foggiest," answered the elf.

He ran his gaze over the vast cellar.

"We'll be back, I hope," he said.

"How do you intend to get us across?" asked Alejandro.

"I'm getting there," said Petrus. "That is the last thing you must know before changing worlds. The mists, the gray notebook, the painting and all the rest—that will be for the other side. For the time being, we'll ask you to drink some tea that's been slightly altered and doesn't taste all that great."

"How do we know that your concoction won't kill us?" Jesús asked.

"Four days ago, Maria and Clara came here for the first time, thanks to this very same tea," Petrus replied. "But they were not alone. There were two humans with them."

"You mean real humans?" Jesús asked. "Not ghosts, or semi-something-or-others?"

"Real humans," said Petrus, "as human as one can possibly be."

"Are they waiting for us there?" Alejandro asked.

"They are waiting for us and, what's more, they are watching us at this very moment," said Petrus. "A priest and a painter, but they are also soldiers."

For some unknown reason, to Alejandro these words seemed to echo those of his tutor, and again he murmured, *empty and full of wonder.*

"It's time, I think," the elf said to Clara.

The young woman smiled at him tenderly.

"I always obey Uncle Petrus," she said, with delightful irony.

She took a few more flasks from her basket, and when she turned to face Alejandro, she smiled at him with just a touch of mischief that said, Here we are, trapped like two fish in a net. To fall in love in the middle of a war, what a mad idea, he thought. For the second time that night, he laughed out loud. Petrus cast him a suspicious glance before holding up his flask: it acted as a prism, and the sparkling of the dead flickered in every direction through the cellar.

They all drank their gray tea.

For several seconds, nothing happened. The brew tasted vile, of fermentation and decomposition.

And they waited a few more seconds.

Life was split into two equal parts that went to crash on either side of infinity, then re-bonded under the sky. To Alejandro and Jesús it seemed to last forever, and yet to be occurring outside of time. In the second when the world faded away, images had scrolled past their inner gaze—fields, lakes, fine-weather clouds with the faint outlines of beloved faces. Above all, they had the sensation of eternity being transmuted into a journey, and they could have stayed in limbo forever to take that journey with neither movement nor duration, suspended in an infinite space devoid of place or shape. Finally, everything ended abruptly in a great sensory void. Now they couldn't take their eyes off the spectacle unfolding before them.

Beyond the red arch of the bridge of mists, beneath a black sky, an old wooden pavilion overlooked a valley of white trees. In the entire motionless scene, the only colors were the white of the trees and the black of the sky, and the crimson bridge like a splash of blood in one's vision.

Alejandro looked at Clara and knew that she was beautiful.

Is she beautiful?
A splash of blood in one's vision

Book of Paintings

亡霊

GHOSTS

Whatever shape you give them, it's useless to deny the existence of ghosts. If few humans encounter them outside of their imagination, that alone suffices to show how much they live among them.

How do we know what happened in ancient times? Because we know inherently. The blood of ages runs through our veins like a river, and as long as we pay attention to the earth and the sky, that blood will convey the heritage of those people who came before us.

It's not magic, it's not a chimera. Who could forget the first line ever drawn, when it came time to paint the landscape of the world?

快活

GAIETY

Clara had not always been mischievous and joyful. For far too long she had been confined to the fallow regions of the heart, and only laughed for the first time when she turned eleven. But love and war had immersed this solitary soul in a gaiety of the sort everyone will surely need, if it is true, as a great man wrote one day, that gaiety is the most amiable form of courage.

The company who had come from the land of humans stood on the bridge of mists beneath an inky sky shot with light. The day was emerging from darkness and lit up the landscape. At the heart of this landscape was the red arch of the bridge, radiating with untold strength. Unlike the world around them, the creatures of flesh had preserved their colors.

"I don't understand what I am seeing," Jesús said.

"You are seeing the essence of our world," Petrus said. "Once you see it with the eyes the tea will give you, it will appear more normal to you."

"More tea?" muttered Jesús.

Beneath their feet the wood was vibrating slightly.

"Welcome to Nanzen" said Petrus.

Alejandro was stunned by the black sky. It was as if it had been wash-painted, and his gaze could follow the lazy, shimmering ripples as they merged with other magnificent figures. From this liquid ink came the light of dark lacquers, to which the invisible grooves of a brush gave a clear texture. Although Nanzen, with the exception of the bridge, was entirely black and white, the sense of nature there was more concentrated than elsewhere. The whiteness of the trees revealed their structure, without concealing their overall beauty, and in the center of this arboreal arena stood the Pavilion of the Mists. It was at the mercy of the wind through its paneless, frameless openings which were arranged asymmetrically, although the building itself was square. This broken rhythm surely led to a melodic vision of the landscape; the more one's gaze wandered aimlessly through the spans, the more the panorama took shape, in keeping with the most beautiful music; but if you asked the two men what they were seeing, they would simply have answered: an old bandstand at the mercy of wind and rain. The veranda all around had acquired the patina of age, and Alejandro understood that the building was not a vestige of the past, but the spirit of that past—neither rhyme nor reason, he thought again, before he was seized by another realization.

"The lines are perfect," he said out loud.

And he thought: the proportions of this rickety refuge are absolute.

The red bridge reigned over the austere territory. The arch was veiled in thick mist, and radiated a form of unfamiliar harmony.

"The bridge of mists is the bridge of natural harmonies," said Petrus. "It holds the elements of our community together. But it also brings about the union and synthesis of our worlds."

He broke off.

"You will hear the whole story," he said then, "but for now we must not keep our welcome committee waiting."

And indeed, leaving the pavilion, the delegation was coming to greet them, and I owe it to my integrity as a chronicler to mention that Alejandro and Jesús stood there speechless. One woman and two men, escorted by four creatures as absurd as they were splendid, were making their way along a path of black stones. Further along I shall relate the impression the woman made upon Jesús, but just then he was completely absorbed by the emotion of discovering elves in their native environment. Taller than humans, they seemed to be made up of different species that blended with one another in a slow ballet of metamorphoses. At the head of the delegation came a white horse that was also man and wild boar, *becoming* each of its constituent essences in succession. The blond man with glacial eyes changed into a snow-white horse, then his nostrils were transformed into a broad, steaming snout, he grew horns, and now he was a wild boar, finer than any Alejandro had ever seen in his territory for major hunting. Intermittently, the reflected light of an ancient waterway passed over the creature's face, and through a clearing in the mist Alejandro could see that the bridge spanned a silver stream with wild grasses growing on either side. The elf had about him the same fragrance of eternity that filled the young general with the greatest reverence. The second creature in the escort, a brown-haired man whose horse, a moment later, seemed made of quicksilver, inspired the same respect. His coat glinted with great beauty, a beauty preserved by the fur of the hare into which he was ultimately transformed—beige and brown, extraordinarily silky, and rippling with gentle quivers.

"The Guardian of the Pavilion and the Head of the Council," said Petrus.

What land is this, that creates leaders like gods? thought Alejandro.

"That is the impression the high-elves generally give," murmured Petrus.

Behind the masters of the mists, two elves displayed their fine human features and their lustrous coats of wild horses, while the third species turned out to be a squirrel for one, and a polar bear for the other. One was not overcome with deference in their presence, and it seemed to Alejandro that in comparison with the high-elves they must be minor elves, but their beauty was perhaps all the more moving in that it was instilled with innocence. Now Petrus advanced onto the descending arch of the bridge, and Alejandro and Jesús followed him, disrupting the enchantment to notice how, surprisingly, they were growing accustomed to the black sky. When their elfin companions stepped onto the path of stones and were transformed in turn, they could see that they all contained an essence of man and horse, and that Petrus, in addition, became the prettiest, most jovial, potbellied squirrel one could ever hope to meet. Then he gave his place to a little chestnut horse with lovely thoughtful gray eyes. Next to him, Paulus also turned into a squirrel and Marcus became a large brown bear. Just as they all regained their human form, a strange garment covered their bodies. It looked like a soft, organic cloth shot through with ripples which ceased the moment the human part of the elf vanished. It was difficult to identify the fibers the cloth was woven of, but it adjusted to the body while preserving the glow of the animal, and Jesús would have liked to touch its light and flesh.

As for Alejandro, it was the path that led to the pavilion that fascinated him above all. The stones were wide and flat and reflected the trees in the hollow below, as they were actually above the stones. There were no trees along the lane, but the flagstones radiated a swinging of branches in the wind which gave an impression of walking beneath thick foliage. Alejandro stepped onto the first stone and was surprised by the invisible, stream-like wave that went through the mineral hardness of its surface.

"Soon you will see liquid stones," said the adorable chubby squirrel Petrus had once again become.

Behind the four elves, a priest in a cassock brought up the rear of the delegation. His face was open and magnanimous, his form freighted with a paunch that attested to his delight in earthly pleasures. Although as a rule Alejandro did not like priests, he immediately took to this one, as did Jesús, who revered the men of the cloth, whence we may conclude that they had not met just one sort of man in the Church, for there are so many sad souls there, but also true scouts who set off to explore unknown lands with no aim to enlighten any other consciousness than their own. Above all, the priest's good-natured contours couldn't hide his gaze, that of a man who had observed and, upon observing, grown. He was walking with one arm around another man's shoulder, a tall, very handsome man, the same age as the good father—perhaps sixty or so—and this man, according to Petrus, used to be a painter. The man smiled at them with the sort of elegance that is born of the mockery one reserves for oneself, and the equal and opposite consideration which, on principle, one displays toward others: Alejandro and Jesús liked him, too.

The young woman was raising her hand in welcome. She gave off an air of singular authority, although her appearance was frail; her hair and eyes were brown, she was rather thin, and very distinguished, her skin was golden, her lips the color of fresh blood. Beneath the skin on her face there were fine veins that radiated in concentric circles from the bridge of her nose. There were moments when these veins were paler, to the point of fading and disappearing altogether. Then they returned to throb gently and darken her serious features. All at once she smiled, and Alejandro saw that she was smiling at Clara.

Turning to one side, he looked at the young woman and she took his breath away. She was smiling back at Maria; in her smile, he saw compassion and sisterly love, and his own passion was heightened still further. Now he knew that he would have to pray late into the night, no longer to die in honor, but that this flame would not fall to the enemy—how could I bear its loss? he pondered, and thought less of what he was feeling than of what Clara incarnated. And this was how Alejandro de

Yepes, in his thirtieth year, was awakened to love. Neither the self-sacrifice of combat, nor the pledge to shed his blood down to the last drop, nor allegiance to the land of his ancestors, nor Luis's poetry, nor Miguel's ideas had ever shown him the way so clearly, and if he'd thought he was close to it when he stood before his dead, what was always missing was the echo of a sigh. Now the fact that he'd always taken and never given seemed so obvious to him that shame rose to his cheeks. He'd already sensed this, briefly, in the cellar, when he felt that he loved because he felt uplifted. But the smile Clara had given Maria tore like a raging wind at the last ties binding him to his former life, while he clung to the yearning to give with which she filled him, a yearning that was transforming the parameters of his heart one by one. Now he understood Luis's lesson, the restlessness that comes from enthusiasm when passion has the power to bathe us in calm waters: this passion had made him cease to notice whether Clara was beautiful—never diminishing his desire for all that.

The delegation from the alliance of humans and elves, now a few steps away, came to a halt. Close up, the beauty of the elves was almost unbearable. It emanated from the perfection of human and animal forms commingled in their slow choreography of mutations, but also from the manner in which the elves expressed their emotions, in the form of faint emanations that traced drawings in space—and, whether it was pride, sadness, weariness, goodness, mischief, or courage, a symphony of ethereal sketches was created, intelligible in the way that abstract paintings are intelligible, and this made their deepest hearts transparent to humans. Alejandro looked at Petrus and was stunned by the etchings which the only alcoholic squirrel in the civilized world was sending out in the air in leaping bursts. There was courage there, candor and obstinacy, irreverence flirting with ribaldry, but also a procession of juvenile aspirations bathed in ancient wisdom, in such a way that, through this consensus of lightness and depth, Petrus the minor elf actually appeared to be great.

"Am I seeing things, or do they have their heart written on their brow?" murmured Jesús.

Then the two men got down on one knee to greet the elves from the land of mists and their human companions.

Jesús Rocamora, as he bent his knee, got the impression that he was returning to a semblance of reality. The stone was lukewarm, and he liked the trembling of organic life. The first minutes had been a succession of shocks: the absence of colors, for a start, the young brown-haired woman, then at last the elves themselves, in all their fantastical multiplicity. Now that he was getting used to the black sky and the trimorphic creatures, the true impact of the change of worlds became clear to him.

"Welcome to Nanzen," said Maria.

She had a deep voice that evoked some elusive memory. For an unknown reason, he recalled his only encounter with Luis Álvarez, during the second year of the war—their one brief meeting, in a January of endless frost and exhausted soldiers. At the end, Luis had recited three lines to him. While some men are not cut out for words, that doesn't mean they cannot be found by a poem that has searched the stars for them; that will be their loyal companion on days of glory and in times of hunger from that day on. These three lines were all that Jesús would ever attain in terms of literature, but at least he'd recognized them from the very start as his own. After reciting them, Luis had added:

"They're special, because I knew them before I ever composed them."

"Don't you always have to know ahead of time what you are about to compose?" Jesús had asked.

Luis had laughed and replied:

"If you are a good craftsman, perhaps. But if you want to be a poet or a warrior, you have to consent to a loss of self."

In this mourning
Liquid soul
I sleep clothed in clouds

The lines had carried Jesús into a great, white silence. At the heart of the silence, a sensation was being born and, although he couldn't have explained why, he read it as the announcement of his redemption. Then it passed, and if Jesús sometimes thought of the three lines, it was when he despaired of ever understanding their effect upon his life—now, a young woman, her face stitched with tiny dark veins, was standing before him, and the poem became flesh, embraced as it was by passion and a woman's grief. Jesús was a strange mixture, as we all are. Because of his childhood by the lake, he believed that life is a tragedy, and the fact that he'd fled made him feel obliged to endure it without complaining. He was a Christian because he had spent time with his priest, a righteous man left sublime and powerless by his obstinate desire to pray, and from him, he inherited the belief that the crosses one bears can compensate for an act of disloyalty. He bore his own cross without bitterness, with a cheer astonishing in a man of duty and remorse, along with a healthy heart and a lust for life that kept him from being crushed by his burdens. But while he might not know what Maria had experienced in life, he knew the pain of it, the perfume of regret; he thought that the mist from the lake of his childhood had gone up to that black sky to relieve them both of their sorrow; and that Luis's poem, in a way, explained why they had met and, similarly, linked their fates. Of course, as a man who was as impermeable to introspection as he was to poetry, these were not the words he was thinking, and it will surprise no one to learn that, in the end, it could all be translated by a single thought in which he invested all his hope: *we will suffer together.*

"My name is Maria," she said again.

She turned to the man who was also a gray horse and a hare.

"My father, given his authority over the Council of Mists, asked me to greet you here," she said.

"Welcome to Nanzen," said the Head of the Council in turn.

"Welcome to Nanzen," said the man who was also a white horse and a wild boar. "In my capacity as Guardian of the Pavilion, I am honored to meet you. You are those we were not expecting, but it seems Yepes has a role in the history of our bridge."

Alejandro and Jesús stood up straight, and realized that they no longer found it incongruous to be conversing with a horse or a hare.

"How should we call you?" Alejandro asked.

The Head of the Council smiled.

"That is always the first question humans ask."

He let out a quiet modulation which was not exactly a melody, but a liquid sound, rather, where an ancient stream flowed.

"That is my name," he said.

He addressed his fellows in the same natural musical language which bathed Alejandro's and Jesús's spirits in a summer rain. It was very beautiful and harmonized so closely with the landscape that Nanzen now made them feel dizzy.

"But we also like the language of humans," continued the Guardian of the Pavilion, "and we are not averse to borrowing their names. To you I shall be Tagore."

"Solon," said the Head of the Council.

Jesús, who was no more enlightened about the former than the latter, looked at Maria. When the guardian had resorted to the language of elves, he saw in her eyes the gleam of the tall trees reflected on the flagstones, and in this way, he understood that invisible foliage lived inside her, its memory so enduring that it sometimes turned into a vision.

"Like you, I grew up in a poor region," she said, "but you could see very beautiful trees there."

She turned to the painter and the priest and said:

"Here are two men who used to know those trees."

The men came forward and held out their hands to Alejandro and Jesús.

"Alessandro Centi," said the painter. "In Italy, they call me Sandro."

The priest took a sudden unexpected little bow.

"Père François," he said. "I am glad our paths have crossed."

Jesús made this sign of the cross.

"Are you French, Father?"

"I am indeed," said the priest.

"Are we in heaven?" Jesús asked.

Père François looked at Petrus and laughed.

"If we are, the angels are awfully strange-looking," he said.

Then he became serious again.

"To be honest, I don't know if all this is real or if I'm dreaming."

"Those who drink know that reality resides at the bottom of a bottle of amarone," said Petrus.

"I'm the only one who can say what can be found at the bottom of an Italian bottle," declared Sandro.

"Ecstasy," said Petrus.

"And tragedy," added the painter.

Maria, addressing the entire company, made a gesture of invitation toward the pavilion.

"In the name of the Council of Mists," she said, "may I invite you to have tea with me?"

She bowed slightly to Tagore and led the small group along the path to Nanzen.

*

Nanzen. As they made their way toward the Pavilion, they saw below them a valley of tall trees, their tops veiled in mist. The pavilion was built on a promontory and elevated on pillars planted in thick moss gleaming with dewdrops. Worn steps led to a veranda that ran all the way around the old bandstand. When Alejandro stepped onto it he felt a brief, intense vibration. He went immediately behind Tagore, Solon, and Maria. The rest of the delegation followed, with Clara and Petrus bringing up the rear. From outside, the building seemed rather cramped, and Alejandro and Jesús were surprised to find it was big enough to accommodate them all and still project a feeling of spaciousness. As they left the veranda to go inside, they could sense they were going through an invisible vestibule, and now the sounds of the outside world were stifled. Oddly, Alejandro found the tranquility of the place seemed to match the nature of the mist in the valley, woven from the same evanescence, where a deep, vital breathing could be felt. All around, through openings that set off discrete portions of the panorama, the landscape unfolded in a succession of images. In the background, the red bridge, squeezed into the narrow space of a little window, revealed only the rising section of its arch; this confined perspective suggested the abstraction of a red stain upon the surface of an inky lake. Visible through other openings, further enhancing the tableau, was the splendor of trees and the mists in their successive rebirths. Every swirl of mist, every branch yielding in the wind, every mottled streak of black sky relentlessly produced the highest configuration of beauty.

The polar bear showed everyone where they should sit on the floor. Tagore and Solon sat across from each other to preside over the cenacle.

"Quartus, at your service," said the polar bear with a slight bow.

"Hostus," said the other minor elf just as he was being transformed into a squirrel.

He added:

"We are today's assistants."

The wooden floor was bare, apart from a faint silvery dust left undisturbed by their footsteps. A slight breeze traced swirling arabesques in the dust. On one of the walls of sand, a band of light-colored cloth, the only visible adornment, was decorated with unfamiliar writing as beautiful as a drawing and made with ink like that of the sky. Between two views onto the trees in the mist, against the wall on the side of the valley, was a bench covered in cups, teapots, terra-cotta bowls and a few rough-hewn wooden spatulas and ladles. Earthenware tea jars stood in a row under the bench. Next to them, on a brazier on the floor, a cast-iron kettle was whistling.

The only sound or motion in the room was the boiling of water and the dancing of silver dust. Quartus and Hostus set down two little cups of differing size and shape in front of each guest, then Quartus brought a teapot to Tagore along with a bowl and one of the tea jars. From it, the Guardian of the Pavilion took out a sort of crumbly brown cake and broke off a small piece. Hostus dipped a ladle into the kettle and Tagore poured a first splash of water onto the crumbled tea, which he set aside in an earthenware bowl. Then the assistant brought him another ladle of water and, as with the first spoonful, he poured it onto the tea leaves.

The guardian let out a sudden soft trill and everything changed. The power of ritual confers a rather stiff dignity upon humans until the moment it develops into a trance and, causing them to leave themselves behind, gives them the strength to grow. In Nanzen, the elves hadn't abandoned their nonchalant air, but their gaze showed they were conscious of the beauty and vanity of the world, the certainty of darkness, and the desire to honor whatever it was that, in spite of war, kept creatures standing tall under the heavens. Time passed, empires crumbled, people perished; at the heart of this disaster a fragment of the sublime was hidden; it was a serious moment, yet not solemn, deferential without being formal, and joyful, however grave the hour.

The silvery reflection on Tagore's face intensified. Something welled inside him. It was an intangible transfiguration, but Alejandro recalled the way Luis Álvarez would turn handsome when passion lit up his puny, ugly self and, in that light, made him more dangerous than an assassin. Now he looked at Tagore, no longer splendid, suddenly dangerous. Where did they gain such strength? he wondered. Looking around him at the austerity of the pavilion, with its ink calligraphies, its silver dust, and its views onto trees and mist, he found the answer in himself: from beauty.

"And, in its wake, fervor," murmured Petrus on his left. "Take note that one can also achieve it through poetry or, better still, amarone."

Solon looked at him and kept silent, laughing softly to himself.

Tagore poured tea into the first cup in front of each guest. When he sat back down, he raised his cup to eye level but, to the surprise of Alejandro and Jesús, he then transferred the contents into the second cup. They followed his example and, like the others, raised the empty cup to their nose.

They had imagined they would smell some rare perfume, but they were overcome with a fug of dust and cellars. There were so many layers of memory and childhood sensations here that Alejandro and Jesús relived long-ago adventures, when the cellar opened doors leading to an enchanted land, a place of moss and hiding places where they could hope without hindrance and travel without ever going anywhere, a land of undergrowth, and storerooms where dreams were metabolized, a land blessed with that inexhaustible time which the next day would run like water through one's fingers—they breathed in the tea, wishing that it would never end, while the magic of the empty cup wove its way through the years. Now they saw themselves in the forest of the time when they were no longer children. A downpour soaked the branches and the earth dripped and steamed in newfound brilliance; the smell of wet pathways rose from the ground with a telluric spirit that recalled that of their youth. Alas, they had to make their way in life, and mature, and the boys became men in whom faith in infinity was transmuted into the awareness of death. However, as they leaned out of the window at the fortress, toward the rain-drenched courtyard, General de Yepes and his major breathed in the pungent fragrance wafting toward them and over them, between heaven and earth. We have gone back through time, thought Alejandro, just as the cup lost all smell, and with it the intoxication of seeing the world through the prism of years gone by.

"It is customary for one of us to recite a poem before we drink the tea," said Solon.

Alejandro thought of the words he'd received from Luis's ghost, and a very old memory came to him.

"In my country, there is a song we sing at funerals, in a dialect of Spanish no one can speak anymore," he said. "It's an old poem from Extremadura which the women brought to me long ago for my dead."

And, suddenly understanding the old idiom, he recited the last two lines.

To the living the harvests to the dead the storms
And then everything shall be empty and full of wonder

A prolonged murmuring spread among the elves.

"Those are the very words someone wrote here this morning," said Solon, pointing to the cloth on the partition of sand. "Usually we write the poems down after we have recited them, but today an invisible hand got there before us."

"I don't understand a thing," said Jesús, who was beginning to have pins and needles in his legs, and was wondering if they would ever get around to drinking.

Tagore smiled, put down his empty cup, and drank slowly from the full cup. The taste of the tea was subtle, and retained none of the aromas of dust and cellar. Rather, it tasted of the affability of days and the relaxing interval of twilight; nothing changed, nothing became, the tea was drunk, the universe was in repose.

A few seconds went by.

Alejandro blinked.

Before them, in the middle of the room, an earthenware bowl had appeared.

Its irregular edges gave birth to a consistency of light that was striking and powerful. The creator had preserved the rough texture of the earth from which it was made, but the shape was extremely elegant. The sides were straight and tall, without tapering, nor were they regular, but sculpted with a jagged surface, slightly flatter where the lips would be placed. Touches of dull silver here and there conferred a patina of time, although, goodness knows how, it was clear to all that the bowl had been fashioned the day before. If someone had asked Alejandro and Jesús what they were seeing, they would've replied, a simple earthenware bowl, although they were conscious of the fact that they were gazing at the work of time, and not only the work itself but also the simplicity of feelings it commanded. What sort of art is this which incorporates the imperfection of wear and urges us to be modest and pure? wondered Alejandro. Beauty is caught in the trap of a voluntary erosion where we can contemplate our entire existence, to such a degree that all that is left to do is live on effacement, earth, and tea.

"I saw this bowl in a dream a long time ago," said Maria. "That very bowl, precisely."

"For as long as the pavilion can remember, the writing of the poem has been followed by the appearance of a bowl," said Petrus. "They are all splendid but this one has something more that thrills the heart."

Tagore took it to each guest in succession. When it was Alejandro's turn to drink from it, he thought he could feel the softness of Clara's lips where she'd placed them before him, and he welcomed the faint, sweet taste of the tea on his tongue.

The guardian went back to his place.

They waited in silence.

Life was flowing. Life was drifting. Life was expanding, about to burst its banks. What were those lights in the forest? The world had changed and they could no longer see a thing. Inside them, the river was swelling, heavy with jewels. Were these pale flowers? Stars upon the surface of the dark waters?

Then the water flowed over the dark banks and, in a stormburst, Alejandro and Jesús discovered the world of the mists.

In this mourning
Liquid soul
I sleep enclosed in clouds
To the living the harvests to the dead the storms
Then everything shall be empty and full of wonder

Book of Prayers

Other

E very major story is the story of a man or a woman who leaves behind the distress of the self to embrace the dizziness of the other.

For this journey, one needs the song of the dead, the mercy of poetry, and the knowledge of the four Books.

The Book of Prayers.
The Book of Battles.
The Book of Paintings.
And the fourth Book which, at this point in the story, we cannot yet name for fear it might be misunderstood.

This is the story of a few souls who, in war, knew the peace of encounter.

WRITINGS

The world of the mists had several languages. The elves communicated among themselves through the modulations of streams and breezes, and those who had stayed at the pavilion in Nanzen could speak every language on earth. For a long time, they did not have writing, but when the desire came to them, they chose one form of writing in particular.

There were two reasons for this.

The first had to do with a human country where people wrote that way. Like the land of elves, it was surrounded by an emptiness of turbulent seas lost in fog, and it reflected the theory of the ancient poet who said that the land of the living was merely an island surrounded by mist or by the waters of a great dream.

The second reason was more essential: not only was this writing beautiful, but in it one could admire the flight of dragonflies and the grace of wild grasses, the nobility of drawings in ash and the great whirlwinds of storms.

Hence, one can understand why we were tempted to leave some writing upon the silk in Nanzen, since beauty, nature, and dreams are, if not our exclusive preserve, at least our daily bread.

What We Are Looking At

The territory of the elves unfolded before their inner gaze. Just as the perfume of the empty cup had opened the doors of the past to Alejandro and Jesús, the tea had transformed their mental space, and they were partaking of a vision that did not belong to them, but which caused the landscapes of the mists to parade through their minds with fresh new colors.

"There is someone in my head," murmured Jesús.

The sky was blue or golden, the foliage was bursting with green and tawny colors, mingled with touches of orange and purple; the bowl had taken on a gray patina enhanced with veins of old copper—this renewal filled Alejandro and Jesús with joy, as well as an unexpected nostalgia for the black sky and white trees.

"Once someone has seen the structure of beauty they can never look at things in the same way again," said Sandro. "I still wonder whether it sharpens your vision or burns your eyes."

"Where have these visions come from?" asked Jesús. "I feel as if I am simultaneously here and there."

"From the tea and the good offices of the guardian," answered Hostus, "who has the power to see what is far from him and to share that vision with us. We are together here and with him there. We can look at what is before us and inside us at the same time."

"Until now, the Guardians of the Pavilion came to us from

the two high families, the wild boars and the hares, who are more powerful in contemplation and in prescience," said Solon. "The lower houses of squirrels and bears, however, are more lively and agile in action."

"So squirrels and bears fight better than the others?" asked Jesús, looking at Tagore, who had closed his eyes and did not seem to hear them.

"Not at all," said Petrus, "wild boars and hares are great warriors. But they're not great when it comes to their senti-mentality, and with them, the urge to fight comes from reason-ing, whereas with the squirrels it springs from the enthusiasm in their hearts."

"If they're not busy drinking," said Marcus.

"Along with the bears," added Petrus.

And to Alejandro:

"The high-elves are the aristocracy of this world, but it doesn't mean the same thing as in your world. I was a sweeper for much of my life and I am as highly respected as a guardian of the pavilion."

"Sweeper?" said Jesús.

"Moss sweeper," said Petrus.

"What makes an aristocrat, then?" asked Jesús.

"He is responsible for others," answered Solon. "He shoulders the burdens of the community. Having said that, history has shown that certain squirrels have more spirit than all the hares put together, and that they can shoulder burdens that would crush many a wild boar."

"Is it possible to see any place in the universe from here?" asked Alejandro.

"Any place at all," replied Solon. "And if you would kindly take a look at what Tagore is about to show you, I will try and tell you the history of the mists."

"Then, perhaps we could find out what role we have to play in it," said Jesús.

They all fell silent as yet another landscape unfolded in their minds.

"Katsura," said the Head of the Council.

Until that moment, trees and mist had succeeded one another with monotonous grace. Now the guardian's guests could intermittently glimpse wooden pavilions, the outline of high mountains, or even the contours of strange gardens. Then the vision broke through the fog and slowly came to rest at the foot of Katsura. It was a large city surrounded by peaks, with low dwellings set in terraced rows on what should have been the slope of a hill—however, despite their efforts to make what they were seeing conform with what they knew, they were compelled to face facts: Katsura, the capital of the elves, the chief town of the province of Snows, backed onto a void, clung to a flank of mist the way other cities cling to a mountainside. As far as the eye could see, there was a similar magic of landscape and buildings poised upon layers of vapor. The world was afloat on an ethereal gauze and the vast city shone forth, even perched on a void. Never had human eyes gazed upon a more admirable panorama, for the wooden structures bathed in mist were humble and perfect, as in Nanzen, and floated between the sky and the light mists in a sanctuary of mystery and cloud. And also as in Nanzen, verandas ran around the gray-tiled houses, some of them tiny, others more vast and similar to temples. One in particular was striking. In front, there was a great rectangular courtyard covered in snow and planted with trees, their dark branches sprinkled with snowflakes as if at random. On these wintry boughs, twisted and knotty like those of old fruit trees, delicate flowers had bloomed, pink or red around their light stamens, with round petals braided with scarlet and white. And so, the blood of the corollas, the dark wood, the glistening of the snow: the fine season and the cold one sharing their love on the austere, bare branches, made these claw-shaped branches somehow necessary, so that one's gaze, all along—leaving the heart to endure its ecstasy—could pick the flower that had emerged from winter. A gust came to die in the enclosed courtyard and the petals, strained, seemed to swoon. Then, as they rose again in a graceful arabesque, the wind transformed the air into a brush and gave the scene a brilliance and disposition that supplanted all preceding scenes by way of beauty.

"What are those flowers that bloom in the snow?" asked Alejandro.

"Plum trees flowers," replied Clara. "An essence that yields no fruit, only perfume in winter."

"The headquarters of the Council of Mists," said Petrus, pointing to the building with the rectangular courtyard. "It also houses a large library where I used to work as a sweeper. There is lovely moss beneath the snow, and sand walkways that are cleared daily of dead leaves."

"What do sweepers do in winter?" asked Jesús.

"They read," said Solon. "But that part of the story is for later."

Alejandro focused on the vast valley beyond the city. Now and again, stolen from a patch of mist, a handful of gray roofs could be seen hanging on the line of sky. Everywhere there was the same snow, the same purple flowers on barren branches, the same swaths of steep mountain—and from one summit to the next, one tile to the next, one flower to the next, a painting was created the color of the first Nanzen, a play of ink and blood between darkness and light. Everything floated, the mist coiled upon itself, and the world sparkled in successive facets.

"Sometimes the mist decides to cover the universe, with the exception of a single bare branch," said Petrus. "Sometimes it contracts and we see the greatest possible proportion of things. But we never encompass all of them."

"Everything rests on a void," murmured Jesús.

"There are islands of land suspended in the mist," said Solon.

Hostus brought the bowl to each of the guests for a second time. Alejandro was surprised by the new taste of the tea, strong and pungent, with the hint of an unknown spice against the perfume of a white flower.

"Our tea opens and develops like wine," said Petrus. "There are vintages and cellars for aging. The one you are drinking today is over two centuries old. With each sip, you move forward in time, in the secret of stones, in the life of the earth."

Alejandro looked at the light cloth where, earlier, the poem had been written, and it seemed to him that the writing had changed. Some characters looked like human figures, others like trees or even flowers, and he was beginning to get used to their strange shapes, to make out the gist of the meaning—but his hunches were fleeting and slipped away the moment he thought he was about to grasp them.

It came stealthily, like a rustling of cloth or a ray of light. Was it around them? Was it inside them? A moment ago, they had been alone, now there were a multitude of them. When he used to haunt his cemetery, the young Alejandro heard the voices of the dead in an echo that seemed to come from the depths of the earth, but this time presences seemed to emerge from the mist in a way that is hard to describe, for humans are strangers to the community of the spirit, to the impalpable ties of those who, although they may not have their own body, do at least know the union of consciousness. Every existence in these lands acted in accordance with the mist, lives which, although they did not speak or appear to each other, could sense one another through osmosis.

"The mist is alive," said Jesús with a sigh.

"Let's just say it is the breath which brings the living together," said Petrus.

"It is by regulating the harmony of the mists from the pavilion that we assure the continuity of our world," added Solon.

"I thought natural phenomena were self-regulating," said Jesús.

"Our existence rests on an inhabited void, an osmotic medium we must alter so that it will answer the needs of our community. The mists are the web of eternity, and however slow our evolution might seem to humans, we live in time. And so, we transform the mists thanks to the properties of our tea, the power of temporal alteration without which the mists would ignore us. We drink our tea and the mists obey, the mists listen and we are together."

"How do the mists listen to you?" Alejandro asked.

"The guardian greets the mist and retransmits its message to the community," answered Solon. "The tea grants him this power to welcome and, in return, informs the mist of the elves' needs."

"He greets the mist?" asked Alejandro. "I thought you altered it."

"Welcoming is already a way of altering," said Solon, "it is even the highest possible level of altering reality. Few of us, however, are capable of this, to the level the mists require, and it is not by chance that the most powerful guardian the elves have ever had came to power during this era of total war. Without Tagore's empathy, I think we would already have foundered."

"Without his empathy for the mists?" asked Alejandro.

"His empathy for the whole, of which we are a fragment," said Solon. "Everything is connected, everything is attuned."

"Not everything is transformed into its opposite," said Alejandro. "Human beings do not become rocks."

"No," said Solon. "But they can hear the sorrow of stones."

On seeing that Alejandro, disconcerted, had fallen silent:

"Those who cannot hear the sorrow of the world cannot know themselves in their own sorrow."

"In that case, I wonder what your opinion of humans might be," said Alejandro.

"Most of you do not hear stones, or trees, or animals—our brothers, although they live in us elves the way we live in them," said Solon. "You see nature as the environment you share with other beings; for our kind, it is the principle that makes them exist—not only them, but everything that has been and that shall be."

The effect of the second sip of tea was making the presence of the elves more intense. For Alejandro and Jesús a thousand impressions were leading to a cacophony of images—they experienced the sensation of a vertiginous plunge into a valley of trees, and they realized they were leaping from treetop to treetop, until they landed on a new branch. Before long, it became a breathless race through a pre-human forest where the light of the sun struggled to enter. Low to the ground, the race lasted a long time in the exhalation of dead leaves, borne on the delight that the sap beneath the bark was also that which flowed in their blood. Suddenly, everything was illuminated and they were above fields of shrubbery with tight foliage, trimmed in vague rows across gigantic expanses. From these undulating stretches of green dunes, where furrows of mist reflected furrows of crops, there came a perfume of the sacred, familiar to Alejandro from cemeteries and battlefields. As they flew for a while over these plantations, the presence of the elves from the community grew ever more intense. They are never alone, thought Alejandro—it was as if he could feel every one of these foreign sentient beings without having met a single one, and deep in his chest he felt the piercing of a stake, both familiar and strange.

"These are the Inari tea plantations," said Clara.

He looked at her and the stake caused his heart to bleed.

"That is what the presence of those who do not suffer from

solitude does to those who are alone," she said. "The tea plantations carry the presence of the community."

"So tea is a sort of telepathic elixir?" asked Jesús.

"There are two ways to drink tea," said Petrus. "The ordinary method of each elf, which connects us to one another and keeps our bonds alive. And the extraordinary method, which takes place in the pavilion. It's the same tea, but Nanzen grants it other powers."

Tagore's vision changed and they saw a lagoon, above which the mist delineated a channel. Propelled by some invisible force, barges without sails drifted slowly across the lagoon, making their way between walls of fog that rose like high banks of clouds, and moved forward along the weave of the mists.

"Circulation between the major islands is one of those powers," said Petrus. "When the channel opens, the mist turns liquid and it is possible to sail there, like on a river. In peacetime, there are locks of mist that open and close at set times, but the Guardian of the Pavilion can change them as he sees fit. One of the great battles of this war has been over these shipping lanes. We have to intervene continuously regarding the configuration of passages, in order to bar the way to the enemy."

"I can't see any oarsmen or sails," said Jesús.

"Everything in our world is propelled by intention and vision," answered Petrus. "Through the tea, the guardian and his assistants visualize the destination, and transmit it to the boatmen."

The spectacle shifted yet again, and the slow procession of ships vanished, to be replaced by a peculiar garden. Can we even refer to it as such, something that contains neither flowers, nor trees, nor earth? Devoid of the charm of verdancy, it was an enclosure consisting entirely of stones and sand. On a flat expanse furrowed with parallel lines, a few rocks of varying shapes and sizes formed isolated summits in the sea. On the horizon of the shore other rocks rose in a miniature range of peaks, sculpted by the powers of earth and time. Everything was motionless, but the sound of the surf could be heard; everything was inanimate, but one sensed that the landscape was alive. I cannot imagine a more peaceful spot, thought Alejandro, and he felt a sense of relief that eased the lacerating pain of the stake. He turned to Jesús; stunned, he saw a tear flowing down his major's cheek.

"The stones are liquid," said Jesús, almost beseechingly.

"What do you mean?" said Alejandro, failing to understand.

He looked closely at the stones and suddenly he saw it, too. A few tongues of mist billowed over the garden, and wherever they had been, the rocks had turned liquid: they preserved their form by passing from solid granite to a quicksilver lava. All around, the sand was becoming a lake, shot through with the sparkling of gems before it returned to its hard mineral surface—thus, the sand and the stones not only represented the water and the mountains, but also incarnated the solidarity of states of matter, and Jesús Rocamora, gazing at the scene, was taken back to his early life.

"We are a world of incessant metamorphoses," said Solon. "We are transformed into horses and animals of the earth and sky but, in the past, beyond the three essences, we were every species at once."

"Vapor turns solid, rock turns liquid, and you will also see plant life becoming fire," said Petrus. "This is only possible because we live at the heart of the mists."

"What is this garden called?" asked Jesús.

"The garden of heaven," answered Petrus.

"Heaven," murmured Jesús.

Another tear trickled down his cheek.

"In heaven, then, everything is changed into its opposite," he said.

"The opposite is still the same, but in its extreme form, for everything proceeds from one and the same matter, with multiple facets," said Solon.

The garden of stones disappeared and an indistinct shape appeared on the horizon, perhaps a terraced city or a high cloudbank—what are we looking at, wondered Alejandro. But they went closer and it was indeed a city of wooden houses, surrounded by undulating fields where more tea was growing, although the plants did not undulate as gently as in Inari, and the leaves were colored gray, and cold.

"Ryoan, the city of the enemy, surrounded by its plantations of gray tea," said Petrus.

It was as vast as Katsura, with the same buildings surrounded with verandas, the same tiled gray roofs, the same trees with red flowers. There was the same beauty in the snow, the same encounter of seasons on the hospitable dark branches but, despite this, it was a horrible sight.

"There aren't any mists," whispered Jesús.

"There are *no longer* any mists," Solon corrected him. "They were once the most beautiful on earth and I don't know a single one of us who wouldn't have given his life for such glory. But Ryoan was crushed by the enemy and now you see the sad result. Everything has become rigid, the void is being filled, we are losing our life force and our connections, we cannot breathe and the community is disintegrating."

They stood for a moment facing the fallen city, picturing its erstwhile splendor, while once again, Alejandro felt his life spin upside down. The discipline he'd imposed upon himself in order to speak for his dead on the battlefield, his enduring solitude in spite of friendship, his castillo crippled with murder and poetry, the war and its abject processions—in the end, everything was being borne along on the flow of an unknown river that released an uninterrupted outpouring of debris inside him. If the sobriety of ink and whiteness in Nanzen seemed familiar, and if the humility of the earthenware bowl had transported him, it was because they'd made the bare structure of his life visible to him; and so, through the magic of feeling the impalpable presence of the tribe of elves all around him, the inhabited mists had offered him the pathway to the other—when he went deep inside himself and accepted his own destitution, he received in return the sweet delight of the encounter. Was it the presence of the elves that served as a balm and healed his grieving heart, or was it that his love for Clara had opened him to the possibility of receiving? I ask the question, but it hardly matters, for great power is a chimera inside us that either elevates us or kills us, since living is nothing more than being able to forge ahead in life by telling oneself the right story. The presence of the community of elves was, to Alejandro, a stronger remedy than the sufferings of the past, and Clara's smile completed the transfiguration. The stake was plucked from his heart and borne away on the waters of the river.

Jesús, too, gazed at the enemy city. With the strength of the mist, his faith had taken on a new dimension. The fact that the mist brought the breath that turned the stones to water made it the messenger of his redemption. The liquid rocks could change dishonor into honor, betrayal into a gift, and damnation into salvation, while this alchemy required the barrenness of the void. Moreover, we know that Major Rocamora, although he was not a man of words, was nevertheless a soul whose behavior could be affected by three lines of verse, and we weren't surprised that he was open to the grace of moving stones. Might I add, as I have an undeniable affection for these men, that the young General de Yepes and the young Major Rocamora, driven by their renewed hope that suffering might be transformed into fervor, had just ventured onto a path rarely used by humans. It has been marked out by the breathing of the void, which removes the mess that burdens us—however, we must not simply feel it in ourselves, but also discover it all around us, in the erasures in which true beauty is born, through the unique branch of a world engulfed in fog or through an earthenware bowl more spare than the trees in winter.

"What does the new poem say?" Alejandro asked Clara.

"I cannot read their language," she said, looking at the light cloth.

"*The last alliance*," said Petrus, who had turned toward the wall where the ink inscriptions were glowing faintly.

After a pause, he added:

"Separation is an illness, union is our way of life and our only chance. That is why we are founding our wager regarding this war upon new alliances."

He gave Solon a questioning look.

"We will speak of the prophecy later," said the Head of the Council.

Petrus remained silent and Alejandro said:

"So you are doomed to drink tea until your last breath."

The elf gave out a long sigh.

"That is the entire question of this war," he replied. "You have seen the color of the tea plantations around Ryoan. That ash gray comes from a noble rot which is eating at the leaves through an entirely natural process. All it will take is one degree more of humidity and a fungus will develop on the tea plants. You have something similar with wine, do you not, and it yields magnificent vintages? Simply, here, the consequences are fatal, and it is unfortunate that we did not realize this earlier. But this blindness, like all the rest, is due to the powers of gray tea."

"Fatal?" said Alejandro. "Everything we have seen of the tea up to now is that it makes drunkards sober and opens the door to humans to enter this world."

"Those are simply a few pleasant side effects," said Solon. "It is because of the power of gray tea that the enemy built his bridge and his pavilion and kept them invisible for a long time."

Tagore's vision rose in altitude and they discovered Ryoan's bridge and pavilion on the other side of the city. The construction was similar to the ones in Nanzen, except that the wood had been coated in gold leaf. The arch had the same curve and the same elegance as the red bridge, the pavilion had the same appearance of chaotic openings and immemorial verandas, but there was no more mist to be seen there than in the town of Ryoan itself, and everyone gazing upon this gilded splendor was cloaked in a feeling of deepest dissonance.

"The bridge can be crossed thanks to the power of the gray tea," said Petrus. "It is thanks to the tea that Aelius is conducting his war and accelerating the decline of the mist he claims to be saving. You will note that the enemy's strength resides in a substance that is easier to produce than any weapon on earth."

There was a moment's silence.

"That is why we have made a radical decision," said Solon.

The images vanished. Tagore opened his eyes and Alejandro felt a pang of anguish. Without knowing why, he recalled the words Jesús had uttered long before, the evening after the battle when they sat conversing on the shady little plateau. The best strategist, he had said, will be the one who looks death in the eye and sees what he must not be afraid of losing.

Tagore nodded his head.

"We will destroy the tea plantations," he said. "All of them, down to the last one, at dawn on the coming day."

Who knows what we are looking at

The Book of Paintings

TEA

Though elves loved poetry, they didn't make up stories. Those who are on good terms with the world have little need of works of the imagination, particularly as the tea served the same purpose as wine and human fiction—that of rooting the community in its earth and in the spirit of its members.

Can one conceive of a life without fables, or novels, or legends? One would have to endure, relentlessly, the burden of being oneself; there is no distance between consciousness and dreams, no way to escape from the naked truth; but in return, how great the ecstasy of living in the intimate glory of things.

However, when the elves began to notice the decline of their world, this gave rise to renewed resolution. That is surely how the temptation of Ryoan was born, whereas others came to think that an alliance between tea and wine could perhaps save them from disaster.

空

Void

It is said that everything came into being from the void, the day a paintbrush traced a line separating earth and sky.

Poetry is the proper balance of earth, void, and sky; murder comes into being when it is forgotten.

One must travel light, said the ancient poet. Humans are weighed down with so many burdens! The mists of Nanzen could be so beneficial to them!

GENESIS
1800–1938

The practice of storytelling is a strange thing. The day before the great battle of this time, in the sixth year of the deadliest war ever endured by humans and elves, at a turning point between epochs, the likes of which only two have ever existed in the history of the humans of the West, I must take a shortcut in order to continue the tale. Just as the earth never appears so vast as after the tide, stories and fables require the ebb and flow of the seas—and so, just as the waters are changing, a simple shell is revealed which on its own knows how to embrace the entire cosmos. It is our eyes, our ears, our feelings and our knowledge, and it is to that shell that we must turn for light in the darkness.

Here it is, then, slightly less than a century and a half ago: our lonely shell at the moment when the great tide of kingdoms is ebbing.

There were not many elves as modest in appearance as Petrus, nor many destinies as brilliant as his. In fact, it seemed at the outset his fate was to remain as obscure as the woods and the good family of squirrels into which he was born. The Deep Woods, to the east of Katsura, were a region of mountains and forests inhabited by terraces of thorny pine trees, whose branches reached skyward from their twisted trunks, to form a sort of parasol, so elegant you could weep. Nature had created them in great number, then planted them one by one in the rocky surface, choosing each location as if it were the setting for a jewel. Then the entire scene was cloaked in mist, and as it emerged from the void it revealed a landscape of peaks crowned with pine trees that seemed to be writing upon the sky. The Deep Woods were highly valued by the community of elves and, bathed in the majesty of high-altitude fog, they went there to admire the rising and setting of a sun that glorified every branch and every engraving of foliage. From one summit to the next the elves proclaimed the beauty of the sight, and Petrus grew up with these dawns and twilights that rustled with sounds and poetry. The ridges stretched beyond space, against a golden backdrop sketched with the curve of pines.

There are many mountains worthy of such moments of wonder, but none can compare to these. Fortune had decreed they would be vertiginously high and narrow, and wherever one looked, the slender mass of summits bathed in an ocean of clouds. At times, the trees, set on a single salient peak, were as delicate as lace in the great mossy void. At other times, the entire range rose above the cloudbank and offered up its succession of peaks. But what ultimately enthralled one's vision was not the unending succession of undulating summits, but the fact that they overlooked a vaporous mass that seemed to give birth to each slope before leaving it with the kiss of a pine tree. Once lost in the sight, where the mystery of creation seemed to have found refuge, it was to encounter simply one's own self; as if one were a mountain in a storm that turned the world on its head then restored it to the hollow of its own consciousness; and this was what the elves of every province came to seek in the Deep Woods, traveling great distances to stand in the morning to face the mystery above them. Later they would recall the hard rock, which was smooth and affable in places and sharp as a blade in others, and again they would see the landscape of the Deep Woods, the velvet mists, and the beauty of the mountain range, as if it were their own internal landscape.

Quite logically, the province was largely inhabited by elves that were also squirrels, bears, and eagles, who feared neither the steep crags nor the dizzying heights. The villages seemed to have been transported through the ether before being deposited on their high plateaus; and then all was hidden, revealed, and so on, to infinity. And so, everything that was true for the world of elves in general was true here a hundred-fold, given the fact that these colossal spires reaching for the sky reserved for the mists valleys that were no less colossal, gigantic expanses where the hand of the elf could not be seen. From Mount Hiei,[2] all you could see on the horizon were three needles floating on the magma until, suddenly, ten more broke through the surface, and you felt reborn. The mountains, rising

[2] Pronounced "He-ay."

out of nothing, hovered suspended over this absence; through the force of the void, spirit and rock sketched a *pas de deux* on the summit of existence before turning back to the original nothingness; and these games of hide and seek, of incessant birth and dying, gave the mountain in return the shape of consciousness that it had lacked until then.

It was in such a land that Petrus—who was not yet called Petrus—was born and grew up. He retained a sincere affection for the realms of mountains and the poems of dawn. Lulled by the affection of his family and the favor of the great mists, his first decades were filled with enchantment and love. Far from the sound and fury of the rest of creation, the squirrel elves made up a peace-loving house. They didn't write poetry, but they gladly partook of the poetry of others and, although they thrilled to the speed of flight, they could remain motionless for long stretches of time. While they were frugal in nature, they knew how to entertain extravagantly, and even though they were far away from Katsura, they were never the last to reply to a summons from the Council. The surrounding landscape described them as well: as obscure as their woods and as noble as their mountains, they wandered in peace there, among treetops and cliffs, and didn't suffer from either metaphysical dilemmas or from any longing for unknown horizons.

Despite the idyllic landscape, Petrus's youth had been quite turbulent. Among his numerous relations he was unique because, ordinarily, all elves are identical: their human form is handsome and dignified, their horse is noble and thoroughbred, their third animal is ideally proportioned, but here we must face facts: our hero doesn't correspond to the norm of the species. Shorter than his brothers, he also had more padding, which had grown, by adolescence, into a little belly, the likes of which had never been seen on any local lads, and, year after year, he grew chubbier, and the fine features of his kin melted into a round mug. It's true that he had the most remarkable eyes in all the Deep Woods, and his mother had eventually come to believe that Petrus could be summed up by a pair of silver pupils. In reality, it was not only his eyes, but above all his gaze that was so striking, and the contrast between his chubby face and the pensive twinkle of his eyes meant that everyone around him grew irresistibly fond of him, so much so that the only elf in the mists who had a perfectly ordinary appearance had a special gift for arousing the affection of his peers. But others followed him not only because they loved him, but also because they wanted to protect him during those adventures where he oughtn't go on his own, for fear of losing his life. The mists had never seen a clumsier elf: he had almost lost his tail by getting it caught between two boulders, something which in all the memory of the Deep Woods had never happened, and it had earned him the torment of remaining trapped in his squirrel essence until his appendage was completely healed (and he was forced to nibble hazelnuts which—another oddity of his nature—he only moderately enjoyed, and this added to the pain he felt in his poor crushed tail). It must be said that his rescuers, once the fear that he might be seriously injured had been set aside, had some difficulty in restraining their laughter as they set about moving the boulders. Three days earlier, the same Petrus had almost killed himself, about to take a squirrel leap just as he'd decided to change into a horse, and he'd only been saved thanks to the thick carpet of fresh pine needles, where he landed with a stunning lack of grace. Icing on the cake, for no apparent reason he often tripped over his own tail. To slip on his own tail! For an elf, this was as unthinkable as turning into a cauldron. In short, the patent conclusion to be drawn from all this—even if one couldn't really understand why—was that Petrus would go from one disaster to the next, but his lucky star would save him, every time.

*

Naturally, his awkwardness and appearance were only the tip of the iceberg. What lay below the surface was a mind configured like no other, completely indifferent to the matters of mountains—perpetual rebirth, merging marvels, and so on. The morning of his first hundredth birthday he gazed glumly at the sparkle on the summits of jade-lacquered pine trees and thought that it would be impossible for him to live any longer in this sublime boredom. His usual sidekicks were there with him: a ravishing squirrel and a tall brown bear, full of the graceful, powerful vivacity Petrus utterly lacked—and, turning to them as they became lost in silent admiration of the landscape, he declared:

"I can't take it anymore, I have to get away."

"And where would you go?" asked the bear, tearing himself away from the splendor of the vista.

"I'll go to Katsura," said Petrus.

"You'll get yourself killed ten minutes into the trip," the other squirrel pointed out, "and if you survive your own bad luck, you'll pick the wrong channel."

"It doesn't matter where I go," Petrus said obstinately. "I just don't want to end up like some old pine tree on a peak that's never seen the world."

"But the world is inside you," said the bear, "in every pine tree, every peak, and every boulder you see."

Petrus sighed.

"I'm bored," he said, "so bored I could die. If I hear one more poem about twilight I'll make a point of throwing my horse into the void of my own free will."

In the distance, they could hear the modulation of a voice as supple as bamboo, as crystal-clear as a stream, and saying something which, in the language of humans, meant roughly:

Dark woods on the edge of mist

My friend the pine
Whispers to the twilight

"Right," said the bear, placing his paw on Petrus's shoulder, who was holding his head in his hands and shaking it gloomily, "don't torment yourself like this. For every problem, there's a solution."

The solution was what Petrus had stated. He had to leave. Inside him rumbled a call which his hundredth birthday made irrepressible, and the very next day he left the Deep Woods in the company of his two sidekicks—without his mother knowing, because she would have tied him to a tree—and without the slightest idea of what he would do in Katsura.

"We'll go with you as far as the capital," said his friends, "then we'll come back here. We can't reasonably set you loose on the world without an escort."

If ever there was an epic journey, this was it. There can be little doubt that without his guardian angels—whom you will recognize as the future Paulus and Marcus—Petrus would have gotten lost and killed a hundred times or more. His distraction and awkwardness were compounded by the fascination of the journey. Never had he breathed like this, never, since leaving the Deep Woods had they been so dear to him, and never had he understood their message so clearly. Distance was enlightening, as it clarified the scene he'd gazed upon all his life in vain, and gave it meaning through magic and nostalgia. Again, he saw Mount Hiei and its spire pointing toward the sky with a pang in his heart as delicious as it was wrenching, and he was astonished that it had taken this departure for him to feel the fullness of being in every rock and every pine needle, in a whispering friendship, touched by the mystery of the living. Four days after they had left the territory of the Deep Woods, he felt a moment of regret so sharp and painful that he came to a halt in the middle of the path, stunned at the sensation of ecstasy this wound had given him. They'd just reached the region of the Southern Marches, a short cold plain where the mist glided like seagulls above the shore. This was the last stage before the first channel, since they were reaching the edge of the earth and would soon have to call on the services of the boatman. They had already been circling the abysses of mist on which the mountains stood for a long time, but soon there would be no more path and they all thought excitedly about their first passage through the locks. They'd never left home, and Paulus and Marcus had to confess they were enjoying this adventure. Now, however, Petrus was standing stockstill in the middle of the path, overcome and radiant, and so oblivious to everything around him that he could have walked on the tongue of a dragon and never realized.

The channel was one of the smallest in the mists, for the Southern Marches and the Deep Woods had the lowest population density in this world. However, when they came within sight of the estuary, the spectacle was phenomenal. The black earth stretched lazily between its bands of fog, then came up against a mountain of mist that rose toward a sky so high it never seemed to end; there were no more bearings, no sense of distance, only an intuition of infinity that split any scale of vision wide open.

"Who knows what we're looking at," murmured Petrus, emerging from the abyss of his thoughts to dive into the abyss of the channel, no longer able to tell reality from madness.

At the tip of the estuary they came upon others aspiring to cross, waiting and drinking tea at the way station. A little otter elf, not yet twenty years old, was serving the travelers. Petrus, who didn't feel at all like drinking, collapsed on a chair and sat there without touching his cup—which was a great pity because the tea served at the estuary of the Southern Marches is prepared according to a very special method, with a view to ensuring the comfort of the voyage.

For the time being everything was calm. They could hear the cries of birds, they admired the fast-moving mist, the black earth, the pilgrimage trails. Seated at right angles to infinity, the travelers conversed placidly among themselves. The elves' osmotic life and their immersion in the cosmological dimension of the world have made them a species that is unfamiliar with solemnity. Humans only resort to solemnity because in everyday life they are small, but under certain circumstances are called upon to raise themselves up to an unaccustomed level of the soul. But elves, as a rule, are tall, since in their hearts they respect the presence of wholeness, and they have no need to raise themselves up or to let themselves go. And so, while they were waiting until it was time for the channel to open, everyone sipped phlegmatically on their tea, at the foot of immoderation. The paneless windows in the way station looked out onto large sections of lagoon and sky, mingled like so many charming pictures—however, since the weather was mild on that late autumn afternoon, everyone stayed out on the veranda to make the most of these nuptials of earth and sky.

The channel of the Marches opened twice a day, at daybreak and again at roughly five o'clock in the afternoon, in order to serve Hanase,[3] the main town in the province of the Ashes, in what was, give or take, a slow four-hour crossing. From Hanase there was another lock to pass through before they reached Katsura. Shortly before five o'clock, the voyagers saw the father of the little otter come in, for he was also the boatman. His equine incarnation, with its robe flecked with shimmering light from the water, was transformed into an otter with an impressive build. His human features seemed to have

[3] Pronounced "Ha-na-say."

changed in substance: while preserving their shape, they had become liquid, illuminated by that tremulous light one finds beneath the surface of the water. Was it from living in these desolate Southern Marches, where the earth had become the shore, and the sky had turned into the sea? His physiognomy represented some essential immersion, the original wave through which we are no longer objects, but flow—who knows what we are looking at, thought Petrus again, ruminating on a failure to merge with the flow of mist which left him, frustrated and unhappy, on the banks of the river where his fellow creatures were frolicking.

"Well, damn," he murmured.

Now the channel opened. It's crucial to remember that everything was ordained through Nanzen, and in Nanzen, by the pavilion, and in the pavilion, through the agreement between the guardian and his mists. In those days, the guardian was a wild boar elf who was about to begin his four hundredth year of service, and who was intimately acquainted with the currents of his world. Thus, everything unfolded at a pace that was unequalled in harmony; the channel opened, the mist which had hitherto risen to the heavens now coiled inward and dissolved into a liquid carpet where barges appeared, moored to a wooden pier; finally, everything became stable and everyone, connecting to the mist, set off at a march behind the boatman. Petrus, absorbed by his metaphysical ruminations, morosely afflicted by his sentiment of exclusion from the great brotherhood of elves, only half paid attention as he followed along behind. Moreover, for him to understand the boarding maneuvers, he should have drunk the tea at the way station. But because he hadn't, and was ignorant of the instructions the others had received, he did everything all wrong: instead of staying in the middle of the pier with his eyes down and walking in a straight line to board his barge, he veered off slightly to the left and, still in a glum mood, cast a sullen look at the mist.

A fleeting sensation of dizziness suddenly tipped him over the edge of the pier. There was a hellish *splash* which caused everyone to turn around, while the boatman gasped with disbelief, but before Paulus and Marcus could say a word the elf, ordering them to stay still, called out into the mist for help.

"Don't be afraid," he said to them.

A moment passed in total silence. The voyagers, trying not to feel dizzy, concentrated their gaze on the spot where the unfortunate elf had disappeared. After a long while, there were ripples on the surface of the passage, and Petrus slowly rose above the mist, imprisoned in a net held in the mouths of four silvery dolphins. The contrast between the squirrel's distraught expression—his tail stuck in the fine mesh of the net, thus preventing him from transforming himself—and the smiling grace of the large dolphins was so striking that Paulus and Marcus, after an initial effort, were no longer able to contain their laughter. The squirrel's face was also painfully squeezed by the net, and was dripping pitifully. His fur was drenched, and he looked like a poor hairless critter set to dry by the fire. The dolphins pulled the sides of the net together so that he could be hoisted up onto the solid wooden pier and, exhausted and dying of shame, there he collapsed, wheezing like a turbine.

"In the five hundred years I've been doing this job, I've never seen such a thing," said the boatman, his otter face still wearing the same flabbergasted expression as his human face had the moment Petrus fell.

"But you do have nets," Marcus pointed out.

"For baggage," he replied, "in case they get knocked over or there's wind. But for an elf!"

Petrus continued to blow like a whale.

"Thank you, my friends," he croaked to the dolphins, breathing heavily.

One of them swam up to him and, raising his silver snout, let out a shrill arpeggio, before going back where he had come from.

"Mist dolphins," murmured Paulus. "I'd heard of them, but actually seeing them is something else entirely."

"There is a great population in the mist," said the boatman, "and my best friends are there."

Then, to Petrus:

"Perhaps you too are fated to have strange friendships."

Petrus would have liked to answer him, but he'd gotten his paw stuck between two planks on the pier and was trying to work it loose as discreetly as possible, which in fact led to frenetic wiggling that revived Paulus and Marcus's laughter. Finally, he achieved his aim and, springing up, took with him a centuries-old slat of wood as he did.

The boatman looked at him with stupefaction.

"Good," he said after a moment, "let's go now."

Marcus and Paulus escorted their waterlogged friend, and everyone was able to board. There were six of them in each barge, and four boats in all. The boatman had taken his seat in the boat with the three friends, joined by a pair of deer elves. The mist was lapping faintly at the side of the boats and Petrus, who'd ended up in the bow, was catching his breath. After his fall, in the seconds before the arrival of the rescuers, he hadn't felt any real fear. The mists in the channel had the texture of air and water combined, the resistance of a liquid in which he could breathe, and this aqueous, gaseous weave aroused in him the awareness of a time when the living dwelled equally on earth and in the sea, in an airy existence made of oxygen, sunshine, and water.

"We dwell in the atmosphere," he thought, as the boatman closed his eyes and the crossing began.

He gave a sigh and hoped for a well-deserved rest. It would

have been magnanimous, indeed, if he could have stayed with his thoughts about strange friendships and cosmological fluidities. The mist was rising with streaks of gray iridescence, as if composed by a painter with a delicate touch, using here a light brushstroke, spreading there a wash in successive layers of dark ink. There were moments when the flows of mist rose all at once toward the sky, and clustered together in a tasseled cloud. Then everything grew lighter, and in the clarity after the storm, as if a brush had divided the world in two, one could make out the perfect line of the horizon. As a rule, Petrus enjoyed these demonstrations of cosmic painting, for he appreciated the beauty of the universe, and his gaze differed from that of his peers: he felt that this beauty was calling for *something else*, whereas his fellows wanted nothing more than the beauty itself, but he had no idea what that something else could be. Often, when in his Woods he gazed at the summits dotted with their ineffable pine trees, he could sense an undulation trying to emerge, vibrating lightly in the air with each twilit poem, but then it dissolved, for lack of whatever it was that was missing and which, he could tell, was missing in him, too. And while in the poetry there was some of this mysterious restlessness, the manner in which the lines agreed with an outside world from which he felt irrevocably separate left him dissatisfied, deprived of the instrument that would at last have enabled him to *experience* his moments of ecstasy.

So, he had believed that the crossing would provide a respite for him, give him time to become himself again, and the early moments had seemed to keep that promise. But for a while, now, the barge seemed to him to be rocking a great deal; above all, he could feel the stirrings of nausea, and that did not bode well.

"Do you feel sick, too?" he whispered to Paulus.

"No," replied the elf, astonished.

Then, with consternation:

"You don't feel mist-sick, I hope?"

"Feel what?" asked Petrus, alarmed.

Paulus looked at him with trepidation.

"Mist-sick. Travel-sick. Did you drink the tea at the way station? Normally, you shouldn't feel like this."

"No, I didn't drink it," said Petrus, now frankly worried. "I wasn't in the mood to sit drinking tea."

"What's going on?" asked Marcus, coming closer, "Why are you whispering like conspirators?"

"He didn't drink his tea," said Paulus wearily. "He wasn't in the mood."

Marcus looked at Petrus.

"I cannot believe it," he said, finally.

And, divided between exasperation and pity:

"How do you feel?"

"Horrible," said Petrus, who didn't know which tormented him more, nausea, or the prospect it could get worse.

To make things worse indeed, a few hours earlier, on leaving his pine forests, now more beloved than ever, he had stuffed himself with herb pâté (something he adored) and some of those sweet little red berries that can be found at the edge of the Southern Marches (and which he was mad about). Subsequently he had felt terribly sleepy, which had made the last leg of the journey quite difficult. Now there could no longer be any question of sleeping, because the pâté, the berries, and a few older remains of cranberry compote were fighting for the honor of coming out first, while Petrus, looking all around him in horror, saw nowhere that he might reasonably dispose of them.

"You're not about to throw up now, are you?" whispered Marcus in a hiss of irritation.

"Do you honestly think," gasped Petrus, "that I have any choice in the matter?"

His fur had taken on an interesting greenish tinge.

"Not in the barge, please," said Paulus.

"Above all, not in the mist," said Marcus.

He sighed with pity and weariness.

"Take off your clothes," he said, "and do what you have to do in them."

"My clothes?" said Petrus indignantly.

"Stay a squirrel or a horse, whichever you prefer, but take off your clothes and be as quiet as possible," answered Marcus.

Petrus wanted to answer back, but he seemed to suddenly think better of it, and his companions understood that the dreaded moment had arrived. Once he'd changed into a man, he turned modestly to one side and removed his clothes, baring his pretty little round white buttocks, which were sprinkled with freckles. Then he changed into a squirrel. What is about to follow will remain forever in the annals of the mists, for no one had ever seen such a thing and, above all, *heard* such a thing. Vomiting is very rare among elves, for they do not indulge in excesses harmful to the smooth workings of the organism, and so the event was shocking in and of itself. But you must know that of all the animals, squirrels get it over with most indelicately. Consequently the other three elves turned away with horror the moment they heard the first rumblings of release.

"What's going on?" asked the boatman, while Petrus was apocalyptically spewing his guts out.

"He's mist-sick," answered Paulus.

"I'm sorry," hiccupped Petrus between two bursts of pâté.

The boatman and the two deer looked at him, stunned.

"Didn't he have tea at the way station?" asked the boatman.

No one answered. For a moment, they could see that the boatman was piecing a series of concordant clues together and, gazing at the finished picture, finally understood that he was dealing with a madman. Just then, Petrus let out a final spasm and the boatman laughed so hard it caused the entire barge to shudder, bursting the deer's eardrums. His laughter gradually subsided and then, looking at the pale squirrel clutching his clothes close to him, he said:

"Well, dear friend, I have no doubt that an interesting destiny awaits you."

And we know he was right about that. At present, however, the voyage had become a nightmare, and Petrus's stomach, emptier than it had been in decades, was now regurgitating nothing more than a little bitter bile and the shame of having soiled his clothes.

"I won't kill you," Marcus said, "that would be letting you off too lightly."

But Petrus shot him such a pathetic look that he softened his tone somewhat.

"I hope this has taught you a lesson," he sighed, in the end.

As for Paulus, he was far more positive.

"I'd never seen one of our kind throw up," he said, showing a lively interest. "It seems really horrible."

The crossing continued at its slow pace, rocking Petrus with nausea. The others enjoyed sailing through the mist. The boatman had closed his eyes and the barges moved along smoothly, in close collaboration with Nanzen. It was an hour for prayers, and all the elves knew this, without ever having learned as much. Immersed in the inhabited void of the mist, in symbiosis with the living creatures of the world, becoming the vapor that conveyed the message, and, beyond, turning into water, air, mountains, trees, and rocks, the passengers were lost in gratitude for the great cosmic mix. That is how our prayers that do not require liturgy are recited, and how our hymns are sung, when the point is not to worship—if praying, as I believe, really means loving life. The barge plowed its way through the mist, life turned gently back in on itself, and everyone nestled in the furrows of the mystery of being there.

Then the journey was over. The channel began to close over again behind the barges and they could see a pier on the shore similar to the one in the Southern Marches.

"You will get off first, and go straight ahead," said the boatman to Petrus once they'd docked. "Here there are no dolphins, but there are divers who don't want to jump in just when the passage is closing over."

Petrus, obeying conscientiously, hopped as fast as he could toward the shore and collapsed, panting, before he even knew where they'd landed, and it took his breath away.

Directly opposite, Hanase sat at the top of a hill of mist so thick it seemed to be lifting the city skyward. Gray particles, rising up from gardens of trees and rocks where smaller, rounder shapes could be discerned, floated upon the scene.

"Hanase," said the boatman.

Everyone stood silent and motionless on the shore. In keeping with ritual, he added:

"The dead must tend to the living."

And they stayed there, silent, honoring in their hearts those who had passed away before them.

The dead must tend to the living
The living shall know strange friendships

Book of Prayers

ASH

Ash is the boundary of matter and dream, the world made visible in near-evanescence.

祈

PRAYERS

Is the Book of Prayers the oldest book of all? Some think it requires the prior violence of battles. But those who hear the great clouds speak and the breathing of trees know that the first breath is also the first prayer, since no one can fight without first taking in pearls of air.

Like a day slipping between two clouds of ink, like an evening sighing in the weightless mist, wrote the poet. The breath that brings the world to life is necessary to this relaxation from the world—the ecstasy that helps humans to escape themselves, and the magic allowing the world to enter gracefully into them, are the literal text of the first oration. In this impalpable trance, they breathe in unison in the mingled air of the living and the dead, and thus they know what their fathers before them fought, and painted.

An Iris from Ryoan
1800

Hanase, the City of Ashes, the second sanctuary of the mists.

"I seem to recall that the year we studied the four sanctuaries, you were snoring at the back of the class, after stuffing yourself with redcurrants," said Paulus.

"Ah yes, the four sanctuaries," said Petrus, struggling with a vague memory buried by digestion and naps.

They set off. Night was falling, and the lights on the hillside were coming on. Petrus could think of nothing but a good bed and something to fill his stomach, and he found the straight path to the city monotonous.

"The four sanctuaries," he murmured, nodding off and tripping over his tail.

Behind him, Marcus gave a sigh.

"Oh," said Petrus again, stopping short, "the four sanctuaries, Hanase, the City of Ashes."

"Well done," said Marcus, giving him a thump.

"I mean, now I remember. But I'm almost certain that I was asleep during that lesson," said Petrus, captivated by the mechanism he'd just discovered, and beginning to suspect that his awkwardness and distraction could also be his genius.

For now, along the narrow strip of land, the evening mist sighed to the rhythm of lazy twists and turns; although it was almost pitch dark and they couldn't see any trees, the passage was shrouded in those shadowy scatterings of light formed by foliage in good weather, and their nocturnal stroll was resplendent with the lightness of dragonfly wings falling from invisible branches.

"The transparencies of the way to Hanase are renowned," said the boatman, coming up to Petrus. "They are said to be even more beautiful than the ones in Nanzen. Whatever the case may be, they both share the memory of the origins."

"The origins?" echoed Petrus, who was thinking of other things.

He had a headache and everything was muddled again.

"The memory of trees," said the boatman, looking at him, somewhat puzzled.

"What does that have to do with origins?" muttered Petrus out of mere politeness.

The boatman stopped in the middle of the path.

"What do you mean, what does it have to do with origins?" he asked.

"Forgive me, my mind was elsewhere," said Petrus. Suddenly wrested from his thoughts, he didn't understand a thing, but didn't want to get in trouble either.

The boatman began walking again.

"There are some, nowadays, who forget the origins," he said, with a mixture of anger and sadness; "it does not bode well."

"Would you be so kind as to close your trap until tomorrow?" muttered Marcus.

"I was thinking of something else," Petrus replied, "my head is upside down and my stomach is empty."

"He's thinking about eating," said Marcus, turning back to Paulus.

"By the way," said Petrus, "the memory of trees, the whispering of pines, the breathing of the world—I had my fill of all that in the Deep Woods, don't start on it again here."

Paulus tapped him curtly on the head.

"Shut your mouth," he said, "I don't want to hear you blaspheming."

Petrus rubbed his scalp reproachfully.

"What is this city of the dead, anyway? If someone would tell me, maybe I would shut up."

Paulus sighed and, working his way toward the front of the procession, went to speak to the boatman.

"Could you tell us where there might be a teahouse open at this time of night?" he asked.

"I'll take you there," said the boatman, glancing with dismay at Petrus. "You can also sleep there."

But after a short silence, he gave a smile that spread from ear to ear on his silken otter face.

"At least you don't get bored with this one around," he said.

Before long, they arrived at the gates of Hanase. The streets were narrow, but as they walked up toward the top of the hill, they passed large gardens where gray flakes were rising, then enveloping the city. It was dark in those enclosures, and they could just make out the shapes of trees and rocks, and other, rounder shapes, from which the ashen sequins seemed to be wafting. Petrus, who had forgotten his headache and his hunger, followed his companions in silence, absorbed by the unusual atmosphere of the city. They passed a crowd of elves wandering through the halo of cottony particles, along the sides of beautiful houses where wooden verandas were adorned with low tables and comfortable cushions.

"Pilgrimage houses," said the boatman to Paulus, pointing to one of them. "You could have spent the night there, too. But I think your friend needs a more robust experience."

At the very top of the city, they stopped outside a dwelling plunged in darkness. On the wooden sign to the right of the entrance they could only make out the sign for tea.

"The oldest teahouse in Hanase," said the boatman.

"I hope they have room," said Marcus. "I'm exhausted."

"It's Nanzen that ordains the flow of tea," said the boat-man. "There is always room."

He bowed amiably.

"Now I shall leave you," he said.

And to Petrus, half-derisive, half-kindly:

"Good luck, my friend."

The three companions, now on their own, looked at one another.

"Do we have to knock?" asked Paulus.

"Would you rather sing a serenade?" replied Petrus testily.

He was hungry again and he felt a shooting pain in his head. Raising his hand, he prepared to knock.

Before he had time to complete his gesture, the door sound-lessly slid open to reveal a vestibule perfumed with an aroma of undergrowth and iris. On the dirt floor, three large flat stones, freshly rinsed with clear water, invited them to move forward into the darkness. At the back of the entrance, an ele-vated wooden floor led to a doorless opening, enhanced with a short, two-paneled curtain bearing the sign for tea. It had been calligraphed in a style whose name our friends didn't know, but I may reveal it, if you like, because it matters to the beauty of the moment: and so, drawn in the style of wild grasses, the sign for tea invited them to enter. Beneath their bare feet the water was like the ford of a river. In an alcove on the right, an incense stick gave off its fragrance of fresh breeze and humus, wrapping them in a veil of iris and moss.

"I love irises," murmured Petrus (who was not only a stom-ach, but also a nose).

They sat down on the edge of the floor and waited for the soles of their feet to dry. Then they headed toward the opening and, crouching down, crept under the curtain.

In front of them was a long corridor; on either side, closed sliding doors; all around, the dull, gentle sound of rain on stones, although it was dry in the building and there were no signs of the rainstorm, apart from its resonance. The soft melody, however, making its way into the recesses of their hearts, made them feel like crying. They followed the corridor as far as another opening marked by a curtain printed with the same sign. Beyond it was darkness. Paulus, the first to crouch down, went under the cloth, and Marcus and Petrus heard him cry out from very far away.

"I'll bet you that on the other side we'll fall into an endless vortex," murmured Petrus.

"I'm surprised you know that word," said Marcus.

Behind the curtain was a dark vestibule, where it seemed to Petrus all his senses were on the alert; then the scene that had caused Paulus to cry out was revealed to them.

They were standing on a podium overlooking a garden. The moon had risen and illuminated the entire scene, with the help of stone lanterns where torches had been lit. Three earthenware bowls awaited them on the floor. Beyond them was the garden. A stream wound its way to a pond where the dark sky was reflected. Crowning the motionless waters were the bare azaleas of winter, their branches reaching out in battle order, and they offered the eye even more joy than the summer generosity of their flowers. All around the pond was a beach streaked with parallel lines. In a few places, they could see the leaves of a heavenly bamboo plant standing above the furrows on the shoreline; in another spot, three rounded stones added commas to the text of the sand. Further still the moon, streaming with a weave of light, polished the leaves of the maple trees. But although the garden was very beautiful, it did not derive its substance from its natural elements: at the end of the pond, a bronze basin tossed light ashes up into the twilight; they flew into the ether like moths, rising slowly from the bowl into the sky.

"It is a funeral urn," murmured Petrus.

"It is a funeral urn," said a female voice, causing them to turn in unison to see a snow-white mare smiling amiably at them.

She changed into a female hare, her fur sparkling with moonlight, iridescent with silvery shimmers. When at last she became a woman, they could not take their eyes off her timeless face, a delicate mother-of-pearl that seemed to have been dusted with a transparent cloud, and this eternal beauty, and the exquisite texture of her complexion, left Petrus with the impression of an unfamiliar, grandiose world.

"The boatman asked us to receive you this evening," she said.

And, to Petrus:

"If you will give me your garment, we will wash it."

His fur turned crimson.

"You will be more comfortable as a man, to drink tea," she said.

Then she added:

"Apparently the boatman likes you."

Petrus, in torment, handed his soiled clothes to her, and she disappeared behind the curtain.

Paulus and Marcus looked at him and guffawed.

"Luxury cleaning," said Paulus, mocking.

"You offloaded your puke onto the most beautiful creature in the universe," Marcus pointed out.

"I didn't do it on purpose," said Petrus, wretchedly.

"That's worse," said Paulus, "that means you'll do it again."

They gazed silently at the garden. Stones had been laid on the bed of the stream in order to create the loveliest melody, and now the scene was lulled with its special music. This type of activity had always bored Petrus as much as tea calligraphy and flower arranging, along with pottery and singing, that were part of a young elf's education for an unbelievable length of time. He got pins and needles in his legs when it came to art lessons, and his only consolation was the presence of flowers, which he loved passionately. Most of the time, alas, he had to make do with looking at some unfortunate peony withering on its stem before it was stuck in its vase beneath the tea poem. But whenever he tried to complete the exercise, which meant he rummaged at random in the floral display, the professor looked vexed and, shaking his head, murmured some vague excuse before grabbing the flower from his hands.

"You just put a white tulip under an ode to three scarlet camellias," Paulus said to him. "Can't you try and read, at least?"

"If only we could eat them," sighed Petrus in return.

In fact, he did nibble at them now and again, in secret, for not only was he crazy about the perfume of flowers, but also their taste, and he knew all the ones that were edible. You must understand the extent of Petrus's extravagance: elves do not eat much in the way of flowers or leaves, any more than, by nature, they eat any part of an animal, since the former are the source of life and the latter are their brothers—and so a feast of that kind was tantamount to devouring the very cause of their existence or worse yet, devouring themselves, and Petrus was always very careful to hide when he indulged in his vice. Clover, violets, and nasturtiums featured in the trio of his preferences, but he wouldn't turn his nose up at a wild rose, either, and they grew in abundance around the family home, because his mother knew of nothing more refined than their fragile corollas above their black thorns. As Petrus feared his mother more than any other secular power on earth, he was doubly mindful when pillaging the woods. As a result, he was never caught, and remained awkward when it came to subjects that did not interest him, but crafty and furtive when his desire was aroused.

This time, Petrus was sensitive to the charm of the stream. Night was deepening and something inside him was slowing down. A flake landed on his paw and he gazed at it with curiosity.

"No one knows who we are looking at," said the hare elf, startling him.

He looked again at the ash, so light and potent in its near-immaterial state.

"Are they our dead?" he asked.

She handed him his clothes.

"They are our dead," she replied.

Petrus regretfully allowed the ash to fly away and he took his clothes back, covering himself just as he was transformed into a man.

"You are a high-elf," said Marcus. "This is the first time we've met a representative of your house."

She motioned to them to sit down by the three empty bowls. A high-elf, thought Petrus, that is why there is an invisible burden on her shoulders and a perfume of hidden worlds all around her. Maybe that's what I am looking for.

"It's not what you are looking for," she said. "Your destiny is elsewhere, but I don't know how to see it. Unprecedented things are happening in the mists these days, and we have become attentive to unusual circumstances. Perhaps you are one of the pieces of this strange puzzle that is being assembled."

Paulus and Marcus adopted the expression of the well-brought-up who must not be rude, and Petrus himself, although flattered, seemed doubtful.

"Puzzle?" he asked courteously, all the same.

"The Council issued a new alert yesterday in several provinces where the mist is in difficulty," she said.

"Has it affected Hanase?" asked Paulus.

"As you were able to see from the lock, our mist is intact," she replied.

A shadow passed over her face.

"The day it is affected, we can bid farewell to this world."

She made a graceful gesture with her right hand.

"But these are merely passing nighttime thoughts."

They saw that the bowls had been filled with a golden tea that flickered with the same light as the bronze sides of the basin.

"One of you must choose a flower and recite a poem," she said.

Marcus looked mockingly at Petrus.

"Would Mr. Puzzle feel up to honoring his studious past?" he asked.

Astonishingly, Mr. Puzzle did feel up to it. Was it the strangeness of the situation, the hollow feeling in his stomach, or the touch of the flake of ash—it seemed to him that the inanity of his years of schooling was being driven against the cliffs of the present moment, releasing a trembling corolla from its gangue.

"I would like an iris," he said.

An iris appeared, lying between the bowls, smaller than those you are accustomed to seeing in your gardens, its white petals dotted with pale blue, its heart deep purple, and its stamens orange.

"A Ryoan iris," she said. "They are to be found mainly in the province of Dark Mists, but one can also occasionally come upon them around here. In the tradition of the worlds, irises are messengers, flowers of annunciation."

"The tradition of the worlds?" asked Petrus. "What worlds?"

"The world of elves and the world of humans," she said. "I have studied the human symbolism of flowers, and it is similar to our own."

"Are you acquainted with the world of humans?" said Petrus.

"No," she replied, "you can only see it from Nanzen, but I

used to belong to the Council's community of gardeners. In my moments of leisure, I went to the library to read books about humans and flowers."

"Humans really exist," asked Marcus, "they're not just a legend?"

"A legend?" she said, surprised.

"It's hard to believe in something that only exists in your thoughts," said Marcus.

"Existence is not a variable given," she said. "Reality is the place where hunger and faith, life and death, dreams and flowers all come together and blend. A tree, an elf, a note of music, a chimera born from the night—everything exists while proceeding from the same matter, and all is displayed within the same universe."

She fell silent and Petrus suddenly thought of a poem, which he recited to those gathered there.

The mandate and the realm
In the heart of an old woman
An iris from Ryoan

Paulus and Marcus looked at him, stunned, but their hostess closed her eyes and was contemplative for a moment.

"I cannot see everything your poem is invoking," she said. "There are the living, the dead, and strange friendships."

"I saw . . . I saw peculiar images," said Petrus.

He tried to grasp one of them as it was slipping away, like flowing water.

"There was a faint sound from another world," he murmured, troubled.

She looked at him thoughtfully. After a moment, she made the ritual gesture of invitation by placing her hands, joined at her fingertips, on the floor, and bowing her face toward them. They greeted her by bowing their heads in turn and raising their bowls to the sky. Then they drank. The moon sparkled and sent a silvery flash through the ashes. The tea tasted of clay and chalk turning into dust and dirt.

"I've never drunk anything like this," said Paulus.

"This tea is a thousand years old," she said.

"A thousand years?" gasped Marcus. "To what do we owe the honor?"

"To the boatman, and Nanzen," she said.

"I didn't know that a simple boatman could prevail upon Nanzen to serve a thousand-year-old tea to three traveling strangers," said Paulus.

"A simple boatman? The channel that connects the Marches to the Ashes is one of the most ancient in this world," she said, "and it is always remarkable elves who seek to be in charge of it. Moreover, otters constitute a very particular lower house, engendering some of the most extraordinary characters in the mists."

"Why is that?" asked Petrus.

"If you will just take another sip," she replied, "you'll see why."

They drank again from their bowls. Ever since Paulus and Marcus, still under the effect of the tea from the Marches, had landed on the shores of Hanase, they'd been hearing the distant sounds of the dead all around them, mingled with the effervescence of the living. The first sip of the thousand-year-old tea, making its way to as yet untouched layers of empathy, had transformed the dull echo into a faint clamor, which the second sip evolved into a symphonic uproar. For Petrus, however, who had emptied his last flask from the Deep Woods long before they'd reached the departure lock and, consequently, had no longer been receiving much from the mist for a good while, there was nothing miraculous about the first sip at all, but the shock of the second one was so intense that he thanked the heavens that his stomach was empty. You must understand how the voices of Hanase's dead resonate. Their song delivers no message, there are merely ashes mingled with air—and this snow into which past lives have been diluted transforms reality into a vague music, a drifting threnody that enters each elf as much as he flows into it, that melts the limits of his being to dilate it beyond what is visible, and transforms the world into a fluid place where the living and the dead move together.

"I feel like I'm swimming," Petrus finally managed to say, clinging to his bowl.

"That is the lesson of the ashes," she said. "We are all mixed together in the same air. You felt nauseous because you passed without transition from an awareness of the borders to the intuition of the mixture."

"Is that where this sensation of being immersed comes from?" asked Petrus.

"Everything always comes from contact with everything else, through immersion into the vaporous matter. It is through that matter that we can mix with others and be transformed without losing ourselves; it is also through it that life and death are mingled. The thousand-year-old tea simply made this fluidity more perceptible to you."

After a moment, she added:

"Otters swim at the border between earth and water, and live in the heart of the memory of sharing."

The vision of an old, wrinkled face crossed Petrus's mind, then vanished.

"Do humans have the same appearance as us?" he asked. "I think I just saw the old woman in the poem in my thoughts."

"I saw her, too," she said. "It would definitely seem that you are destined for strange encounters."

"It's just a vision," said Petrus.

She did not reply.

"Does the path to the lock preserve the memory of vanished trees?" asked Paulus.

"Of all living things, trees best incarnate the reality of mutations," she said. "They are the motionless vectors of the genesis and transformation of all things. The transparencies of the path are made from the invisible presence of trees long dead, but which, like ashes, live on with us in another form."

They mused for a moment on this transparency beyond death.

"What does *to be with* mean if one is no longer conscious?" asked Paulus.

"What we are before our birth and after our death," she said. "A promise and a memory."

"For the living," he said.

"For the living," she replied. "Those who have passed are fully fledged members of the great people who are entrusted to us, and the duty to respond to their call is what we call the life of the dead."

"Is that what the high-elves do?" asked Petrus. "Respond to this call?"

"Some are born to assume responsibility for other creatures," she said. "That is our realm, and our mandate, the ministry that gives life to the powers of death, to their territory and legacy. This eternity and this responsibility are henceforth incumbent upon you, because today you have drunk from the thousand-year-old tea."

The garden glittered with shards of moonlight. The sensation of immersion was growing stronger. They drank a third and last sip of tea. Petrus, in spite of his dislike for metaphysical effusions, let himself go to the peace of the mixture and wondered how the ashes were moved to these bottomless urns. At funerals, the bodies of deceased elves were burned, but he'd never known that they were subsequently taken to Hanase. They were scattered from the deceased elf's favorite mountaintop, and then disappeared from view forever.

"Nothing disappears forever," said their hostess. "The ashes are brought here by the mists. The bottomless urns are what is left of the eternity they passed through before returning to mingle with the time of the living."

"So, the dead are alive?" asked Paulus.

"Of course not," she said with a laugh, "they are dead."

Petrus smiled. Indisputably, the trip was improving. His nausea had left him and the shock of the second sip of tea was dissolving into the third. He drifted nonchalantly about, and heard the tumult of the dead without attaching any more importance to it than to the twilight poems from his Woods. The fact she'd laughed at the thought the dead could be alive reinforced his indifference toward mystic effusions. And yet, he thought, I can hear the song of the dead more clearly than I can feel the presence of the living.

She got up.

"Your beds are ready," she said.

But before taking her leave, she said to Petrus:

"In Katsura, you will go to the Council library and you will introduce yourself as a friend of the Wild Grasses."

"The Wild Grasses?" he repeated, surprised.

"It is the name of our establishment," she said.

They bowed deeply, finding nothing to say that was equal to what they had just experienced.

"I hope you will forgive us our peasant ways for not knowing how to thank you," said Marcus finally.

"Only now is the true experience beginning," she said.

She waved her hand toward the bottom of the garden.

"Your quarters are on the other side."

And then she was gone.

They stood for a moment in silence gazing at the scene. A cloud drifted on a patch of moon and the world's rhythms had slowed. The ashes rose toward the heavens in lazy swirls, the melody of the stream became more languid, and the light on the maple leaves stopped glistening. As for the song of the dead, it expanded still further, deeper, more solemn—such peace, suddenly, thought Petrus, and he felt the spirits of repose enfold him.

"Shall we go?" said Paulus.

There was no visible path to the other end of the garden, and they had to resign themselves to walking on the sand. But although they felt as if they were sinking into it, their steps didn't disturb the lines. The further they went, the more the distance seemed to increase, and the maples as a whole looked as if they were retreating and growing larger. Above all, there was a different quality to the air in the garden—sharper, giving clarity to one's thoughts. Perception gained in precision, and crossing the enclosed space became a journey. But a journey to where? wondered Petrus. Or to whom?

Suddenly he knew he was heading toward someone, that every step was taking him closer to their encounter, and that he had come to this place solely for that purpose.

At last they reached the end of the garden. On the other side of the row of maple trees, standing on pilings driven deep into the black water, a wooden platform awaited them for the night. As they went closer, the sounds of the garden were stifled, and they felt as if they were entering a bubble of silence. Then the garden behind them also vanished, and they found themselves on a moonlit island, lost in the middle of a dark lagoon. There was not a breath of air; in harmony with the rhythms of the earth, the stars refrained from twinkling. Summoning their courage, they went up the steps; on the floor of the platform, the ripple of an invisible stream swirled around their ankles.

However, all that interested them were the mattresses set out for the comfort of their night. Soft and thick to look at, they were made of moving ash.

"Ash mattresses?" murmured Petrus.

"Night of the dead," Petrus heard himself reply, just as colossal fatigue came down upon their shoulders.

If only I could reach that mattress, he thought, before taking another step and collapsing onto his bed of dust.

It was a strange night, where he wandered in his dreams along a path lined with tall trees, aware that he was stepping on human ground. Whether the light was different or there was a sense of negligence in the woods—a sort of fantasy about the copses and passages, as if they'd been trimmed and traced at random—one could sense a presence there, and its nonchalance was pleasing to him. The path led to the edge of the trees, and came out to face a landscape of verdant hills. In the distance, two sparkling little lakes; all around, vineyards nestling into the landscape; below them, a village in a valley. Thin lines of smoke rose from stone houses with steep, tawny roofs; judging by the tender green hue of the vegetation, it was springtime; seasonal flowers were breaking through the freshly turned earth of the plots. There was an abundance of the veined, purple hellebores much appreciated by elves as the end of winter draws near; but there were also daffodils, tulips scarcely opened and crunchy as oatcakes, and grape hyacinths interspersed with crocuses and cyclamens. Above these lovely carpets, tall irises formed battalions in charge of overseeing the gardens. Their lower petals were puffed out in a hanging curve which seemed to form a face with velvet cheeks, from which a bearded tongue emerged. These were taller, more complicated irises than the ones in Ryoan, with something inexplicably martial and slightly ridiculous about them, but they spread all around them the same fragrance of annunciation and message, turning each plot into the guardian of a secret. They're growing vegetables that will ripen in summer, thought Petrus, and you can smell the simples which perfume and heal. After a moment, he added: this is a dream, but it is all true, and I can go on ahead without fear of waking. He began walking toward the village. In the blue sky, a little tasseled cloud went by and a breeze began to blow. It caressed his nostrils with the perfume of the tulips, mingled with a touch of lemon balm; the path wound through the springtime trees and he was intoxicated with this unusual display of nature. Here, anything is possible, he thought. When he reached the first houses, he thought again: this countryside is my landscape.

Then everything faded, because the old woman in the tea poem was coming toward him, her arms laden with wildflowers. She was smiling in the spring light and Petrus liked looking at her aged face, like parchment beneath her headdress with ribbons the color of forget-me-nots. Borage flowers matched their azure cheer, and there was a brisk, mischievous charm about her appearance. She went by him without seeing him and he decided to follow her. After a moment, she paused by a row of pink irises, then went into a farmyard. She glanced over her shoulder, went up the steps to the entrance, and disappeared inside. Petrus stood there for a moment, petrified. Reality was transfigured by this brief gaze, which he alone had seen, into a succession of scenes bathed in an unreal light. He now knew that the old peasant woman had given birth to a daughter, and that daughter to another daughter who, in the future, would conceive her own daughter in turn, until the line of women ended with the arrival, in the fifth generation, of a much-loved son. He knew that the last-born girl would inherit the science of simples from her ancestor, and that the true encounter would be that of the last female descendant, not yet born. And so, the theater of worlds was revealed to him. Gigantic fronts covered an entire continent, endless smoke rose toward the sky, armies gathered beneath a sky of storm, and the much-loved son lay dying on a field littered with corpses. He stood for a moment gazing with horror at this rumbling apocalypse until, without warning, the scene changed. In the sweetness of a summer twilight, tables had been adorned in the garden with large June irises, and a female voice was saying: *the lovely evenings around Saint John's Day*, then, after a silence: *go, my son, and know for eternity how much we love you.* How is it that I can understand her language? he wondered, and at that very moment he woke up. He raised his hand to his heart. Everything is in the dream, he thought; landscape, love, and war. He recalled the words of the hare elf: *the day the mist of Hanase disappears, we can bid farewell to this world*—and was overcome by a premonition of coming disaster. Come now, he said to himself, I'm raving. But before the last vestiges of the dream could dissipate, he thought again: there you have ecstasy and tragedy beneath a beribboned headdress. Finally, he was fully awake.

They thought they were resting on mattresses of ash above black water, but they'd slept on layers of cool grass right on the floor of the very first platform. It was raining, and the garden was gleaming. What the showers do to the garden, thought Petrus, and in the world; here, they pass by, they concentrate the universe. Abandoning himself to the music of water falling upon water, he delighted in this liquid encounter, where the ordinary time of the living was erased.

"It is time to go," said Marcus, "the first channel to Katsura is about to open."

They stood up and looked at one another.

"Did everyone dream of great things?" asked Paulus.

The other two nodded their heads.

"We'd better get going," said Petrus, "I'm hungry and I want to drink as much tea as possible before the departure."

He suddenly felt it was urgent to get under way and, looking one last time at the pond, he thought: everything is beginning.

They went back down the corridor they had taken the night before, went again through the vestibule fragrant with iris, and came out into the street in dazzling sunlight. There was no trace of the garden's warm, melancholy rain. All around whirled ashes, stitched with clarity by the morning light. Now that they were going down to the lock, the crowd grew thick and, at last they reached the grand channel that led to Katsura. As it opened out before them, huge and grandiose, a hundred barges appeared.

"We are late," said Petrus, before rushing into the way station building, where a host of steaming teapots awaited them.

He took long sips of a black tea that tasted of chestnut, before gobbling down a tray of little tarts dripping with honey. Paulus and Marcus, who followed at a more leisurely pace, nibbled decorously on a few mouthfuls of pumpkin mille-feuille, and after that they went out and stood at the back of the line on the pier.

The barges could accommodate a dozen voyagers, but as they quietly boarded the last one, they found themselves alone with two wild boar elves accompanied by one of their piglets. Petrus scrupulously followed the instructions of the boat-men—otters, beavers, and seagulls—who were overseeing the maneuvers with a watchful eye. Fully satisfied that he'd accomplished his task, he collapsed in his designated seat.

Then the barges set off in the liquid mist, and they departed without knowing that now, they were traveling in the company of their dead.

Brothers, do not forget the mandate and the realm
Sons, in the heart of an old woman an iris from Ryoan

Book of Prayers

死者

THE DEAD

Elves can understand their dead without envoys, since they welcome everything that has been and ever will be by means of tea and mist. Thus, every elf stays in the second sanctuary at least once in his life—whether he knows it or not, he will go there.

Released from the desire to live, the dead do not wish to weep and do not wish to laugh. They cultivate emotion without appetite, and joy beyond conquest. They know how to uncover meaning that is not drowned in thirst. And it is through this quest, detached from necessity, that the intuition of the beauty of living can be born.

But few men understand now the wisdom of immersion in ash.

PAINTINGS

In Petrus's dream, the theater of worlds was lit by that cold, pure light that has inspired the most beautiful works of art. Paintings are the motionless translations of our moving dreams, which in return bathe us with the clarity of paintings.

No one will be surprised to learn, therefore, that a canvas painted in Amsterdam in 1514 played a decisive role in this story. It had to do with the first bridge between the worlds, but also with murder and its immeasurable consequences.

One must be familiar with the light and landscapes of the North to understand this singular artist's decision to settle in Amsterdam, for he could just as easily have gone south, east, or west, since from the pavilion he'd been given a free rein to begin his human life wherever he desired.

Finally, one must be acquainted with the history of humans and elves to understand what he decided to paint, and to penetrate, beneath the visible surface, the invisible sparkling.

The invisible sparkling behind the transparency of tears.

Wild Grasses in the Snow
1800

They set off, unaware that they were now traveling with their dead. The journey from Hanase to Katsura, the capital of the elves, would take six hours, and Petrus intended to have a pleasant time along the way. He'd drunk the tea from the Ashes and filled his stomach. Moreover, the sight of the hundred barges gliding over the liquid mist had been well worth the trip. The barges advanced ten abreast, forming a magnificent display in the wide channel. And so, I find myself enjoying the sight, thought Petrus, surprised by this contemplative mood, attuned to the memory of the tea-house. What really happened there, I wonder, he thought again, recalling the night of the dead. Finally, he set aside his orderly thinking, and let himself go into the gentle trance of the voyage. No one spoke, the boatmen only voiced brief instructions regarding the passengers' comfort—it could go on like this forever, thought Petrus and, suddenly weary, he yawned noisily.

"There are six hours less ten minutes of crossing remaining," Marcus pointed out.

"Six hours less ten minutes of potential disaster," muttered Paulus.

"I drank the tea," said Petrus, offended.

Paulus studied him skeptically, but Petrus was already lost in the new vistas the channel offered.

In the monochromatic setting of the mist, wild grasses had

sprouted, spindly and sublime in an airy dishevelment, and they looked as if they'd been penned with black ink, as they stood stark against the whiteness of the décor in irregular groups, some as bushy as copses, others no more than three sprigs bending gracefully, like the necks of mourning women.

"The name of the teahouse," he murmured.

In the evanescence of the world, the grasses evoked the lines of a text. They were unbelievably graceful, because they rose out of the mist with no sign of their roots, but what intrigued Petrus most was that the black tufts could be read like calligraphy. This beauty of the handwritten poetry which, up to now, he'd always found deadly dull, now seemed vibrant and full of meaning to him. Something was calling him, and for the first time he felt *penetrated* by figures from without; their enigmatic tale promised far greater delights than any he'd found in the poems he knew from his youth. For elves, you see, have too much respect for the living kingdom ever to constrain it; they allow their woods and their pastures the freedom to grow as they see fit; consequently, their inner gardener is merely the servant of nature, a prism refracting and sublimating nature. But one thing Petrus knew for certain was that there was something about the channel's wild grasses that couldn't be summed up either by the freedom of natural things nor by any intention to magnify them—shimmering inlaid with a touch of adventure; a mystery that delighted with its perfume of enchanted revelation. Perhaps that something is inside me? he wondered, and for the second time in as many days two lines of verse came to him.

Wild grasses in the snow
Two children of November

I'm turning into a poet, he thought, amused. Two children, that's not elfin, it's human, he reflected. Suddenly, everything disappeared, the channel was empty once again, and he felt orphaned. Go on, he thought, I'm not good at crossings. He wedged himself into his seat to have a nap, but an image suddenly came to his mind, so clear that it caused him to sit bolt upright. A little girl was walking toward him, wrapped in an iridescent veil that drifted slowly around her. Marcus looked at Petrus, raising a questioning eyebrow, and the apparition vanished. However, it stayed in his mind and again he saw the serious little face—ten years old, perhaps—the dark golden skin, her mouth like a stain of new blood. Then the vision was gone.

"Everything all right?" asked Marcus.

He nodded, and eased into his seat again. No one spoke; before long, he dozed off.

He awoke with a start, driven by a feeling of urgency. It seemed as if he had slept long and deep, and he hoped the journey was nearly over.

"You slept for a good two hours, snoring like a trumpet," said Marcus spitefully. "So, we couldn't get any sleep."

"Two hours?" echoed Petrus. "So there are four more hours to go?"

"Apparently snoring doesn't affect the ability to do math," said Marcus to Paulus.

"I'll never last," said Petrus.

"What do you mean, last?" asked Paulus.

"I have to do something about the tea I drank," he replied, looking all around him.

Marcus and Paulus studied him with consternation.

"How many cups did you drink?" Marcus finally asked.

"I don't know," said Petrus, annoyed, "maybe a dozen. You're not about to reproach me for being conscientious?"

"A dozen," echoed Paulus.

"Didn't you read the signs?" asked Marcus.

"Was it too much for you to read the signs?" asked Paulus.

"We were late," said Petrus, "I wasn't about to waste time reading poems."

There was a silence.

"They weren't poems?" he asked.

Marcus and Paulus didn't reply.

"I didn't read the signs," he said. "I was busy drinking."

"And eating," said Marcus.

"Otherwise you would've learned that because of the length of the crossing, they recommended drinking only one cup of tea," added Paulus.

"It's highly concentrated," said Marcus.

"And the toilets are at the way station, to be used before departure," said Paulus.

"But usually we don't need to explain that to anyone other than elfkins," said Marcus finally.

When Marcus said, "highly concentrated," Petrus began to suspect something.

"Did you see the grasses?" he asked.

"Grasses?" said Paulus.

"The wild grasses," said Petrus.

"There were no wild grasses," said Marcus.

Petrus registered his reply with interest, but his bladder, alas, now required all his attention.

"I can't possibly hold it for four hours," he said, beginning to sweat like a pig.

"Well, you will have to," said Marcus.

"That's a superelfin feat," said Petrus, "I can't."

Paulus let out a whistle of irritation.

"Not on the barge, in any case," he said.

"And especially not in the mists," said Marcus.

Then he gave a sigh.

"Take off your clothes," he said, "and do what you have to do inside them."

"My clothes?" said Petrus, horrified.

"Then you'll just have to hold it," answered Marcus.

Petrus felt so pitiful, and the prospect of soiling his clothing yet again was so disgusting to him, that he wanted to
believe he could do the impossible. For ten minutes, he wrig-
gled like a worm on his seat, changing from horse to squirrel,
then man, unable to find either a position or a shape that might
bring him some relief.

"If you make yourself sick on top of it," said Paulus, exas-
perated, "that wouldn't be very smart, either."

Petrus was about to reply when he noticed that the young
wild boar elf was looking at him with interest. All I need is a
spectator, he thought, annoyed. The boar's parents had fallen
asleep, but their offspring was watching him with his lovely
brown eyes fringed with rebellious eyelashes and, in spite of
the urgency of the moment, Petrus took note of the roundness
of his young snout, the delicate line of the stripes on his back,
and the adorable neatness of his silky hooves. How could such
a pretty animal become so ugly when it grew up? he wondered—for although the wild boars of the mists are a more
handsome species than those to be found on human earth, they
are not particularly refined, either. Petrus was already not
crazy about hazelnuts and acorns, but the thought of digging
in the ground to feed off them turned his stomach (moreover,
like his fellows, unless circumstances dictated otherwise, he
only fed when he was in human form, and he even suspected
that his horse self was allergic to forage).

The young wild boar, captivated by his contortions, was still
scrutinizing him unabashedly.

"You drank too much tea," he said, "I saw you at the way
station, you were really thirsty."

"I wasn't thirsty," snapped Petrus.

"I can give you a vase," said the boar, ignoring his answer.
"It's a present for the Head of the Council. If you like, you can

borrow it, you can empty it when we arrive and give it back to me discreetly. Your clothes wouldn't be enough," he added, realistically. "So that's why I thought of the vase."

There was a prolonged silence, then Paulus cleared his throat.

"That's very kind of you," he said, "but we cannot do that."

"And why not?" asked the piglet, turning into the most admirable little human specimen you could ever meet.

His blond hair was perfectly matched by his blue eyes, which were virtually impossible to look away from. Was it the fact they were so light, almond-shaped, magnified by sweet lashes that were also blond, and garlanded with perfect brows? Or were those eyes so beautiful because of the spark that migrated from those artfully drawn pink lips, lighting an exquisite fire in them? The young elf was smiling at them, and it seemed as if the world was glistening, so much so that Petrus, bewitched by such an endearing face, briefly forgot his torment.

"A vase intended for the Head of the Council cannot be used as a urinal," continued Paulus.

But he couldn't take his eyes off the splendid young face either.

"It won't diminish its beauty," said the boy, and he smiled again.

Marcus, Paulus, and Petrus, lost in that smile as if they were in a forest carpeted with periwinkle, all felt their resolution give way at the same time.

"It simply isn't done," said Marcus, in a final effort at decency which lacked all resolve.

The elfkin reached for the vase, which was wrapped in a soft poppy print fabric and stamped with family seals in flat tints of ink. Elves have two seals, that of their animal self and that of their personal house. The seal of wild boars, in tribute to the species' preference for nocturnal life, consists of a waning moon above a tea plantation. Added to this was the piglet's own family seal, a spotted iris against a background of tiny stars. Said piglet checked that his parents were asleep, and he went over to the threesome, whose will was as weak as their reflexes. There was a hypnotic fluidity about his movements, and while he was removing the vase from its cloud of poppies, Petrus, Marcus, and Paulus looked at him dumbly. He set it down before them.

"It's an urn," murmured Paulus.

It was indeed an urn, of light, changing bronze, alternately fawn, gray, brown, or, finally, a milky comet white.

"It comes from the oldest bronze foundry in the mists," answered the elfkin. "We came to Hanase for it, and we are taking it to Katsura to give it to the Head of the Council."

"I thought that urns didn't travel," said Paulus.

"Only bottomless urns," he replied.

He changed into a colt, a ravishing bay colt—but however adorable he might be, the spell that had bound the threesome was broken, and Petrus shook his head as if emerging from a dream.

"I appreciate your offer," he said to the colt, "but I cannot accept it."

And as the moment was dire, and he didn't think he could wait any longer, he took a few steps toward the back of the barge, turned to one side and, revealing his white buttocks, removed his clothing. Then he turned into a squirrel and relieved himself as discreetly as he could. It felt so good and so wretched that he could have wept twice over, and in the end, in fact, it was tears of gratitude that came, because in addition to the remarkable relief, a miracle had occurred: the more he wet his garment, the faster it dried. The supple cloth absorbed the liquid, creased, then dried. When he'd finished his business, he didn't dare get dressed again, but he waved the cloth in front of Paulus, Marcus, and the colt.

"Well, I never," said Paulus. "When it rains it doesn't dry that quickly."

"I'm astonished we didn't know this before," said Petrus, "it would have spared me a few very nasty minutes."

"You must be the first elf who has ever urinated in his clothing, that's why," said Paulus.

"It's cosmic," said the colt, turning into a piglet.

Once he was human again he wrapped up the urn and laid it at his parents' feet. They were napping quietly, and Petrus was surprised that this pair of peaceable high-elves had given birth to such a subtle little monster, for he didn't doubt for a moment that the blond boy was as handsome as the very devil. Once the enchantment of his smile and sky-blue eyes had waned, Petrus felt a fleeting intuition of danger, and now that the young elf was coming back toward them, he still felt an unease, something the boy's dazzling face couldn't dissipate.

"Which province are you from?" Marcus asked him.

"We are from Ryoan," he replied, "which is why we have the iris on our coat of arms. My father is the Council emissary for the province of Dark Mists. He presides over the permanent assembly and is in command of the regular units."

"Is it customary for envoys to offer urns to the Head of the Council?" asked Paulus.

"Ordinarily," said the elfkin, "we give presents to everyone in the upper chamber. But this is an election year and we thank the departing head with personal gifts."

"That's right," said Marcus, "I'd forgotten, the Head of the Council has been serving for four hundred years."

"It's a historic moment," said the elfkin, "when you reach Katsura it will be bubbling with excitement."

"So there will be a new guardian in Nanzen," said Paulus thoughtfully. "If I'm not mistaken, he will be appointed by the Head of the Council, then voted on by the new councilors."

"I will go to Nanzen someday," declared their traveling companion straight out.

Marcus laughed.

"How can you know that?" he asked.

"I will be appointed Guardian of the Pavilion," replied the elfkin, "and I will be the master of Nanzen."

They looked at him, flabbergasted.

"Desire makes destiny," said the little high-elf. "In the meantime, we will support our champion."

"Who is this champion?" asked Petrus.

"A high-elf hare from the Dark Mists who is running for office for the first time, against a high-elf hare from the province of Snows, who is already on the Council."

"Ryoan versus Katsura," said Paulus. "Our Deep Woods are not about to give rise to a leader."

"All it takes is a little ambition," said the elfkin. "Don't you want to be part of history?"

"We are members of lower houses," said Marcus, "I suppose that explains why we have so little appetite for power. History, on the other hand, belongs to everyone. And I didn't know that you could call a candidate a champion."

"We've never had a more unusual candidate," said the elfkin. "He doesn't belong to the inner circle of councilors, even though he does come from another prestigious lineage, that of the Council's master gardeners. He is so brilliant that in only two hundred years he has managed to obtain the endorsement of the councilors. Now he has his eye on the ultimate office."

"Will your family vote for him?" asked Petrus.

"My family and many others. The elves are afraid, they need a daring leader to fight against the new dangers of our time."

"New dangers?" echoed Marcus.

The other elf looked at him as if he'd just stepped out of a dusty closet.

"The day before yesterday the Council issued a new alert regarding several provinces where the mists are in difficulty."

"Yes," send Paulus, "we already heard about it in Hanase. What does that have to do with your daring leader?"

"My father thinks this is only the beginning of a long death, and that we need someone who will not be afraid to face the causes."

"And what might these causes be?" asked Petrus.

He was in a bad mood from being stuck in his squirrel essence, and he could feel the defiance growing inside him. The young elf turned into a piglet while taking his time to reply. He lowered his lashes graciously and when he looked up again he said in a conspiratorial tone:

"Humans."

The other three looked at him aghast and he seemed pleased with the effect he'd had.

"How could humans have anything to do with the fluctuations of the mist?" asked Paulus, puzzled.

"It's a long story," said the piglet.

He wanted to continue, but suddenly something shook the barge violently. A murmur of astonishment spread over the channel and the boatmen closed the communicating canals. The shock woke the piglet's parents, and when they found their son in the company of the threesome, they came over, smiling, and bowed amiably. In their human shape, they were indecently good looking, as dark as their child was blond.

"I hope our young chatterbox hasn't been too much of a bother," said the father.

"Not at all," said Paulus politely.

"Quite astonishing, that sudden jolt," said the mother, frowning.

She had a deep voice with something of a drawl, which Petrus liked.

"Your son told us you are from Ryoan," said Paulus. "I've heard it's an incomparable city."

"You are very welcome there," she replied, "we are always happy to share the splendor of our dark mists. May I ask where you are from?"

They didn't have time to reply because new instructions required the passengers to remain seated and the three wild boar elves returned to their seats. But after a moment, as nothing particular was happening, everyone began once again to enjoy the gentle pleasure of being on the water. As for Petrus, he was thinking. *Perhaps you are one of the pieces of the puzzle that is being assembled*, the hare elf at the teahouse had said—and, indeed, he felt as if they had drifted into the center of a game that was beyond them. Even though the wild grasses in the channel were hallucinations, a product of his exaggerated consumption of tea, they disturbed him as much as real writing would have done. *And even if they are chimeras, shouldn't they make us see something?* he wondered. Then, exhausted by all these incongruous considerations, which were giving him a headache, he fell asleep. But before nodding off he had one last thought: what an adventure! And as he slipped into sleep, he smiled.

At last they reached Katsura.

"Our first real lock," said Paulus.

The boatmen woke the travelers shortly before the channel began to close again behind the barges, which stayed motionless on a patch of liquid mist while other mists, to the rear, returned to vapor. Facing them was the void of still more mist: the lock. The boatmen sought their positions in successive adjustments of a few centimeters, the channel grew ever narrower, and before long the boats were lined up side by side on the last square of liquid in the world. No sound, no movement; the mist coiled on itself as time was suspended and everyone held their breath. Not a single native of this world was ignorant of the fact that the lock at Katsura was dangerous, and although it had not happened in five centuries, a distracted mooring maneuver could throw barges, boatmen, and voyagers into the void from which none would return.

After a long while the boatmen relaxed, just as a sound came to their ears, and the mist lifted to reveal, far below them, the great city bathed in light. They went slowly down toward Katsura, following a vertical trajectory which had given its name, the Well of Mist, to the lock, a well of half a league that was used ten times a day in both directions by one to two hundred boatloads of pilgrims. It was the middle of the afternoon and the November sun shone above the gray roofs. There was no sign yet of the lovely soft snow that covers the province from the end of the year until the first days of April; plum and maple trees blazed with their autumn colors, and from above, Katsura looked as if it were on fire; tall gingko trees added amber touches, like will-o'-the-wisps frozen in flight. Beyond them was a landscape of trees in fog with a few isolated villages here and there, but what dominated were the vaporous mountains the city backed onto. They overlooked the snowy peaks that circled the city and created such an imposing lofty landscape that Katsura seemed to be floating there like the survivor of a shipwreck. Closer inspection of the city revealed it to be more solid and firmly anchored than rock, because the mist, in contrast, gave it a vigor that no solid ground could have conferred. As the descent continued, the mist grew ever larger and seemed to muster a force that would have been threatening were it not for the beauty and harmony it shared with the rest of the landscape.

At last, the docks came into sight. The disembarkation zone was just before the city, offering a new perspective that was equally dizzying, for what could be more breathtaking than this spill of wooden houses interwoven with the most beautiful trees on earth? The trees were set among the buildings in a random order that to Petrus seemed not unlike the wild grasses in the channel: thus, his first sight of Katsura was also under the seal of a text waiting to be deciphered.

At the heart of the city and its wonderful garden, the astonishing proportions of the headquarters of the Council of Mists immediately caught one's eye. There are few important buildings that fail to correspond to the image of what they are, places of celebration or of power whose appearance sets them apart from ordinary places. But the Council headquarters managed to be the heart of that world and still prove humble and whispering, its low-lying wings and hidden courtyards apportioned according to a secret, asymmetrical plan. There were surely shady patios there, the murmur of water from a fountain on a birdbath, a dark, cool room from which the Head of the Council could look out at the moon, and so on, to infinity, in the labyrinth of this noble house that diluted any evidence of power in vibrant humility. From where they stood they could see all this, and everyone saw it just as they did, and that was the intention of the founding fathers of Katsura—that one could only reach the city after discovering it from on high, then observing it from below, before giving up on either perspective to embrace that of meditation.

Disembarkation began, and Petrus, with his clothes under his paw, diligently followed the boatmen's instructions. Katsura enchanted him, and the air he breathed seemed brisker than elsewhere. On solid ground, they bade farewell to their traveling companions.

"Good luck," said Paulus to the piglet, just as he was again turning into a blond angel, "may your quest lead you with wisdom."

But the elfkin was looking at Petrus.

"I have a feeling we shall meet again," he said.

The family of wild boar elves turned away and walked off casually, but Petrus felt a chill, something he couldn't put his finger on.

"What's the plan, now?" Marcus asked.

"We're going to the library," said Paulus.

"That's out of the question," said Petrus, "I need to find a roof, for a start, then wash my clothes, and get a little sustenance."

"Sustenance?" said Paulus. "Stuff your face, you mean. That is out of the question. You need to pay your respects on behalf of the Wild Grasses first. I don't want you to go off feasting before you've done your duty."

"My duty?" asked Petrus. "What duty?"

"Oh," said Marcus, "you're right, what does one owe in exchange for a thousand-year-old tea?"

"Do you think an unwashed squirrel is the best ambassador for a session of introductions?" Petrus protested.

But Paulus set off, followed by Marcus, then Petrus, who between sighs dragged his feet morosely as he followed his companions.

His torture, however, did not last long. It took barely ten minutes to reach the first houses and the labyrinth of little streets that rose up toward the Council headquarters. What an enchanting city! thought the friends, as they discovered the cobblestones, warm and soft beneath their paws, and majestic trees along shady passages, and pretty houses with their windows concealed by bamboo blinds that combined transparent and opaque effects. Little moss gardens ran all around the verandas, and their small size gave rise to a feeling of depth which Petrus, after a moment, attributed to the distinctive elements that gave each house its charm—here, a smooth, hollow stone where rainwater collected, there, a sudden shower of heavenly bamboos, or over there, a dialogue between a maple tree and an azalea. All around them were the terraces of high, misty mountains, and a skyward gaze revealed their undulating crests, but they were also visible straight ahead, at the end of a narrow street ending on the void. Here and there a bouquet of trees would vanish beneath a cascade of mist then come back in sight, while the gauzy mass that had engulfed the trees, denser and more imposing than an iceberg, dissolved or unfurled in search of more foliage. Where the houses were concerned, however, by virtue of the equilibrium of the world of mists, which requires that elfin constructions remain visible, the only things that disappeared, intermittently, were the sunny slopes of a roof, a mysterious veranda, or a door decorated with a hanging vase of violets.

By the time they came in sight of the Council headquarters, Petrus had forgotten that he was annoyed and hungry. The noble house was preceded by a large, rectangular courtyard planted with hundreds of plum trees and crisscrossed by pathways of light sand. It was surrounded by a delicate moss that broke like a wave at the walls of the enclosure, which made the edges of the garden seemed mobile, uncertain, and in spite of its mystery the place seemed open to the flow of that world.

They stood for a moment silently contemplating the tide of plum trees.

"I can only imagine what it's like when they're in bloom," murmured Paulus.

A host of elves strode along the passages admiring the trees. The next day would be winter, but that November afternoon, the soft air gave the impression that autumn would never end and, from one languid moment to the next, one warm flow of light to the next, they would remind themselves, not to forget to love. Oh, how I would love to love! thought Petrus, brushing his paw over the fringe of a ribbon of cool moss. Oh, how pleasant life is! thought Paulus and Marcus, smiling vacantly. Such a lovely autumn! Oh, love! thought the elves on the pathways, and the message was carried, beyond the Council, the city, the mountains, a message born of trees and seasons which kept this world together.

They could have stayed in the warmth of that dream of love for a long time, but a hare elf was coming to greet them.

"We were informed of your arrival," he said when he stood before them.

The three friends bowed, and Paulus and Marcus took on their human form.

"If you will come with me," said the elf, "I will take you to the library."

When he noticed what Petrus was holding beneath his paw, he asked:

"Is there a problem with your clothing?"

The squirrel in which Petrus was stuck blushed to the tips of his ears.

"Unfortunately, it, uh, got dirty during the crossing," he stammered.

The hare elf's face lit up with surprise, but he commented no further.

"Let's go," he said, and they followed him along the main path that led to the Council headquarters.

Access was through a gigantic gate reinforced by tall, circular pillars. The vigor that emerged from these columns of dead trees, after an immemorial life, was phenomenal, and stepping over the raised edge at the bottom of the gate, the friends placed their palms on the pillars. The surface was rough, streaked with centuries and shot through with deep dissonances. Across from the entrance, a wooden veranda ran all the way around another, smaller, rectangular courtyard which was planted with the same plum trees and carpeted with the same cool moss. Tall, open doors faced them and on either side.

"The north door leads to the high chamber and the quarters of the Head of the Council, the west door to the inner gardens, and the east door to the library," their guide informed them. "By inner gardens, I mean the ones where it is possible to walk about, but there are others visible from inside the building."

They headed to the right and, passing a great many elves, went past the wooden partitions adorned with long banners of silk and printed with the emblem and motto of the Council. Beneath an ink drawing of snowy peaks in the mist one could read *I shall always maintain*, written in the hand of every leader from the dawn of elfin times. Petrus lingered for a moment by one of the pen drawings. Through an optical illusion, its curves also formed a line, in such a way that one's gaze moved constantly from the tenderness of the rounded signs to the austerity of a single brushstroke. The hare elf paused in turn.

"It is said that this was drawn by the hand of the elf who witnessed the birth of the bridge," he said.

He was about to add something when he was interrupted by a movement near the north door. A group of elves emerged, and everyone drew back against the partitions to let them go by. They turned left and came up to meet our foursome.

Two hare elves were marching in the lead. They were clearly the candidates for the supreme calling, for each one of them was followed by a number of other hares as well as imposing wild boars. The elves in the escort had the bearing of their respective high-elfin houses, an accentuated gravity to their gaze, and a way of moving that implied excellence—but this, already striking, was nothing in comparison to the allure of the two hares at the head of the procession. Ordinary elves move about the world, thought Petrus; but the world adjusts to the movements of those two. As they came forward, they quickly turned into their constituent species, and it was troubling to see how much their animals resembled one another. The hares' fur was ermine-like, until they turned into horses with a white robe glinting with bronze. The muscles beneath their skin caused the velvet robe to ripple, and now and again it shimmered like a landscape of hills in the distance. At other moments, the cloak seemed made of pure silken snow, and one could really believe that the two candidates were brothers by blood.

Everything changed when they took on their human appearance. The taller one had thick white hair despite his age—three hundred years or more—brooding gray eyes that flashed like thunderclouds, a hard face with marble features, a hooked nose, high eyebrows, and prominent cheekbones. Given this face sculpted in hard rock, he seemed both young and old at the same time. His demeanor was nonchalant, but haughty, his gait fluid and controlled, which suggested strength and will—an elf like this can carry the mists on his shoulders, thought Petrus. He turned to look at the other elf and felt his heart leap. Oh, love! There can be no lovelier creature in this life! he thought. A mane of copper hair flew from the creature, his ice-cold eyes sparkled, and his milky complexion gleamed in an etching that roused trembling and desire. One couldn't get enough of this mixture of crystalline purity and fiery heat, a vision that was both frightening and warming. Unlike his competitor, he seemed insolently young, and Petrus, dazzled by the fact that so much beauty and vigor could be concentrated in a single being, told himself that he must be the head of the Council gardeners. His porcelain skin reminded Petrus of the elfkin they'd met during the crossing, but he walked with a feline self-confidence, the suppleness of a predator destined for combat. To be honest, there was something warlike about him that was surprising in an elf who devoted himself to the noble practice of gardening, and bit by bit his initial bedazzlement faded and Petrus was overcome by the same sensation of danger he'd felt with the piglet. The group drew level and Petrus's gaze was drawn to one of the boars in the retinue. Sweetness welled up in him like a stream with impetuous currents of youth, wiser than ancient rivers, and Petrus was almost more intimidated by the depth of his silver gaze than by the aura of power of the two hares.

This was the first encounter between Petrus and the elf who would soon become the greatest Guardian of the Pavilion ever known in the mists and who, one hundred and twenty years later, would father an extraordinary child called Clara. At that moment, the wild boar exchanged a brief glance with the storm-eyed hare that attested to an enduring friendship. Then they walked past the foursome and disappeared onto the veranda. After a moment, passersby on the veranda whispered among themselves, then returned to their business.

"What a shock," said Paulus.

"You were lucky to see them," said their guide. "This was the last council meeting before the start of the campaign, each one of them will now return to his stronghold."

His brow creased with concern.

"There has never been a more fraught election," he said.

"Who is your champion?" asked Marcus.

"Champion?" echoed the elf. "Are you for the garden? Their partisans use that term."

"I didn't know that," said Marcus. "We are from the Deep Woods, we know little about what goes on here."

"The distribution of the professions of faith will only start tomorrow, that's true," said the hare. "You will have a better idea of who is in the running once you've read them. As for me, I've been serving the library for five hundred years. I know who my candidate will be."

"So it's Katsura against Ryoan, the library against the garden?" asked Paulus.

"What garden, I do wonder," said their guide. "That which shines does not maintain."

"Aren't you concerned about the decline of the mists?" asked Petrus, recalling what the piglet had told them.

"Must we adapt our behavior because of that concern?" replied the hare. "We are not a warlike species, and our leaders shouldn't be warriors."

"The champion of the garden is a warrior?" asked Petrus, surprised.

"The best of us all," answered their guide.

He wiped his hand across his brow.

"But the war is mainly in his mind."

"I'm curious to see what his gardens are like," said Paulus.

"You'll see an example at the library," said their guide. "And perhaps you will think that purity is not always the best ally of the heart."

He motioned to them to go ahead, and followed them into the room.

The room extended over three thousand square feet, protected by large picture windows that looked out onto the inner gardens. Bamboo blinds could be adjusted at varying heights depending on whether one wanted to meditate on the floor, or read at the tables set up below the invisible shelves. In the center of the room, scrolls and tomes were suspended in the air, neatly stored on an immaterial frame.

"There aren't any walls," thought Petrus, "just windows and books."

"And readers," said the hare, with a smile.

And so, he understood why he had come.

Wild grasses in the snow
Two children of November

Book of Battles

保

MAINTAIN

The candidates' professions of faith were disseminated throughout the entire territory of the mists one hundred days before the election, in which every elf over the age of one hundred could take part. Later, in the provinces, assemblies would be held, where the programs could be discussed. On the day of the election, Nanzen would tally the votes and the Guardian of the Pavilion would come to Katsura to announce the results.

Let us agree to call our candidates of the moment the councilor and the gardener respectively, and let us hear a few words about their vision for the future of the mists.

The councilor's profession of faith was magnificent, for it was written in the style of the wild grasses, with a melodious turn of phrase that resonated in every heart. The hare elf of Katsura may have appeared cold and austere, but his prose and manner were warm and kindly.

I shall always maintain, he wrote at the end of his speech. More unexpected was the phrase that preceded his motto: *the older our world gets, the more it is in need of poetry.* When was the last time anyone had read the word *poetry* in a leader's profession of faith? I will leave this question to the historians and, for the time being, look forward to this tribute to the spirit of childhood.

権力

POWER

I nversely, the gardener's profession of faith reflected none of the brilliance of his person. It was as devoid of heart as he seemed to have been fashioned with love, and as drearily dry as he was insolently youthful. One must be glad of this lack of subtlety in the prose, when the elf was such an expert in the conviction of his gaze and his acts, since it would cost him this election and the next one, thus demonstrating that the mists were not yet prepared to sacrifice their multi-millennial soul.

Elves are less inclined than humans to act under the influence of fear, for tradition, with them, is not opposed to progress, nor is movement opposed to stability. When the gardener wrote, *I shall be the protector of the continuity of our culture against the threats of modern times*, he could not hope to win over a species used to thinking in circular terms. Some even suspected that he was driven—perhaps without even being aware of it—by that force that undoes more than it maintains: a thirst for power.

However, he was right about one thing, and it would soon earn him enough partisans to build an army: the mists were declining and it was becoming ever more difficult to keep the avenues of this world together.

I have come here to read, that's the message, thought Petrus, who two days earlier would have thought it extravagant that messages could be spread throughout the world.

"I'll take my leave of you now," said their guide with a bow, "someone will be coming to look after you."

The three friends stood there for a moment, but no one came, and they went over to the large picture window to admire the garden.

It was a centuries-old jewel, embellished over time by the Council's successive gardeners, an elite respected among the mists because each one of them had completed an interminably long apprenticeship, kept up a permanent commerce with trees, and made art that worked with the legacy of the ages—all things the elves believed were vital and to which they devoted themselves by tending their gardens and respecting their trees. The enclosure of the Council was sealed with a velvety moss that covered the roots of specimens so old that on the very ground they formed a miniature landscape of valleys and hills. On this late autumn day, the maple trees were ablaze; in the foreground, all along the building, a strip of sand streaked with arabesques gave the garden its waves; beyond it began the ocean of greenery. Here were a few azaleas that had already lost their leaves; there, heavenly bamboo in bunches of red berries; and everywhere, those pine trees that are pruned over the centuries until they have taken on a singular shape—

their essential form, which is found inside and requires a gardener who will listen to what the tree is whispering to him,
while winds and storms speak only to its bark. They resembled
the trees in the Deep Woods, but at their extremities the contortions of their dark branches produced needle fascicles,
trimmed by the gardener's art to form delicate lashes, and
against the dry wood they seemed to be winking, while singing
a hymn that was refined and graceful—it was something to see,
the openwork wings reaching out from the bare, rigid tree
trunks, then branching out in the air like figures so graphic
that for the third time in two days Petrus wondered whether
the world were not murmuring a poem in his ear.

In the middle of the scene, the mercury waters of a pond
reflected the heavens and the branches, but it took Petrus a
moment to understand the strangeness of what he was seeing.
He had to blink several times to adjust to the aberrant color
scheme that lost its hues in the water, reflected back as black
branches on a gray mirror of waves. From this alloy of metal
and ink a ballet from the foundries of the universe emerged,
where the streaks of pine trees performed a monochrome choreography on the liquid silver. Harmonizing with the scene
were stones of various shapes and sizes that formed ageless
mineral promontories and bridges along the shore or above the
surface of the pond. There one knew the fraternal flow of rock
and river; there one felt the tremor of a powerful vision, of a
dream of mountains and shores—this is the essence of our
world, thought Petrus, and the dream is so lofty that it will
never die.

Beyond the pond, a lane bordered with slopes of bamboo
led to a gate with a thatched roof. Ryoan irises had been
planted there, and were nodding at winter camellias that had
just bloomed, set in rows along the avenue and flanked, to the
rear, by tall bamboo and slender maple trees. The Katsura
maples are particularly elegant, because the capital of the elves

is sheltered from strong winds by the rampart of its mountains of mist. Thus, the leaves are the same as everywhere, so delicately carved that their veins and edges form a living lace; but the absence of storms means that that the branches do not need to strengthen to resist the gusts, they remain slender, can bow to the breeze, languid dancers. A swarm of mist rose, slipped between the branches, then evaporated, swirling lazily on itself, and the friends mused it must be a pleasing thing, to come and admire this garden during the long winter. Similarly, they supposed there were other jewels within the annexes to the central building, for through the leaves and needles they could see its verandas. To the left of the pond, the picture windows offered a glimpse of a sunlit room and, to the rear, a raised, interior garden consisting of three large stones set on gray sand. They seemed to have been tossed in the air to fall again at the perfect distance from each other, and the precise form and precise gap between things must certainly be known to achieve such perfection: Petrus did not doubt that it was the work of the young chief gardener. It had the same sparkling purity to it as his very person, and Petrus understood how one might become fascinated. Those who wish to reach the summit barefoot must have a heaven-sent talent, he thought, astonished at all the elevated thoughts he'd been having since his arrival in Katsura, and mentally he scoffed at himself. This moment of distraction changed everything, and he no longer saw the mineral garden in the same way as before. The arrangement that had so delighted his gaze now seemed fossilized, and the stones emitted a message of death which gave him the shivers. *Purity is not always the best ally of the heart*, their guide had said, and this absence of love, now so obvious, made his hair stand on end.

"It's magnificent," said Marcus.

Petrus saw he was looking at the stones.

"It's cold," he replied.

"It's frozen," said Paulus.

"Yes, it's cold and frozen," said Marcus slowly, as if he were waking from a dream.

"How may I assist you?" asked a voice behind them.

They turned around and found themselves facing a tall female elf with red hair and light gray eyes.

"I am the Council's steward," she said.

Turning into a squirrel, she was such a striking replica of his mother that Petrus, fully aware that he'd left his Woods without saying goodbye, blushed violently from the tips of his claws to the top of his ears.

She looked at the cloth he was clutching in his paws.

"Is there something wrong with your clothing?" she asked.

The crimson squirrel in which Petrus was trapped gave out an indeterminate gurgling sound and Paulus, feeling sorry for him, came to his rescue.

"There was an incident during the crossing," he said.

"That is the first time I've ever heard of an incident involving clothes," she said.

"The same for us," said Marcus, looking at Petrus mockingly.

But when he saw Petrus's despair, he resumed his serious air.

"Our hostess from the Wild Grasses asked this temporarily mute gentle-elf to introduce himself to you," he said.

"Yes, but why?" she asked.

"Were you not informed?" asked Marcus.

"We were simply informed of the arrival from the Deep Woods of two squirrels and one bear," she replied.

Dumbfounded, they fell silent.

"Do you not know, either, why you have been sent?" she said, turning into a bay mare with rounded hindquarters.

She studied them, thoughtful.

"The Wild Grasses never do things without a reason," she continued, "particularly during such a troubled period."

"Might you have some work for me?" asked Petrus, his voice so clear that Paulus and Marcus stood there gaping.

"I don't see what's so astonishing about that," he added, in response to their stupor. "I intend to stay here, and I have to make a living."

"What can you do?" she asked.

It was his turn to stand there openmouthed.

"Well," he said, "I don't know. Anything, I imagine, that doesn't require any particular skill."

"You are not good at job interviews," she said, somewhat put out.

She thought for a moment.

"These days, with the elections, I have enough to do without trying to make sense of all this. I may as well keep you on hand, after all."

She frowned.

"Does he really not know how to do anything?" she asked Marcus and Paulus.

They looked embarrassed and she sighed.

"Can you sweep?" she asked Petrus.

"I suppose so," he replied.

She clicked her tongue, annoyed.

"Tomorrow at dawn, west door," she said.

Then, turning into a squirrel and looking just like his mother when she was angry, she turned and was gone.

"You really have some nerve," said Marcus.

"Are you serious?" asked Paulus. "Do you really want to stay in Katsura and spend your days sweeping paths for the Council?"

"I am serious," answered Petrus in a huff. "I don't see why you won't believe me."

They looked at him doubtfully for a moment.

"Let's go," said Marcus in the end, "let's leave this place, we have to find an inn before nightfall."

They agreed, and set off. Before leaving, Petrus cast one last gaze at the books and scrolls floating in the air, and it seemed to him they twinkled faintly in a knowing farewell.

"See you tomorrow," he murmured.

Finally, they went through the gates and back into the streets of the city.

That is how Petrus's life in Katsura began and, although the time has come for us to proceed more speedily with our tale, and return to the protagonists of the last battle of the war, we must say a few words about those years in the capital of the elves, simply because the world they embodied is now gone forever. For the last seven decades, those who have been in charge of the intrigues of fate relentlessly asked themselves this burning question: should they die to make way for a new era, or had their very world come to its end?

"We always believed that individuals and civilizations perished, but that the species would survive," the Head of the Council would say one day to Petrus. "And what if our species has reached its own limits and is meant to die without leaving a trace? Should we not view this war differently?"

However, seventy years would pass before this conversation took place, and while they may have appeared to be monotonous years, for Petrus they were a constant adventure. Every morning he did his sweeping while he daydreamed, and during the seasons when snow covered the paths and the moss, he worked at the library, archiving scrolls and books. Then he read. Twice a year, during his leave, he went traveling. Sometimes Paulus and Marcus came with him on a joyful escapade; most often, he went off on his own and connected with other good souls he met along the way; and he was certainly the elf with the greatest number of friends in faraway places of all the mists, for the species, as a rule, rarely leaves its native province. In Katsura he'd found a place to live at the top of the town with an old unicorn elf lady with whom he shared breakfast every day at dawn, laughing and conversing. From the window of his room he could see the mist rising and falling over the great city. In the morning, it took on tints of bronze that caused his heart to leap, and he enjoyed those sunrises so much that for all his laziness he would wake up early. When he set off down the deserted streets in the brisk air, he forgot the endless tedium of the task before him. On his way down to the Council headquarters, he looked out over the city as it fanned out below him, at the foot of the snowy peaks and the cliffs of mist. The rising sun fringed them with an incandescent edging that frayed above their dark crest; the streets and bridges of the white city were enveloped in amber fog, great vaporous exhalations that disintegrated above the streams, and it was a long dream of water and wood, in a luxuriance of sunlight. Petrus would stop by the dew-lit trees to perform his devotions to beauty, greeting a bird perched on the stone, the swaying bamboo, the camellias in improbable winter. But there were also dawns when the great blaze from some activity in Nanzen (renovations, or major cleaning in the channels) gave everything a fiery glow. There was wind then, too, and brief hailstorms, which left the city purple and steaming; transparent spears of mist soared at great speed toward the sky; and these tantrums of climate strengthened the proof that his life was in search of some missing intensity. He did not know how to define it, but before long it propelled him toward the channels, and caused him to travel all over the country.

Travel had become second nature to him, and the actual journey became almost more important than the places he visited, although there was hardly a remote corner of this world unworthy of praise.

He loved the province of the Leaves, and the pavilion and

bridge of mists on an outcrop in the distance, but above all he'd been astonished by the density of the forest that separated Nanzen from the rest of the world, with neither channel nor passage to get there. At the way station where travelers could stop and admire the first sanctuary, in the distance, they served a frothy green tea with a grassy taste. There was no backbone to its flavor—a powerful flavor of nothing, a smooth, pale concentrate of forest from before the time of elves, which evoked unusual images to Petrus, in particular a dimly lit scene where, against a background of silky darkness, a glass of water stood next to three forgotten cloves of garlic, and he became convinced that this vision with the texture of a painting came from *elsewhere*, from an unknown land that was calling to him, although he couldn't figure out how to get there.

He also loved the northern regions which, in the mists, unlike in human lands, are the warmest. There, one could hear the constant song of cicadas, and swarms of dragonflies vibrated above the rice paddies; above all, the provender they served there was seasoned with grilled herbs and generous spices. In the south, he'd felt at home in the provinces of the Friezes and the Frozen Sands, where all day long they drank warm honey beside the fireplace. Outside, there were endless beaches and stormy plains, constant wind and glacial islands; and yet, beneath the steep thatched roofs where they warmed themselves as they shared their supper, the elves of those lands had created a very comfortable life for themselves. As a reward for their indoor isolation, they would venture out the next morning into the frozen mist of dawn and, suddenly, it was as if everything had been cleared away and made bright, a powerful gust had chased the clouds away to reveal a huge sky, a profusion of pure sky, a sky so enormous that one was lost in it, a sky where seagulls passed high overhead as if shot there by invisible archers.

This was the world Petrus explored at every latitude and I cannot fully describe the landscapes of mountains and coasts, waterfalls and lakes, volcanoes and prairies. But in every province the same mists could be found, the same trees and the same moss, which give these lands their identity, the same traditions of tea, and the same wooden verandas where one could stand and admire the affability of huge clouds. It was a blessing for the journey, when he still felt out of his mists (as they say in these parts), his status as a stranger gave a logic to this fantasy, and he became a privileged observer of the customs of his fellow elves, painting throughout his travels a picture that few elves have had the opportunity to imagine, and while he might yearn for an elusive elsewhere, he learned to love his people deeply, and their manner of dwelling upon their lands.

For the landscapes of the mists are the alter egos of the souls that incarnate them. Humans, because they separate the seer from the seen, and the creator from the created, cannot understand the nature of this game of mirrors. Elves do not conceive of their lands as portions of the world they might inhabit, but as dynamic forces in which their own energy is released, while the tea gives inner eyes and ears to this great, vital fusion—thus, they could not imagine themselves admiring mere landscapes, but rather, in every valley, every tree, and every garden, the work of the cosmos as a whole, an immense solidarity reverberated to infinity by the mists. This gave rise to a peace-loving population, since the whole would not dream of combatting the whole; elves would be stunned to think one could tell stories, as I am doing, where they could see only landscapes that have been arbitrarily selected from the magma of life. Instead, their days were spent in peace: they drank their tea, which awakens an awareness of the universal mixture; they worked in order to contribute to the proper running of the community; then, once they had drunk their tea and done their work, they tended their gardens, wrote and recited poetry, sang, enjoyed pottery and calligraphy—all activities valued by humans as exquisite forms of leisure, but which, for the elves, constitute the natural continuation of the harmony of the world, flows of action inserted in a flow of mist which, in return, acquires its flesh through these activities. And so, while all this may have delighted the self-respecting elf in Petrus, he also felt frustrated for a reason that the library would reveal to him.

One day when, in the presence of the steward, he expressed his surprise that the books were suspended in the air, she replied:

"These texts and inks are the repositories of the dream of the mists."

Indeed, the dream of the library had the shape of interconnected books that told the history of the mists, scrolls of poetry that celebrated the mists, or parchments that recorded the great deeds of the mists, all of it interspersed with delicate inking that invariably painted trees and mountains in the mist. After decades of reading, he'd had his fill of the misty, elegiac, historical fresco to which all the literature and art of the elves seemed to be reduced, and he despaired of understanding what it was that drove him day after day to keep looking there for that *something* the wild grasses of the channel had once whispered to him, long ago. He did like to read, however, the way some people pray, in the quiet contemplation of a motionless voyage steeped in the value of a reality that real life itself had failed to give him. But this unusual freshness quickly soured, drowned in the endless repetitions of monotonous celebrations, and from all his voyages through channels or poetry, the only thing he gained was a sense of frustration that grew exponentially as the years went by. I have a particular fondness for Petrus, simply because, while I loved the world of elves before the fall, I also understood whatever incongruous aspirations he might have in his heart; one must, in a way, be a stranger to the world to wish to invent it, and unknown to oneself to want to go beyond what is visible.

Do not suppose, however, that he did not love his native land and that, the moment he saw the end was near, he did not feel his heart breaking. It was four decades after arriving in Katsura, while he was on his way to Ryoan for the first time. The channel between Katsura and Ryoan was unstable, by virtue of a topological oddity that had placed the two great elfin cities as far apart as possible in this world, at its highest altitude and at its lowest, and this produced a flow of tension that made the eight-hour boat ride one of the most unpredictable for Nanzen. The channel was often closed and Petrus, after a long series of failed attempts to reach the city, only got there after he had already explored three-quarters of the rest of the elfin territory. After a somewhat chaotic crossing—but turbulence in the channel, once so rare, had now become commonplace—Petrus and his companions landed at dawn at the docks of the fourth sanctuary, and all three now stood there gaping. He thought he'd seen so many marvels that nothing could ever dazzle him again, but he was wrong, for in all the known worlds, there has never existed a more absolute city than Ryoan, and by absolute, I mean beautiful and powerful, but also *impossible.* Although it was entirely shrouded in dark mists, the houses and trees shone like black diamonds. Darkness emerged from light, the world was lit up while an alchemist's filter allowed one to see every object clearly and distinctly, standing out against the background it should have dissolved into. Here there were no mountains, but there were cliffs of mist, as imposing as the ones in Katsura, entire sections standing tall all through the city. These huge gleaming screens ran from east to west, and day and night Ryoan was resplendent in their dark light. There was, too, a liquid silver, a flowing iridescence of the sun in the interstices of darkness, streaming over bridges and silent gardens—all was darkness, all was silver, all was transparency, and the city could be seen through canopies of mist that sparked like power lines. There was a caressing softness to it all, and you missed it once it had moved eastward, then you gratefully welcomed the next wave as it came out of the west.

"It's like a painting in ink and crystal," said Paulus, rousing the other two from their stupor.

"It is said that the brilliance of this darkness knows no rival," said Marcus. "I understand why the elves from Ryoan are proud."

And indeed, as Petrus would declare that first evening, over a mug of honey more refined than any found in other provinces: wandering through the streets of the town was a level one spiritual experience. Earlier on, they had gone past a garden where, on a patch of black sand, a single bitter orange tree grew, and its little white flowers, sculpted against the background of dark mist, looked like stars adrift in the nocturnal ether. Their perfume, which he could taste in his mug of honey, had almost driven Petrus mad, and everything was like that in this welcoming, sublime city, which the three friends did not want to leave.

"Ryoan has this effect on me—like a filter that makes everything seem sharper," he said, again.

He didn't know where this sort of idea was coming from, but each time he had such a thought, it seemed right to him, and familiar, and he would point it out to his two companions.

"It's the effect of the thousand-year-old tea," declared Paulus, setting his mug down. "Ever since we drank it we've been living with our dead, or they've been living with us, I don't know which, but they dignify our private thoughts."

The night before the departure, they went out into the warm twilight. Walking along the banks of the river, yielding to the flow of seasons, trees, and mountains whispered by the current, they made an unexpected encounter. It was only once the elf had come right up to him and smiled that Petrus, addled by the excess of orange flower syrup he'd indulged in at dinner, recognized the blond angel from the channel at Hanase, his complexion more delicate, his eyes bluer than ever, a young adult now and so dazzlingly beautiful that Petrus was (almost) speechless.

"Now I find you just when I'm about to leave Ryoan," said the elf with a smile, "It must be a sign of fate."

They all bowed amiably.

"Where are you going?" asked Paulus.

"To Katsura, through the first channel at dawn," he replied, turning into a wild boar so gracious he made one think of a deer. "I've just been accepted onto the team of gardeners to the Council," he added proudly.

"That's quite a coincidence, said Petrus, "I'm also working at the upper chamber."

"My father recommended me to the head of the garden," said the fine boar, turning into a gorgeous horse.

"He's a remarkable artist," said Petrus politely.

"Who should have been Head of the Council," said the other elf nonchalantly.

There was a moment's silence.

"Our present head has all the qualities required to govern the mists," said Petrus.

"You think this is so because he was elected? Do you believe that the common elf has any idea what the qualities of a leader should be?" asked the horse.

"There are none more common than I," said Petrus, after a moment's silence.

The young elf looked hard at him for a moment then gave that irresistible smile that banished any misgivings.

"I doubt that very much," he said, before bowing gracefully and taking his leave.

But after he'd gone a few steps he turned around briefly.

"I will see you soon," he said to Petrus, in a way that made his blood run cold.

In his capacity as head sweeper, Petrus was witness to the Council's important affairs and backstage intrigue. His subordinate status cloaked him in an invisibility that gave him access to all sorts of information more prominent elves wouldn't be able to obtain, particularly as he was still just as popular as he had been back in his Woods. Everyone liked Petrus, everyone sought out his company, and not a day went by when he was not invited for a drink of maple or rose-hip syrup, to which he would respond favorably if he had finished his reading. Sweeping was an agreeable vocation; the brooms were made of light bamboo and one hardly needed to touch the ground; the job was neither difficult nor tiring, and he took pleasure in leaving a tidy space behind him, cleaned of a few careless leaves. He worked only from dawn to lunchtime, and his afternoons were as free as was his access to all the remotest areas of the headquarters, including the inner gardens which could be reached through the north door, and the Council Chambers. However, the more the time passed, the less he felt like going there. The head of the gardeners had not won the election, but was clearly gaining influence over the upper chamber. Gradually, gray sand came to replace the moss, and the vegetation disappeared in favor of magnificent stones that the gardener's assistants would track down in the four corners of the mists—thus, a visitor to the garden would see, through successive plays of stone and sand, the tide on the shore, eternal mountains, or the unyielding lakes of this world. But these displays were unfeeling, which came as no surprise to Petrus, who was careful to sweep below the picture windows of the upper chamber whenever the Head of the Council was reading out the daily report on the mists from Nanzen. And Petrus overheard the questions on the part of the head of the garden and the curator of the library who, along with the ten councilors, and sometimes envoys from the provinces, had the right to attend the sessions.

He could not have imagined better leaders than those who had been elected. The Guardian of the Pavilion in particular filled him with admiration, with his melodious voice and ageless gaze. The head of the garden never attacked him to his face, any more than he did the hare elf from Katsura who presided over the sessions with elegant authority and a sense of irony that was fairly uncommon among elves. They were giants. They were giants in the service of a world deep in turmoil, because every daily report described the increasing decline of the mist. Moreover, they had to confront the destroyer of the centuries-old vegetation, obsessed with stones and perfection, who was no longer in hiding and was openly campaigning against humans.

"How can you deny the facts?" he asked the Head of the Council. "How can you ignore that their unbearable frivolity is destroying the paradise that was entrusted to them and, through the contagion of the bridge, is also poisoning our own paradise?"

"There are no simple causes or remedies to any illness," replied the hare. "Designating a providential enemy will not save our mist."

"You are deluding yourself with chitchat while criminals are running about the countryside with impunity," replied the gardener.

"Decline is not a crime, but a challenge," replied the guardian.

"Nothing will give us back our mists if we do not act."

And this went on, tirelessly, while Petrus, year after year, saw the elves grow despondent and the words of the gardener infiltrate their hearts, although there was not yet a single councilor who was willing to adopt a radical position regarding the human question.

When destiny takes an abrupt turn, there are no flowers to distract us from it. It was a fine November afternoon and he was reading, ensconced on a soft cushion in a recess in the library, looking out at the only garden that had been spared the mineral mischief of the elf from Ryoan. He read and sighed intermittently, vaguely interested and bored by the autumn elegies in a collection that was part of a great classic of the mists, the *Canto of the Alliance*, where the natural affinities of mountains, forests, and clouds were celebrated over and over. It was illustrated ad nauseam with magnificent ink drawings where, against a background of misty summits, trees gracefully lost their leaves, and birds, joined by the writing of poetry, flew high in the sky.

> *Neither spring nor summer nor winter*
> *Know the grace*
> *Of languid autumn*

He sighed again and, taking the volume with him, went out into the first courtyard where he sat in the sun, his back against an old plum tree. It was very mild and, after a few additional pages of maple trees blazing in the setting sun, he was about to doze off when something in his reading startled him and made him sit up, his heart pounding and his nose quivering. He stared at a camellia flower before him that a gardener from the first shift had left on the moss, not seeing it, went back to the text, shook his head, read it over and over, endlessly.

the rebirth of the mists
through two children of snow and November
the rootless the last alliance

"By the mists," he murmured at last (which, in elfin, is the equivalent of "holy mackerel").

He did not know which was more upsetting, that he'd found in these lines the inspiration of those he'd once spontaneously created, under the influence of the wild grasses in the channel, or that for the first time he was in the presence of such an *unthinkable* text. From his reading, he could swear that this poem did not celebrate anything that existed, did not evoke anything that had ever happened but, on the contrary, described the affliction of the mist and outlined the remedy as if it had anticipated and conceived them. Three lines in an unknown story and life was radiant, in league with a heart swollen with a new intoxication so intense that he could feel that heart pounding fit to burst, and he could no longer see what was there before him—and precisely, there before him, observing him in silence, stood the Head of the Council. How long has he been standing there? wondered Petrus, leaping to his feet. The sun was setting, smoothing the moss in the courtyard with its low-angled light. He felt a chill and blinked his eyes as if emerging from a long dream. He stood there for a few moments before the silent Head of the Council.

"What are you reading?" asked the Head, finally.

Everything that had gathered in Petrus's mind during the hours he'd remained motionless rereading the poem now metabolized and, stunned by the words coming from his mouth, he said:

"A prophecy."

The Head of the Council raised an eyebrow.

"A prophecy?" he said.

Petrus felt as thick as his own broom. Lowering his eyes on the book he was holding in his hands, he mustered his courage.

"A prophecy," he said.

He read the three lines out loud, and every word pierced the cool late-afternoon air like a dagger.

"Where did you find this?" asked the Head of the Council after a moment's silence.

"In the *Canto of the Alliance*," replied Petrus, handing him the book.

There was another silence.

"I don't know how many times I've read the *Canto of the Alliance*," said the Head of the Council, "but I have no recollection of these lines."

Petrus, respectful, remained silent.

"Yet I have the memory of an elephant," said the elf, turning into that hare with the ermine coat that caused crowds to melt with admiration.

He remained thoughtful for a moment while Petrus said nothing, embarrassed and not knowing which stance to take.

"How long have you been working here?" asked the hare.

"Seventy years," Petrus replied.

"You're not from Katsura, are you?"

"I am from the Deep Woods," replied Petrus, "I came here because of a rather peculiar set of circumstances."

The hare turned into a white horse.

"Which were?"

"Well," said Petrus, "I was sent by the Wild Grasses of Hanase."

The horse stared at him as if he'd changed into a slug.

"And what twist of fate took you into the Wild Grasses?" he asked.

"The recommendation of the boatman from the South Marches, who asked the hostess to serve us a thousand-year-old tea," said Petrus.

The Head of the Council laughed.

"Is that all," he said.

Almost to himself, he murmured the name of the boatman in a trill that ended with a plop in the water.

"A squirrel from the Deep Woods, sent by the oldest servants of the mists, and a sort of prophecy come out of nowhere," he continued. "Imagine my surprise to find out only today what's been going on. Do you have something else up your sleeve, by any chance?"

Petrus blushed.

"Just before I arrived in Katsura, I composed a similar little poem about two children."

"Are you a poet?" asked the Head of the Council.

"No, I'm a sweeper."

The Head of the Council changed into a man.

"I'm afraid you are going to have to give up your vocation," he said. "Come tomorrow morning to the upper chamber. I'm going to convene an extraordinary session and you would do well to prepare yourself for a long day."

Finally, he went away, leaving Petrus more dumbfounded and distraught than a broom.

A dream so lofty
Neither spring nor summer nor winter
Know the grace
Of languid autumn

Book of Paintings

聖地

SANCTUARIES

The land of elves has four sanctuaries.

Nanzen, in the province of Leaves, received, regulated, and brought together the mists by means of all the paths and channels.

Katsura, the capital of the elves and the jewel of Snows, was in charge of maintaining the foundations of this world.

Ryoan, at the heart of the Dark Mists, kept the books for the eternity of beauty.

Hanase, finally, the only city of Ashes, maintained the connection between the living and the dead.

The sanctuaries are the secret hearts of a world where the answers to the questions in the great Books are being worked out.

The question of fervor, which Nanzen prayed for every day, that the mist might be saved.

That of courage in battle, overseen by the upper chamber of Katsura.

That of beauty, incarnated by Ryoan's natural paintings.

That of love, finally, the greatest question of all: the dead of Hanase whisper the canto of love, and this canto travels through space and time, and it rides upon the great winds of the dream, and one day it reaches our distant ears.

予言

PROPHECY

The Head of the Council immediately agreed with Petrus's hunch that the three lines were a prophecy. He knew the difference between human and elfin literature, and he knew it was impossible for the poem to be part of the *Canto of the Alliance*—and yet, it was or, at least, it had become part of it.

Elves do not tell stories the way humans do, and they are impervious to stories of *invention*. They sing of their great exploits, compose odes to birds and to the beauty of the mists, but imagination never adds anything to this elegiac celebration. Who would ask for stories in the Great Whole where every event is merely the reflection of the entire story?

As there was no trace in either the annals or the memory of elfin ages of two children of November through whom a rebirth of the mists was said to have come, the poem was an unclassifiable text, which they hoped would prove prophetic. The Head of the Council, who already suspected that the splendid, eternal, and static world of his own kind would be forced to change in order to survive, understood that the sweeper Petrus's epiphany commanded the path to a new alliance.

By Sacred Violets
1870–1871

I t seemed to Petrus from the Deep Woods that he had had two distinct lives: the life before and the life after the moment he read the prophecy. In the first of those lives, there was a broom; in the second, adventure; and he saw his erstwhile voyages and little adventures as leaps of a mouse in a cage.

As if it were meant to happen, that year of epiphanies for Petrus had also witnessed a series of memorable events, bound together by a noose that subsequently seemed to be pulled ever tighter, until it could only lead to war—but anyone who, in those days, could have understood the fabric and the significance of those events would have been very clever indeed. They were, in no particular order: a man's murder, which would send the Head of the Council to Rome; the discovery of a singular painting in which the decline of worlds was sealed; the discovery of the existence of a gray notebook which would change the face of the coming war; and the discovery, by Petrus, of human wine.

Not long after the sweeper Petrus first appeared before the upper chamber and the birth of the idea of an alliance with humans, a conversation took place between the head of the gardeners and his young right-hand man, the piglet from Hanase who was now an adult wild boar. For thirty years, Petrus had been encountering him on the paths of the Council, and their mutual hostility had continued to grow. The initial amiability of the young wild boar had changed to scorn, once he noted the sweeper's lack of enthusiasm for his champion's intrigues. The worship he devoted to his leader made him his most eager acolyte, and they were quite a sight, the pair of them, when they took on their human forms and ambled casually through their surroundings—so handsome, and so evil, thought Petrus, who at times was still unsettled by their dazzling smiles; then he would shake his head and the spell dissolved.

Then one January morning, Petrus overheard this conversation between the two, and he related it to the Head of the Council and the Guardian of the Pavilion. All three of them were standing in the study of the hare elf from Katsura, a tiny little room that opened onto the most marvelous scene. Although he had strolled through many a remarkable garden, Petrus did not know of a single one that offered a concentrated sense of nature the way this one did. That the quintessence of artifice could produce a sensation of such pure nature in a single garden entirely conceived by the mind and hand of an elf, both charmed and stunned him. It was little more than an enclosure of light-colored sand, azaleas, and heavenly bamboo, through which a stream ran, preceded by a hollow stone where birds frolicked. But, however modest it might be, the scene evoked a sensation of the vast world, through a transubstantiation of distances and things, and Petrus had renounced trying to plumb its mystery.

"I tend it myself," the Head of the Council said to him one day, showing him the tools stored along the outside veranda: shears, a little broom, a bamboo rake, and a basket made of woven bark.

And Petrus was not averse to the fact that the gardeners didn't sniff around there. However, the time had come for the report: wandering aimlessly along the corridors in the upper chamber after work, he glimpsed the two cursed souls around the corner of a veranda and, deeming they had a strange manner about them, he followed them, then positioned himself discreetly below the little room they slipped into in order to converse. Apparently, the head of the garden had news from a nephew who, by virtue of the regulations of the mists authorizing families of dignitaries from the headquarters of the Council to travel in both worlds, had recently gone over to the human side, and, in a city called Amsterdam, had found a painting (which did not interest his uncle) and a gray notebook (which interested him greatly), sent them to another city called Rome, then disappeared without a trace. Prior to this he'd come back from Amsterdam a first time without the gray notebook, for he feared the Guardian of the Pavilion might get wind of it, and the head of the garden cursed his own precaution, which now deprived him of the object he seemed to covet. The story, which made no sense at all to Petrus, didn't seem to surprise the other two.

"We always keep an eye on elves who go to stay in the human world," the Guardian told him, "and last night we witnessed the nephew's murder."

"Murder?" echoed Petrus, horrified.

"Murder," confirmed the Head of the Council. "It would seem he wanted to earn human money by selling the painting to an art dealer, and the dealer killed him then made off with the canvas and the notebook. The dealer's name is Roberto Volpe and I'm on my way to Rome to meet him."

"Meet a murderer?" asked Petrus, even more horrified.

"Astonishingly, Roberto Volpe is an amiable, peace-loving individual who, on top of it, just became a father this morning for the first time," answered the Head of the Council.

"What an astonishing business," said the guardian. "We need to take a closer look. Unfortunately, in the commotion over the murder, we failed to determine what Volpe might have done with the mysterious gray notebook. But the head of the garden didn't send his nephew to Amsterdam just by chance, and I bet he knew what he was looking for. So now we have a double quest to pursue: the two children, and the gray notebook."

"Do you think the two are connected?" asked Petrus.

"We think that everything is always connected," answered the guardian. "Including a certain sweeper who was sent to the Council library upon the intuition of the Wild Grasses."

Petrus was speechless.

"There are times we may be blind, but we are not morons," said the Head of the Council. "Apparently you like traveling?"

His expression was sour.

"Still, I'm not sure what I'm offering you is exactly a privilege. This first murder of an elf in human territory augurs a sad beginning but, in these dark times, we must show discernment and audacity."

He exchanged a glance with the guardian.

"Your unexpected discovery in the *Canto of the Alliance* has given us proof that the key of time is to be found in the link between the worlds. I don't know why you told us this so long after you were singled out by the two highest authorities in our world, the Wild Grasses and the boatman from the South Marches, nor why, in the interval, fate went and stuck a broom in your hands, but it would seem you have been chosen for this adventure."

He gave Petrus what seemed to be a rather stern look—or was it solemn?

"I have decided to appoint you special envoy of the mists to the human world," he said, "in charge of the dual quest for the gray notebook and the two children of the *Canto*."

He stood up, signaling that it was time to leave.

"Be here tomorrow at dawn," said the Guardian of the

Pavilion, "and bring what you need for several days' travel, for every kind of weather and every season."

Petrus left the Council headquarters in a state of such confusion that for the first time he went home to the wrong house, then seemed not to recognize his old unicorn elf. Special envoy from the Council of the Mists to the human world! he said to himself, over and over. He didn't have the slightest idea what he would have to do, and the few instructions he'd received had left him mired in confusion. Elves only wear one outfit, which keeps them closely covered at all times, but they also wear capes when it rains, and warm coats in cold weather with added headgear that more or less resembles that of humans. Petrus spent the night trying to put together a bundle then, at daybreak, he stuffed a few belongings at random in the canvas bag he used for traveling. Finally, realizing to his horror that the sun was already quite high in the sky, he rushed to the upper chamber and, without knowing how he got there, found himself in the private study where he'd been the previous day. Before him stood the Head of the Council, observing him with thoughtful intensity. Next to him was the Guardian of the Pavilion, murmuring something Petrus couldn't hear, as sounds vanished into a cottony confusion where he felt his intelligence disappearing as well.

The guardian placed a hand on his shoulder. There was an empty moment while the cotton was endlessly diluted in an icy void. Then they were in Nanzen. The pavilion was silent. Through its windows that had neither trim nor panes, Petrus could see the mist sculpting the trees in the valley. To the rear, at the top of the red bridge, a thick fog was whirling in place.

"How did we get here?" Petrus asked the guardian.

"By the bridge," he answered, handing him a cup of tea.

"I thought it led only to the land of humans."

"The bridge is only visible when it serves to pass between

worlds. Inside our own, it does not require any special material form."

He went to fetch some clothes that were neatly piled on a bench, along with utensils for making tea, and unfolded them in front of Petrus. There was a sort of two-legged sheath, a large, coarsely cut shirt, and a sort of cape with arms.

"This outfit will be suitable wherever you go," said the guardian. "When it comes to shoes, however, it will depend on your destination."

"But where am I going?" asked Petrus. "I haven't a clue."

Then, remembering their conversation from the previous day: "To Rome, perhaps?"

The guardian shared images which made him plop in astonishment upon his squirrel rear end.

"Rome," said the master of Nanzen.

But Petrus couldn't understand what he was seeing.

"These are stone buildings," said the guardian. "Collective buildings, in a way, or houses of cult and power."

"So tall, and so dead," murmured Petrus. "I don't think I'll go there. To be honest, I really have no idea what I'm supposed to do, and for sure I don't know where to start."

"Trust your heart," said the guardian.

For a moment Petrus, uncertain and lost, did not move. Without warning, the face of the old woman with the blue ribbons from his dream at the teahouse came back to him from the depths of his memory, and he saw her coming toward him against a background of little gardens with freshly turned earth. He felt the light presence of the guardian penetrate his spirit and he heard him say, I see her. The vision shifted. Verdant landscapes of meadows and woods went by, and then the vision paused above a village nestled in a valley. His heart pounding, Petrus recognized the stone houses with tawny roof tiles. Snow had covered the orchards, and plumes of winter smoke rose toward the sky.

"That's it," he said, "that's where it is."

The images vanished and the guardian opened his eyes.

"Burgundy," he said. "At least there's no lack of snow there."

An hour later, feeling as much at ease in his human clothes as a squirrel in a tutu, his feet clad in instruments of torture which the guardian had referred to as clogs (stuffed with woolen socks that were unpleasantly scratchy against his calves), Petrus was standing on the red bridge.

"We will not let you out of our sight. When you're ready to come back, all you have to do is let us know," said the guardian.

Finally, he gave him a little purse which contained the money he might need on the other side.

Petrus took a step forward and entered the circle of mist. It was extraordinarily thick and he felt a silkiness against his cheek. And now? he thought, deep down feeling somewhat grumpy. This, I think, sums up our hero better than anything, because his stomach, deprived of breakfast, was now ruining the exquisite frisson of adventure that had been running down his spine. He closed his eyes, took a deep breath, and prepared himself for a long, icy void. A biting blast slapped his brow and he opened his eyes again in surprise.

He was already on the other side. Mercy me! he thought, on seeing the farm from his dream there before him. It was late afternoon and the light was fading. From the only window whose shutters were still open, to the left of the front door, came a beam of lamplight. Just then, someone opened the window and leaned outside, struggling against the icy wind. In the increasing gloom, Petrus couldn't make out her features, but even without seeing her he knew and, his heart leaping, his feet unsteady in his clogs, he took a few timid steps closer. Now he could see the craggy old face, the headdress with ribbons the color of forget-me-nots, and the vitality of a gaze that was both similar to and different from that of the woman in his dream—seventy years have gone by, he thought, this is her great-granddaughter.

"Sweet Jesus!" she exclaimed, on seeing him.

I understand her language, thought Petrus, stunned. She looked him up and down for a moment then, evidently judging him to be harmless, she swayed her head from left to right and said:

"What on earth are you doing, standing there stock-still and stupid? Come into the warm and we'll talk by the fire."

As he awkwardly came forward, still wobbling in his clogs, she laughed, reached for the shutters, which she closed with a bang, then slammed the windows just as energetically. A second later, the front door opened.

He slipped inside and found himself in a large room where a fire was burning in the hearth. There was a small crowd of people, who turned in unison to look at him.

"Hello, friend, what are you doing out in such frosty weather?" asked one of the guests, motioning to him to join them by the fire.

I understand, thought Petrus, but will I be able to speak? But he took the plunge, bowed politely, went closer, and felt the words roll naturally off his tongue.

"I got lost," he said, which was precisely what the guardian had instructed him to say, in any circumstance. "I was looking for an inn for the night, but I must have taken a wrong turn."

The man looked at him with amusement.

"A bow, and a fine gentleman's manner of speaking," he murmured, "but not an ounce of ill intent, for sure."

He thumped Petrus on the back, almost knocking him head over clogs.

"You've come at just the right time," he said, "Cousin Maurice is visiting and we're having a little feast."

He pointed to a man with a tanned, affable face, who gave

a smile and raised two fingers to stroke his temple, briefly—so that's how they say hello on the farm, thought Petrus.

"What's more, our Marguerite is in the kitchen, and that means a sight better food than you'd get at the inn," added the farmer, before placing a tiny glass in Petrus's hand identical to the ones the other men were holding.

He reached for a bottle filled with a clear liquid. Petrus, prompted by some powerful hunch, doubted it was water.

"Doudou's plum brandy," said the man, pouring him a splash of said liquid. "And Doudou never jokes around with serious things," he added, while the others laughed.

He looked Petrus straight in the eye.

"My name is Jean-René Faure," he said.

"Georges Bernard," said Petrus, something the guardian had also suggested, and for a split second he dreamt he might really be called Georges Bernard and stay forever in this farm-house room with its fragrances of paradise.

He'd never smelled such aromas, and he concluded that whatever was simmering in those pots was not what elves put in theirs—there were mysterious smells, powerful and musky, their warm sensuality both disturbing and enchanting at the same time. Just as he was thinking this, Jean-René lifted his glass right next to his and clicked them together, saying, Cheers! And Petrus, glad of a way to remedy the excessive sali-vation caused by the aromas around him, followed his exam-ple, tossing back his head and drinking the entire contents of his little glass in one go.

He collapsed on a bench. Am I about to die? he wondered. A wonderful warmth spread all over him, and he realized everyone was looking at him and laughing.

"This can't be the first time he's ever had a drop?" asked Jean-René, placing a hand on his shoulder.

Petrus wanted to reply, but he could feel tears streaming

down his cheeks. Suddenly letting go, accepting his fate, completely intoxicated by the fire in his gut, he began to laugh, too.

"Thanks be to God!" exclaimed Jean-René, immediately pouring him another glass of Doudou's plum brandy.

And the feast began, and no one was surprised by the presence of the potbellied ginger fellow, who did not seem to know how to put one clogged foot in front of another, but they all immediately recognized him as a harmless, likeable sort, given the candor of his clumsiness.

It was a time for drinking and joking about the day's minor events. When the women, placing the fruit of their concoctions on the table, gave the signal, they sat down; Jean-René recited a prayer before slicing a gleaming loaf of bread, and the cooks served the first of four dishes—or were there ten? Petrus had lost count by the second glass of wine they poured him: it was a reserve, they told him, one they kept for special occasions. He'd liked Doudou's plum brandy earlier on, and at the end of the meal he did justice to the jar of greengages in eau-de-vie opened to round out the experience. As for the wine, it was a brilliant finishing touch, and without it he certainly wouldn't have been able to honor the contents of his plate—which would have been a great pity because Marguerite was reputed to be the best chef in all the low country. Moreover, the provender being served that evening was the product of last week's hunting through the snowy woods where the trees cracked like ice floes and where the animals—caught straight out of their dens, no time even to blink an eye—had the succulent flesh of creatures who hadn't registered their demise. To you who are familiar with human food, I will describe the menu and the adversity this implied for Petrus: in addition to the soup with bacon which was the farm's everyday fare, he was made to suffer duck roasted on the spit, jugged hare, pheasant pâté, the leftovers of a doe terrine, braised endives, potatoes roasted in the fireplace, and a frying pan full of caramelized cardoons. Finally, after the half a cheese (from our own cows, if you please) per guest, they dished up a plum pie with an autumn crabapple compote, accompanied by a sauce that was both sweet and sour, known to refine the palate of any gourmet.

For now, Petrus was gazing at the soup where, among the carrots, potatoes, and leeks, there floated pinkish, off-white bits, and he questioned his neighbor about them.

"Pig, by Jove, pig!" answered the neighbor.

Pig! I can't eat pig! thought Petrus, horrified, picturing the Guard of the Pavilion crammed into a stewpot. But the pinkish morsels seemed to be winking at him, and the aroma was beguiling him like a succubus. After his third glass of wine, he mustered his courage and bit cautiously into the meat. He was met with an explosion of pleasure that dissolved any vestiges of the guilt that had already been diluted by the wines of the arrière-côte. While the fibers of bacon disintegrated on his tongue, he let the juice slip toward his throat and thought he might swoon with pleasure. What followed was even greater ecstasy, and after the sensual delight of the duck on the spit, he had no more scruples about wallowing in carnivorous debauchery. I'll do penance later, he thought, attacking the terrine and its fat and chunks, which either melted in his mouth or resisted his bite in a demonic ballet. It will come as no surprise to learn that the next morning he could not recall having had thoughts so foreign to his culture and his nature, not to mention the fact that he resolved his moral conflict by convincing himself that a stranger must adapt to the customs of the countries he visits, and by deluding himself that the animals had been killed without feeling pain—which forces us to acknowledge the fact that Petrus was behaving in a perfectly human manner. I will leave it to others to judge whether one should be glad of this. After dinner, everyone behaved like humans and natives of France, particularly Burgundians: the men enjoyed their little nightcap, the women tidied up the kitchen, drinking herbal tea, and they honored the dinner with fine compliments. Maurice decreed that Marguerite's pheasant pâté was the most tender in the civilized world, which caused much debate regarding a related existential problem of major importance (the consubstantial dryness of pheasant pâté) then, without batting an eyelash, he asked the chef to share her secret—to which she replied by saying she would rather be crucified alive and left to the crows of the six cantons than divulge the secret to her knack for pâté.

And while Petrus may have enjoyed the evening's fare, the wine had been an experience of another order. A first sip, and it was the land of Burgundy in his mouth, its winds and mist, its stones and vine stock; the more he drank, the deeper he penetrated the secrets of the universe in a way which the contemplation of the peaks in his Woods had never allowed; and while his elfin soul understood a hundredfold this magic born of the alliance between earth and sky, what was human in his heart could be expressed at last. In the dual story for which the winemaker and the drinker were responsible the most marvelous thing, beyond the enlightenment of intoxication, could be found; the vine told a slow adventure, vegetal and cosmic, an epic of low walls and hillsides in the sun; then the wine loosened tongues and gave birth in turn to stories which the prophecy had only foreshadowed. There was talk of miraculous hunting and virgins in the snow, of holy processions, of sacred violets, and fabulous creatures whose wanderings captivated the villagers, absorbed by their last drams of liqueur, while a new life was added to the everyday one, sparkling in the background of what was visible, and opening the freedom of dreams in waking time. He did not know whether he owed this metamorphosis to the talent of his new human companions, or to the exquisite floating feeling that each new glass of wine instilled, but he could sense the death throes of his old frustration that an intangible screen was keeping things from him. Now the screen had been shattered, and he had access to the throbbing pulse of his emotions; the world was radiant, more intense; although he had no doubt that this was possible without wine, the vine and the tale stood together with this transfiguration of levels of reality; and now that, seven decades on, he understood the message of the wild grasses in the channel, he was so moved by it that he stammered something his neighbor had to ask him to repeat.

Everyone fell silent around the table.

Maurice again asked Petrus to repeat what he'd said. They were all staring at him with those soft moist eyes that come from food and the vine, and he mumbled, his voice quavering slightly:

"It would be as if the world was a novel waiting for its words."

How stupid he felt, dismayed by his own syntax, seeing that they were waiting for an explanation. But unexpectedly Jean-René came to the rescue, raising his little glass of brandy and declaring in a kindly tone:

"For sure, what would we do without stories by the fire and old grannies' fairy tales?"

The congregation nodded their heads, sufficiently softened by wine to give credence to this cryptic translation. They cogitated briefly on the matter (but not too much), then returned to their conversation, which was slowed by the prospect of settling cheek on pillow, and snoring off the wine until the next day at dawn.

Still, while they were halfheartedly making their final

comments for the evening, one topic Maurice broached landed on the table like a flying spark and made everyone sit up straight in their chair to enter the debate with passion.

"I say there's no better season than winter," he insisted, without batting an eyelid.

Then, pleased with his contribution, he rewarded himself with a final splash of brandy.

As one might have expected, the trap worked.

"What ever for?" asked Jean-René, his tone falsely amiable.

"For hunting and gathering wood, by Jove!" replied the simple man.

This was the signal for a heated discussion that Petrus only dimly understood, other than that it was something to do with hunts and dogs, timber and orchards, and a divinity in those parts whom they referred to as the whip. It lasted a pleasantly endless amount of time, which he enlivened with a few additional glasses, but in the end (and to his great regret), because it was getting close to midnight and all good things must come to an end, Marguerite took it upon herself to end the discussion.

"Every season is the good Lord's," she said.

Out of respect for the granny, (something to do with her mastery of pheasant), the men fell silent and celebrated their renewed alliance with the courtesy of a final splash of plum brandy. Jean-René Faure, however, who could not ignore the laws of hospitality, asked Petrus what his favorite season was— and Petrus was surprised to discover how easy it was to think, despite his drinking and eating like a Burgundian pig. He raised his little glass to each man in turn, as he'd seen done, and recited the three lines from the *Canto of the Alliance*:

Neither spring nor summer nor winter
Know the grace
Of languid autumn

The others looked at him, astounded, then at each other, eyes shining.

"For sure, if we start with poetry . . . " murmured Jean-René.

They all bowed their heads with unexpected deference. Marguerite was smiling; the women nudged a leftover piece of pie with a final dollop of sour cream in his direction; and everyone seemed happier than the little angels in the great heavens.

"Time for bed," said Jean-René finally.

But instead of taking their leave, the men stood up, their faces serious, and the women made a sign over their breast which, Petrus would later learn, was the sign of the cross. Gripped by the solemnity of the moment, he wanted to imitate them, so he stood up, made the same sign, almost tripped over his own plate, steadied himself on his clogs, and listened to the final prayer.

"Let us pray for those who fell in battle," said the host, "and in particular for the village men whose names are carved on the monument across from the church, so that no one will ever forget them because, though now the fighting's still recent, tomorrow they'll all be gone from people's minds."

"Amen," said the others.

They lowered their heads and stood for a moment in contemplative silence. So they have fought a major war, thought Petrus. Then there was a faint murmur as conversation started up again, and he felt that something was trying to make its way inside him—was it the beneficial effect of the wine, or the dignity of the moment; he could hear faint voices, intermittently.

"Unfortunately, I have heard say that prayers are not enough to knock sense into a man's brain," said Jean-René, placing a friendly hand on his shoulder.

After a pause, he added:

"That is why I go to the cemetery every day to hear what my dead have to say to me."

The simmering echo suddenly exploded in Petrus's head.

"*There was a great earthquake, and the moon became as blood*," he said, then stopped, stunned.

What am I on about? he wondered.

But the other man was gently nodding his head.

"That's it, precisely," he said, "that is exactly what we went through, the lot of us."

Finally, the guests withdrew and Petrus was shown to his room, a little lean-to that smelled fragrantly of hay, where they had prepared a woolen mattress, a soft pillow, and a warm blanket. The visions from the long-ago dream at the teahouse were swirling through his brain, and the horror rumbling inside him made his heart sink, once again. Did I see images of some bygone war or of a war yet to come? he wondered, and then, surrendering his last weapons to the excellent local wine, he collapsed on his bed and instantly fell asleep.

It was a sleep with neither tremors nor visions, a night of existential void that left no memories. On waking, however, he was painfully called back to life, and he more dragged himself than walked to the common room. There was an enticing smell, and a young woman was busy clearing a table where three cloves of garlic lay next to a glass of water and a large earthenware jug.

"Would you like some coffee?" she asked him.

Although he couldn't open his left eye, the first sip did Petrus a world of good.

"The men told me to tell you they send their regards and that you are welcome to stay at The Hollows for as long as you like," she said. "It's the first major hunt of the year, and they couldn't wait for you this morning, but if you're hungry, I can make something for you."

"Is The Hollows the name of the farm?" asked Petrus, politely declining her offer of food.

"It is that," she said, "and has been for longer than anyone can remember."

"Where are the other ladies?" he asked.

She laughed.

"Ladies, indeed . . . " she said before stopping herself, then adding: "They're with the priest at the Marcelot farm, where we heard the old woman won't make it through the day."

And she made the sign of the cross.

An hour later, Petrus took his leave, instructing his hostess to thank Jean-René Faure and to assure him that he had business to see to, but would not fail to come back again soon. Then, stumbling inelegantly in his clogs, he went out into the courtyard. There was not a breath of wind; a vast blue sky was set upon a pure white land; on the branches, pearls of ice twinkled like stars. Not sure what he was doing, Petrus set off down the main road until he came to a large wrought-iron gate. There were stone walls, and pathways in neat rows, and a large rectangle of tombstones and crosses: it was the cemetery. He stood before the graves, ignoring the cruel chill and the searing pain in his head. After a moment, he raised his head and said out loud: I want to go back to Nanzen.

A second later, the Head of the Council and the Guardian of the Pavilion, arms crossed, were gazing at him with an expression devoid of all indulgence.

"I hope you have a headache," said the Head of the Council.

Petrus turned into a squirrel, and he felt how greatly he had missed his animal essences.

"I have a headache," he said, wretchedly.

"*There was a great earthquake, and the moon became as blood*. Where did you get that from?"

"I have no idea," said Petrus.

"Revelation 6:12, although the quote has been truncated,"

said the guardian. "If you are capable of reinventing the human Bible after a few glasses of their wine, perhaps we should think of forgiving you your wanderings."

"The Bible?" said Petrus.

"We are going to have to educate you before we send you back among the humans," said the Head of the Council. "We cannot leave things to chance."

"They are not left to chance," said the guardian.

Petrus looked at him gratefully and, trusting his impulse, he said:

"I have to go wherever there's wine."

The Head of the Council raised his eyebrow, ironically.

Petrus hunted for his words and couldn't find them.

"Wine," echoed the Head of the Council, thoughtful. "We have never paid any attention to it. It never occurred to elves to grow wine grapes, let alone drink it."

On hearing these words, Petrus felt everything come clear in his mind, the way it does in stories and fables, when one grasps what cannot be clearly explained.

"Wine is to humans what tea is to elves," he said. "The key to the alliance is there."

In a time of miraculous hunting
Of sacred violets
Great earthquakes
Beneath a moon of blood

Book of Battles

狩

THE WHIP

The whip is the only true divinity of hunting country. His knowledge of every copse and every thicket is honored. It is known that he leaves at dawn to mark out the path for the hunt, and this silent prayer through the sleeping woods serves him as the finest of matins, rendering thanks to earth and sky and singing the nobility of thrushes.

旅

TRAVEL

If there is one human inclination elves are lacking, it is that of travel.

This inclination, paradoxically, affects humans because of a flaw that makes it impossible for them to *be here*, to find themselves in the simple *presence* of things, and it has molded them into creatures who are both restless and inspired.

Can anyone imagine what immersion in the world combined with an appetite for change would look like? To welcome the void and delight in fantasy? Yes, we can imagine it, and we dream of it, and we pray to the great winds of dreams to take us there.

At the time when Petrus began traveling all over the world of humans, the Head of the Council returned from Rome with astounding news.

"We know who the gray notebook belonged to," he said to Petrus one day when they were both in Nanzen together with the guardian and a handful of his assistants.

He told them how he went to Rome under a false human identity—an orchestra conductor by the name of Gustavo Acciavatti—and, on the pretext of acquiring some Italian Renaissance drawings, he'd met Roberto Volpe. He was normally pleasant company, but the murder had broken him, and his fascination with the painting was eating away at him. At the end of the evening, the elf had followed the dealer into a large room where the curtains were drawn; the painting was hanging on a wall papered in black silk. The Guardian of the Pavilion shared the image and Petrus studied it with curiosity: a sober, intimate scene was unfolding against a dark background; the protagonists' faces were devastated. Now better informed about human religions, he recognized a scene from the Christian New Testament.

"A pietà, like the ones the Flemish painted by the thousand," said the Head of the Council. "Christ in the arms of the Virgin and, in the background, Mary Magdalene and a few grieving followers."

"It's beautiful," murmured Petrus.

He fell silent, prey to a fleeting intuition.

"It's magnificent," said the Head of the Council, "but that is not the painting's only quality. Although I've been studying the art of humans for a long time, it took me a while to understand what I was seeing here."

Petrus blinked and his vision of the painting was turned on its end.

"It was painted by an elf," he said.

"It was painted by an elf. An elf established in Amsterdam as a painter at the beginning of the sixteenth century according to the human calendar. In reality, the first elf to have gone over to the human world."

"I thought the bridge has existed since the dawn of time," said Petrus.

"I should have said, to have gone over *for good* into the human world. To us he'd vanished into thin air, but apparently, he chose to become a man. It had never happened before, we didn't have the slightest idea it was even possible. However, we have no reason to doubt this information, insofar as we heard it this morning from the renegade's father, in other words, from the lips of the previous Guardian of the Pavilion."

"Three hundred years ago the offspring of the former guardian went forever into the human world and no one ever knew about it?" said Petrus.

"I'd summoned my predecessor to Nanzen to ask his advice, and I mentioned the fact that the victim went to Amsterdam in search of a painting and a gray notebook, and he then informed me that his eldest child had transformed the bridge long ago in a way that would allow for permanent passage to the other side, and that afterwards he had settled among humans by taking on the identity of a Flemish painter."

"But why did he hide the fact, not to mention how?" asked Petrus.

"A father's heart is unfathomable," answered the guardian, "and he was surely afraid that others might be tempted by the adventure. This morning, however, he couldn't keep the secret any longer, although he had divulged it earlier to another elf we know—an elf whose family he has been acquainted with since childhood."

"The head of the garden," said Petrus. "They are both from Ryoan."

He looked again at the painting. Why do I know that it was painted by one of our kind, even when I know nothing about human painting? he thought. The picture is telling a human story, but the way it goes to the heart of things is elfin. And yet, there is something else, indefinable, something I cannot put my finger on.

"Why and how did our elf go over to the humans?" said the Guardian of the Pavilion. "His father doesn't know, his son didn't want to see him again once he'd gone over."

"In what way did he transform the bridge?" asked Petrus. "Why didn't that transform our world?"

"In fact, the mists were transformed," said the guardian. "They were already declining, to a lesser degree, and according to my predecessor, this alteration to the bridge regenerated them in a spectacular way. I think the gray notebook contains the answers to our questions, in the hand of our exiled painter."

This marked the beginning of an unprecedented era, where the partisans of the garden gained in influence, the Head of the Council went to Rome on a regular basis in order to meet with Roberto Volpe, and Petrus devoted himself body and soul to his two quests, dividing his time between the world of humans and the Council library. The library contained a section that was closed to the public and only accessible upon special request. But the Head of the Council had placed it at his disposal without restriction or directions.

"Humans know nothing of our existence and we have

always been glad of that fact," he said, entrusting him with the key. "We are a peace-loving sort, and the wars, however violent, with the peoples on the borders have never had the power to destroy the foundations of our harmony. But humans are a warlike species, on another scale altogether than our nasty orcs or our evil goblins."

"Why are they so aggressive?" asked Petrus.

"They are haunted by the notion of their own divinity, and their appetite for war comes from the fact they have rejected their animal selves," he replied. "Humans do not recognize the unity of living creatures, and they consider themselves to be above all other kingdoms. Along these lines, I have come to believe that our woes stem from the loss of a number of our own animals."

"Apparently in antiquity we were not merely triple," said Petrus.

"Our ancestors were every animal at once. One day I shall introduce you to one of these venerable old forefathers."

"A living ancestor?" asked Petrus, stunned.

"That's the big question," answered the Head of the Council.

The *Human Literature* section in the library was restricted but, as Petrus would learn along the way, one could count the requests for special dispensations over recent centuries on one hand. It contained scholarly works about humans written by elves who had lived among them, including Guardians of the Pavilion and Heads of the Council through the ages. But it also contained books written by humans, and Petrus began to read them voraciously; his zeal, far from lessening over time, ended up encroaching upon his sleep.

He could not believe what he was reading. He'd spent so many years yawning over the sublime elegies of his peers, so many years unaware that the object of his quest was to be found in the next room! He devoured essays on the human way of life, where he found the material to plan his journeys to the other side of the red bridge, but it was their storybook fiction that amazed him beyond expression, turning the world on its head, digging tunnels in the marrow of life. As he'd begun to explore the vineyards of France, he chose primarily French novels, and was amazed at how he could understand the language, although he often had to turn to the dictionary because of a lexicon that, to him, seemed to know no limits. Elfin language is univocal and precise; through melodic sounds it represents a natural world devoid of afterworlds, and one can easily match the thing with the word. As for elfin writing, it was borrowed from the earth's eastern civilizations, and consists of lines full of imagery, the polar opposite of the formal alphabets that we in the West use to signify reality. But French, which by the grace of Nanzen, Petrus could read as if it were his mother tongue, seemed to gain in verbosity what it lost in constituent flesh, and he was astounded that a language of such disembodied essence could, paradoxically, be so rich in inexhaustible possibilities. Nothing delighted him more than whatever was *unnecessary*, embellishments serving no other purpose than to be decorative, with which sentences and turns of phrase were saturated, and he wanted to read not only works of literature, but also grammar books and treatises on conjugations and, finally, writers' correspondence, where he would learn how a story is constructed and developed. Then, after relishing the ingeniousness of the language and its practice, he immersed himself anew in a novel, and once again life was illuminated.

"You will feel the same way about other terrestrial idioms," said the Head of the Council, one day when he confessed to his admiration for the French language. "But unbridled invention fails to fascinate me—all that reading you enjoy so much leaves me puzzled. I much prefer human music."

The motionless journey of literature made him see the world in a way he couldn't in the mists, just as it would've been impossible for him to understand the message of the wild grasses in the channel had he not spent the evening listening to legends and tales at The Hollows farm. Like a damp cloth seeping with ink and pigment, human fantasies made the world exude its invisible layers and exhibit them, naked and shivering, in broad daylight. That was the true grace of stories, their complex weave where one never looked at the visible part of the cloth, but rather at a faint sparkling only hinted at in the weft. This ineffable vibration replaced reason and the explanations of the mind when it came to understanding the heart, and Petrus did not see the characters of tales and novels as any less real than the beings he encountered in everyday life, that life which takes place in the motion of voyage and reveals so little about intentions or souls. One thing amused him: he never felt more of an elf than when he was striding through the countries on earth, only to discover that he was definitely human once he returned to his mists. When he was wandering around the vineyards in France or Italy, he thought tenderly of his serene land of tea and poetry; the moment he set foot in Nanzen, he was overcome with nostalgia for humans and their slovenly ways, for their gift at making life luxurious by spicing it up with the hint of imperfection that gave it all its genius. Finally, he was enchanted by wine and, to add a finishing touch to its benefits, the winemakers also told him stories, tales that had their roots in the soil of the vineyards, then rose toward the heavens of desires and dreams. And so, Petrus understood that it wasn't the wine that accomplished a task, the way the elves' tea did, but rather the fictions the wine catalyzed; thus, it was the metaphor, and not the cause of the miracle—however, he refrained from admitting to any of this, partly because he wanted to go on drinking, and partly because what he had begun to suspect at The Hollows was confirmed every time he took a sip from the bottle.

Unlike humans who lose their faculties when drinking, when he drank wine, Petrus found that some of his qualities were enhanced. Of course, he felt the drunkenness that made the world spin toward amiable shores and, like everyone, he would begin to blather on after only a few glasses. But this didn't diminish his ordinary skills, and it even endowed him with a few extraordinary talents, as became evident during a fight he unwillingly got caught up in at an inn in Montepulciano, in central Italy, where he'd been welcomed for the night after a visit to a winery. He was killing time, playing with a last jug of Tuscan wine, and he had no idea why tempers flared, but suddenly the lads had gone for each other's throats, bellowing in dialect and lashing out every which way. Yet, even in the panic, it was easy for Petrus to dodge the blows: the more unsteady he was on his feet, the better he outsmarted the strategies of his adversaries as they whirled their arms uselessly in the air. Well, look at that! he thought, delighted, when a lad twice his height, thinking he'd got Petrus by the collar, crashed enthusiastically against the wall instead. Petrus stumbled in front of another fellow who was plowing the air where he'd stood a second earlier, then he collapsed just in time in front of a third one who wanted to squeeze his throat with his big hairy paws. When the troops had reached the verge of exhaustion and he was the last one standing, he went up to his little room and snored the sleep of the just.

So many fascinating things happened in these stopping-off places where tempers flared that he felt at home, and established a routine. He had come back several times to visit Jean-René Faure and the good souls at The Hollows, and he always took a room at the neighboring Hôtel de la Poste, where the fare was not as mediocre as Jean-René had declared it to be. Still, he never missed an opportunity to dine at the farm when Marguerite was cooking. She excelled at stews and roasts, but she also knew how to work miracles with the sweets from the garden, and he so passionately loved her quince jellies that she would never let him leave without a little basket full of them where, depending on the season, she would also add a few fresh walnuts, crisp apples, or an armful of pink carnations. Then he would go back to the inn drunk as a lord and sit down in the common room, where they would bring him his half-jug of wine. It so happens that in addition to the well-being procured by these last solitary drops, the innkeeper's daughter was blonde, buxom, and smiling. In his native land, Petrus showed so little interest in members of the opposite sex that he'd long believed that love didn't interest him—at least not the sort of love that drove his fellow creatures to declare their ardor, share an open veranda overlooking a little garden of mist, and conceive elfkins who one day would go running among the bamboo and the stones. The young women at the inns, starting with Roselyne-from-the-Hôtel-de-la-poste, made him understand that his past indifference was due precisely to the fact that he loved human women. Picture their first dialogue one evening when Petrus had just come in from a dinner at The Hollows that had lasted longer than usual, due to both a guinea fowl that had been reluctant to cook and a fascinating debate between disciples of Burgundy wine and zealots of claret (the end of said debate is transcribed here).

"Your fondest memory?" Petrus (not yet familiar with the wines of Bordeaux) asked Jeannot (who had a crush on him).

"I don't have any," replied the lad, "but I dream of tasting some petrus, someday."

"Petrus?" said the elf who, that very morning, while pursuing his exploration of human beliefs and religions, had come upon an engraving with the following caption: *Sanctus Petrus ad januas paradisi.*

Enchanted by the coincidence, he added:

"That is my second name."

Then he thought, what am I on about.

"You mean you are also called Petrus?" exclaimed Jeannot, delighted.

From that day on, they only ever called him Petrus at the farm. And so, when he was sitting on his bench in the common room, and Roselyne came to ask him if he needed anything, placing her smile and her white bosom well within sight of his tired eyes, and she added, *what's it they call you, then*, he replied:

"Petrus."

She smiled.

"That's a sweet name, Petrus," she said.

Then she pinched his cheek and added:

"Petrukins."

I owe it to my honesty as a historiographer to say that things did not stop there, and that the next day, Petrus returned to Nanzen with crimson cheeks and a furtive gaze. Roselyne, for all her youth, was not unskilled, and she led him to her room with a disarming, natural ease. There, delightfully candid, she kissed him, long and gently. Her lips had a taste of Mercurey wine and nothing seemed more desirable to Petrus than this serving girl with her ample forms and mischievous gaze. When she undressed and revealed her lovely, heavy, slightly pendulous breasts, he understood that it was her imperfections that were kindling his desire. Her milky skin, round thighs, plump belly, soft shoulders—all characteristics which, in the mists would have been inconceivable and shocking—filled him with lust, and when she placed her hand in his beard this lust became dizzying. When she tore off his clothes and drew him onto the bed and made him collapse on top of her, the exquisite softness of her offered body almost made him swoon with pleasure. As she was giving herself to him and for the first time he was delighting in intimacy with the opposite sex, he thought: right, this is not the time to falter. And, leaning over her face, seeing the delicate texture of her skin, the sweat beading at her temples, the charming flaw of her nose that was slightly off-center, he thought again: I love her smell. Roselyne smelled of the rose perfume she used every morning, but also the sweat of a long day's work, and this mixture of refinement and nature pleased Petrus, and broke all the elfin rules governing desire.

Now he was standing, dying a thousand deaths, before the highest authorities of his world.

"We shall have to find a way to preserve your privacy," said the Head of the Council, who was trying hard not to laugh (which so surprised Petrus that he blushed all the deeper).

"A bit more discretion would do your quest no harm," said the guardian (who was having a very good time as well), "and you have emptied two innocent pillows of their feathers."

There was, in fact, a moment when Roselyne, naked as a worm, had stood up on the bed and, laughing hysterically, had tossed all the duck feathers in the air, above her lovely tousled head.

"I am sorry," said Petrus, who was thinking of jumping out the window.

"We must agree to a signal to help us anticipate the nature of your activities," said the guardian.

They agreed, and Petrus went on with his explorations interspersed with wine and comely young women.

He was in the habit of saying he was traveling on business, and if anyone asked him, what sort of business, he would simply say, family business, because family business is family business, after all, and anyone who tries to stick their nose in it is simply a boor. But the gentlemen he met at the winemakers' did not refrain from divulging their identities and positions, and Petrus learned all about the enterprises and professions on the planet, as well as the splendors of a species he'd learned to love despite all their vanities. One day, when he was at a wine-maker friend's, somewhere in the Côte-d'Or, he met a writer for the first time. He was impressed by his bearing, his mus-tache and his little beard, but surprised by what he heard him saying when he entered the cellar where the great man was drinking and joking with a few others. It sounded like they were exchanging dirty jokes, one after the other, and so on for a good while, and Petrus was disappointed not to hear the writer telling proper stories. Then he forgot his frustration and began to laugh heartily himself. There were a few unforget-table witticisms—*of all the sexual aberrations, the worst is chastity, Christianity did a lot for love by making it a sin*—with, toward the end, a more serious conversation where Petrus was on his own to put his questions to the writer.

"Have you been to war?" he asked.

"I wasn't at the front," the writer replied, "but I have writ-ten about war and I will continue to do so, particularly because the one that is coming will be even more terrible and deadly than the previous ones."

"The one that is coming?"

"There is always a war coming. Always a civilization dying, which the next civilization will refer to as barbarian."

"If everything is doomed, what can we do?" asked Petrus.

"We can drink wine and love women!" the writer said. "And believe in beauty and poetry, the only possible religions in this world."

"You're not Christian?" asked Petrus.

"Are you?" asked the writer, looking at him, amused.

"No, no," said Petrus, "I'm—"

He broke off, at a loss to say what he was.

The writer looked at him, even more amused.

"Do you read?" he asked.

"Yes," said Petrus, "as much as I travel."

"We spend too much time in books and not enough in nature."

"I learn a great deal from traveling, but mainly from books," said Petrus.

"*So, as I did not study, I learned a great deal,*" answered the man. "I wrote that one day in a book no one will read anymore, once flowers wither on my tomb."

"So there is no hope?" asked Petrus.

"It is because we believe in roses that we make them blossom," said the writer. "The fact they end up dying does not change anything. There is always one war coming and another one ending, and so we must relentlessly start dreaming again."

They were silent as they emptied their last glass.

"Do you know who is the first to die?" the writer asked at last, thoughtfully.

Petrus could find nothing to say.

"The visionary," continued the writer. "It is always the visionary who dies, in the first exchange of gunfire. And when he falls in the snow, and knows he is dying, he recalls the hunts of his childhood, when his grandfather taught him to respect the deer."

There was another moment's silence.

"Farewell, friend," he said at last. "May life bring you gaiety, which is the most amiable form of courage."

Petrus often pondered this conversation, and had no trouble honoring its premise—wine and women—and he understood how one could learn without studying. That is the virtue of the novel, he thought, at least for the reader; writing one must be another kettle of fish.

That day, in addition to his meeting with the great writer,

Petrus also received a surprising piece of information from his winemaker friend in la Côte, and he decided to look into it further.

"I recently went to Spain," the winemaker (whose name was Gaston Bienheureux) told him suddenly.

As he said this, his expression grew wistful, which surprised Petrus, who was used to seeing him frank and talkative.

"In a place in Extremadura called Yepes," continued Gaston. "There's a castle there, with an extraordinary wine cellar, and all the winemakers in Europe go there."

He fell silent, took a sip of his *vin d'amitié*, a vintage reserved for friends that he would never sell, and seemed to forget what he'd said. When at dinner Petrus raised the subject again, Gaston didn't know what to say.

The next day, in Nanzen, the guardian shared the vision of a stony, arid plain, broken now and again by sun-baked trees and hills and, on the horizon, a village dominated by a fortress. One hour later, Petrus landed there. It was hotter than hell, and Petrus grumbled at having to wear a bamboo hat that felt itchy on his forehead. Need I tell you that thirty years—which amounts to barely four in an elf's lifetime—had gone by since our hero became the Council's special envoy to the human world? That there is not a trace, anywhere, of the two children of November and snow, and that the entire matter seems to be frozen in permafrost? Patience, however—for everything has been set in motion and is coming together, and one day soon Petrus will find out what to expect from Yepes. In the village, he didn't meet a soul. He went into the inn and, after the torrid heat outside, it felt as cold as the grave, no one came. After a moment cooling down and growing impatient, he went back out and took the steep path that led to the fortress.

At the gates to the fortress, he came upon a young boy who waved at him.

"What fair winds bring you here?" he asked politely.

But the boy barred the way.

"I've come upon the recommendation of a winemaker friend," said Petrus.

"Are you a winemaker yourself?" asked the boy.

"No," said Petrus, who at the time was not prepared to lie.

"I'm sorry, but you must go on your way," said the young guard.

Petrus looked up at the stone walls and studied the narrow windows. An eagle was flying very high in the sky and there was a sharp hardness to the air, but also the fragrance of wonder, a perfume of fury and roses which made him think of the poetry of his mists. *Worlds are born because they die*, he murmured, before waving goodbye to the boy and turning on his heels. Then he remembered another line and, finally, he begged Nanzen to repatriate him.

"*We are all about to be born,*" he said to himself again, upon landing on the red bridge.

He delivered his report on his visit to the guardian and the Head of the Council, who were also puzzled, and it was decided he would go there again the very next day.

But it was at this very moment in the story that news from Rome caused the sky of quests to explode, upending the calendar of actions, diverting Petrus from Yepes, and precipitating a historical decision on the part of the Head of the Council himself.

Roberto Volpe was dead, and he had left all his belongings to his son Pietro, from whom the Head of the Council—still going by the identity, in the human world, of Gustavo Acciavatti, orchestra conductor by trade—had tried to purchase the painting. Pietro had refused to sell it, but they had become friends. Prior to this, Leonora Volpe, Pietro's young sister, had fallen in love with the Maestro, who often came to visit her father on the pretext of acquiring Renaissance drawings. The Head of the Council, who had also fallen in love with Leonora, did not see how he could go against these workings of fate, because this woman's presence had become more vital to him than anything else on earth. Tall, dark-haired, languorous and elegant, she gave a texture to his life that it had always lacked. Her rather austere beauty, without adornment or artifice, gave him a feeling of land and rootedness that contrasted with the evanescence of his misty world; but she also had something of a dancer about her, a languid way of moving that evoked the trees in his homeland. And so, he was going to reside permanently on the other side of the red bridge, although he hadn't uncovered the secret of permanent passage into the world of humans, and had to conceal his elfin nature. The painter in Amsterdam, through the transformation he had transmitted to the bridge, had taken on the genetic characteristics of the species but, as the gray notebook was still unrecovered, for the moment the new Gustavo had to remain content with merely pretending to be a human.

For the first time in the history of the mists, a Head of the Council was resigning from office and calling for new elections. He gave no reason. The world of elves was in turmoil, and resented this man they loved and admired for abandoning ship just as the mists were declining even further.

Naturally, the head of the garden ran in the new elections with a profession of faith that was even more pathetic than the previous time, and his campaign was bitter and ugly. His opponent, a councilor from Inari, in the province of Snows, took after his dear friend who had resigned and strove to win the highest office with the same elegance and ability to distance himself. He was narrowly elected, and now I can refer to him by the name you are familiar with, that of Solon, Gustavo's old friend, but also the guardian's, which he reaffirmed in Nanzen immediately after his accession to the leadership of the Council. I'll wager you will not be surprised to learn that this guardian you have known for a long time was called Tagore by humans; and so now we have caught up with all the elfin protagonists from the beginning of our tale—those who, in slightly less than forty years from now, will welcome Alejandro de Yepes and Jesús Rocamora to Nanzen, fresh from their castillo.

For the time being, however, Solon, Tagore, and Gustavo are working to thwart the enemy's maneuvers. In the person of the head of the garden, baptized Aelius by the opposite camp, the devil is sharpening his knives and rallying his loyal supporters. Does he really believe that humankind is responsible for the extinction of the mists? Who can really know these things? Between the lies our hearts tell us, and the truths we will not admit to, everything has ended up looking like a puzzle where the pieces are mixed and muddled. The fact remains that Aelius's crusade, unable to obtain weapons legally, is now borrowing the weapons it had always coveted, and is conspiring to provoke total war. It is not yet the war that will break out in the human world and last three years, filling the elves of Nanzen with dismay—but the master of Ryoan will find inspiration in it for his own patiently instigated war. A few more years and, once he has gained possession of the gray notebook, he will construct and conceal his own bridge. Then he'll be able to come and go between the two worlds without resorting to the services of a traitor, and will begin to move his pawns on the chessboard of the earth. Appropriately, his first move will be to send his most faithful right-hand man to Rome: the Hanase piglet has become Raffaele Santangelo, the future governor of the capital and subsequent president of the Italian Council, upon the orders of his master in Ryoan.

Every story has its traitors. Our story has one in particular, who wrought so much evil that, out of weariness or sorrow, we shall not speak his name, for he belonged to the respected elite of assistants to the pavilion, and no one had ever witnessed perfidy of this extreme in the mists. He passes information to his master, removes all trace of his passage, executes his orders in both worlds, and delivers the gray notebook by resorting to corruption and murder. Due to a consubstantial impossibility in the species, which has endured despite all its mutations, Aelius will require the complicity of human assassins for his despicable plans. The traitor recruits them, then makes them disappear in a fashion we will learn of soon, the same which saw the murderers in Yepes vanish into thin air without a trace.

The world of mists will be confronted with the first internal division in its history, and Aelius is recruiting new partisans every day, with his speeches filled with anger and fear. I believe this goes to show that something among the elves has been broken, for they'd always been impermeable to fear, doubt, and the question of decline.

Petrus continues to read and travel. Despite his efforts, the guardian cannot get him into the fortress at Yepes, but only as far as the gates, where he is sent away, every time. Marguerite dies of old age, Jean-René of ill health. Petrus makes friends all over Europe, a continent in turmoil, at a time when rumors of war can be heard, despite the pledge that the last war would really be the last. Silence and shadow lengthen and spread like a flood over the continent.

Now it is 1918 on the human calendar, fourteen years

before the beginning of the greatest conflict in the history of elves and humans combined, fourteen years of intensifying intrigue, while the armies begin to form.

But first a night of November and snow.

Worlds are born because they die
We are all about to be born

Book of Battles

薔薇

ROSES

It is said that everything was born from the void the day a brush drew a line through it, separating earth from sky. And so, a rose must have followed, then the sea, the mountains, and the trees.

It is in drawing a line of ink that one makes the earth emerge; it is in believing in roses that one makes them bloom.

So much effort for such mortal creatures, so much beauty doomed to flourish and die. But the battle for the birth of this beauty—doomed to die that night—is all we will ever have in this life.

雪

SNOW

It is said that everything was born from the void the day a brush drew a line through it, separating earth from sky. And so, snow must have fallen, a soft snow that made the chill of the dawning of the world less cruel.

Maria was the lady of snows, of the thawing of bodies and hearts, of light snowflakes and dawns full of promise. It had snowed in the first scene, it would snow in the last, and she wondered if the balm would appease her troubles—the snows of the beginning and the snows of the end are the same, they shine like lanterns along a path of black stones, are a light inside us piercing the night, and fall on the plain where worlds dissolve and take with them sighs and crosses.

OF SOLITUDE AND OF THE MIND
1918–1938

Night of November and snow—somewhere in central Italy a young woman gives birth to a little girl, and in Katsura, the companion of Solon, the Head of the Council, gives birth to their first elfkin, also a girl.

Both newborn babies are miracles.

The young woman's name is Teresa and she will die that same night. The child should never have been born: her father is an elf, and unions between the two species are sterile. It's in Rome, at the home of Gustavo Acciavatti, that Tagore met Teresa, a young virtuoso pianist who belonged to the group of artists and friends, including Sandro Centi and Pietro Volpe, who often met at the Maestro's villa. Solon, Tagore, and Gustavo were childhood friends before they became companions and allies in power—but that was not their only bond, for both of them, among the most powerful elves in all the land of mists, had fallen in love with human women. Who could ever have suspected that one of those unions would produce a child?

In Katsura, another child was welcomed into the world: the infant did not look anything like an elfkin, but rather like a human baby, unable to change into a foal or a doe or any other animal—a high-elf resembling a human child, looking out at the world with her big black little girl's eyes.

Tagore has left Italy to go to the upper chamber where a select council is being held with the councilors Solon can trust. They have been preparing for it since the announcement of Teresa's pregnancy, but they did not suspect the clauses of fate would be so clear. Now the two children of November and snow have been born, and the prophecy will live.

the rebirth of the mist
through two children of snow and November
the rootless, the last alliance

"Rootless ones," murmurs Gustavo, the former Head of the Council, who has just arrived from Rome.

Solon nods. Petrus, recently repatriated from a holiday on the banks of the Loire (and vats of a sparkling wine apt to raise the dead) feels his heart sink (while his head is like a watermelon).

"We have to hide them," he says.

"I will have your daughter taken to the Abruzzo," Gustavo says to Tagore. "There is a presbytery there, with an orchard. Sandro has often spoken to me about the place because his brother is the priest at the presbytery, and he will take care of her."

"I trust Sandro," said Tagore. "Teresa loves him like a brother."

He bursts into tears.

"Loved him like a brother," he says.

Everyone is silent, sharing his sorrow.

"I will take your daughter to Yepes," Petrus says to Solon. "Maybe that is where fate is telling us to go."

In the November night, it is snowing on all the paths of fate.

It is snowing on the steps of the church in Santo Stefano di Sessanio, on the slopes of the Gran Sasso, where the daughter of Teresa and Tagore has been left in warm swaddling clothes, while they wait for the priest to find her. A few seconds later, the priest takes the little bundle in his arms and disappears around the corner of the nave.

It is snowing on the castillo in Yepes where, for the first time, Tagore has been able to gain entrance for Petrus, but for only a minute, alas, after the assassination of the family at the castle. The elf is about to leave for the pavilion again when suddenly it seems to him that the tiny girl is shivering. On an old chest, there is a blanket of fine cambric, and he wraps her in it with care. Then he asks the red bridge to take him to The Hollows. Before long it is cousin Angèle who, on her way to feed the rabbits, finds the tiny high-elf on the steps, looking just like every other little baby girl on earth. Petrus watches as the granny takes the bundled infant in her arms and disappears back into the farm, dries his tears mingled with snowflakes, walks for a while through the snowy countryside, then leaves again for the land where his own kind live.

The night of snow is over, a fine dawn spreads across the heavens, and the peasants of The Hollows discover the embroidered inscription on the poor little girl's white cambric blanket: *mantendré siempre*. A little girl from Spain! they all exclaim in wonder once Jeannot, the son, who was a messenger in the war and went a very long way, right to the bottom of Europe, has confirmed that it is Spanish—and so they baptize her Maria in honor of the Holy Virgin and the words on the fine Castilian linen. At that very moment, in the Abruzzo, the priest's old servant brushes the locks of hair blonder than little springtime grasses from the infant's brow, and marvels at the clarity of her ice-blue eyes which stare at her as if they want to eat her. *Ti chiamerai Clara*, she said.

And so, Maria and Clara, the two extraordinary children, would grow up under the protection of the ordinary souls who had adopted them, and as wards of the trees and mountains in their respective lands.[4] In Burgundy, the coming of the little girl embellished the seasons and caused the crops to prosper, and everyone suspected she was magic—although, deep in their Christian selves, they refused to entertain the idea. But there was a moving halo around her, and they could see she knew how to talk to the trees and the animals in the forest. She was a joyful, affectionate child, who brought happiness to the old grannies on the farm, and warmed the heart of André and Rose, her adoptive parents. They had lost their own children in infancy, and didn't know which saint to thank for the late gift of this child who was so lovely and cheerful. In Santo Stefano, Clara spent most of her time in the kitchen with the old house-keeper, listening to her tales of the Sasso. The priest treated her like his daughter, but he was a man of little depth, for whom she felt polite indifference, and the joy she took in her mountains meant this did not matter. All day long, she ran up and down the slopes and learned the only maps that mattered to her heart, those of the stones on the paths and the stars in the broad sky. The girls grew, one darker than twilight, with brown eyes and skin of honey, the other heart-stoppingly fair, with her sky-blue gaze and complexion like hawthorn blossom—and until they turned ten, nothing noteworthy happened beyond the confirmation of their grace, so that those who loved them could sleep in peace and perform their consecrated devotions before the Lord.

Then they turned ten, and the wheels of fate began to turn more quickly before resuming a falsely peaceful pace. In

———

[4] This is where the story told in *The Life of Elves* begins, covering the period from 1918 to 1931.

Burgundy, the villagers obtained the confirmation that the little girl was magic when a fantastic beast appeared one snowy night—that of her birthday—as they were searching for the child in the dark, for she hadn't come back to the farm. The men found Maria on the hill in the middle of a clearing, in the company of the creature, which initially appeared to be a big white horse, then turned into a wild boar, and finally a man, and so on in a circle dance of species that left them all gasping for breath. Finally, the creature vanished before their eyes, and they went back down to the farm holding the little girl tight in their arms. Now, we know that this was Tagore, who'd come to give Maria the vision of her arrival in the village, because he thought, as did Solon and Petrus, that the powers of the children would be nourished by the knowledge they would gain from their own story as they grew up. The little girl from Spain learned that she'd been adopted and saw her special skills grow ever stronger—for talking to the animals in the fields and shelters, for discerning the pulsations and figures the trees traced in the air of her countryside, for hearing the song of the world in a symphony of energy that no human being has ever perceived, and for increasing the talents of those men and women who shared her life. The day she turned eleven, finally, another fantastic beast appeared before her in the shape of a mercurial horse combined with a hare and a gray-eyed man, whom we recognize as Solon, come in daylight for the first time to meet his daughter.

It was on that day that proof of treason was found. The Head of the Council had been spied on, and the enemy launched an intimidating attack in the form of tornadoes and arrows of smoke. And this confirmed what we had known ever since his cursed soul had passed through the human world and he had become the leader in Rome: Aelius was in possession of the gray notebook; another pavilion and another bridge had been built; he could move back and forth between the two worlds and play with the climate as he liked. The only good thing in all this misfortune was that Aelius had never had any faith in the prophecy Petrus had unearthed in the library and, during the Council sessions, he'd always sat there scornfully disregarding the wild imaginings of that elf from an obscure house. So he was not the least bit interested in Maria, and the little girl was able to stay for another year in the village, carefully watched over by Nanzen and, before long, by Clara.

Clara, the orphan of genius. In the Abruzzo, a piano had come to meet her the summer before she turned eleven, bequeathed to Father Centi by an old aunt in L'Aquila, and brought to the presbytery by Sandro. They set it up in the church and sent for the piano tuner at the beginning of July. The first notes played on the untuned keys sounded to Clara like a sharpened knife, a luxurious swoon; one hour later, she knew how to play and Sandro was giving her musical scores which she executed to perfection, never making a single mistake, and with a technique that caused the mountain wind to blow through the church.

Sandro Centi had been living with his aunt in L'Aquila for nine years. All that remained of his extravagant youth in Rome were painful memories that still woke him at night, to crucify him, heart pounding, on a cross of regret. His entire life had been one of doomed, tragic love affairs and dissatisfaction with his art. He'd been a great painter, but he burned his canvases and stopped painting forever. He'd been madly in love with a woman, and prized friendship as a sacrament, but the woman had died and he turned his back on all his friends in Rome. However, after the episode in the church, he had a messenger take a letter to Rome for him and, at the beginning of August a tall, rather bent man came to the door of the presbytery. His name was Pietro Volpe, he was the son of Roberto Volpe and an art dealer like his father. He was a friend of the Maestro, who had married his sister Leonora, and he had gone through life tortured by the hatred he felt for his late father. He had come all the way from Rome at Sandro's request; he had once helped Sandro build his career, and he loved him like a brother. Clara was asked to play for him on the fateful piano and, the next day, Pietro left for Rome again, with the virtuoso orphan in tow.

Rome, loathsome city. Clara was inconsolable over the loss of her mountains, and now she studied music with the Maestro, who had taken her on as his student as if he didn't know her. Every day, he told her to listen to the stories that were hidden in each score; every day she found it harder to grasp what he expected of her. At the Villa Acciavatti, she saw Sandro, Pietro, and Leonora, the first woman she had ever loved. The rest of the time she was shadowed by a bizarre chaperone called Petrus, who didn't seem terribly in the know about things, and was invariably to be found sleeping off the previous night's wine in a comfortable armchair.

She studied, relentlessly.

The Maestro asked her questions which induced her to describe the wooded countryside or the plains of poplars she had seen in visions while playing, because these landscapes were engraved upon the composer's heart and memory—until, one day, the music opened a path to Maria in faraway Burgundy and, very quickly, she learned to see her, simply by thinking, and to follow every one of her movements, effortlessly. Her magical gaze embraced Maria's companions at the farm, and she grew fond of Eugénie, Marguerite's daughter, but also of André, Jean-René's son and Maria's adoptive father and, finally, of the village priest, who was as different from her own priest as an oak is from a hazel tree.

It was now clear that the two children were miraculous, not only because of the circumstances of their birth, but also because of their own genius. Although elves lose their animal essences on human earth, when they are in the proximity of Maria they appear in all their triplicate splendor. As for Clara, she could see space and beings from a distance, and exercised her father's powers of vision and prescience from outside the pavilion at Nanzen. The facts could not be denied: on human earth the little girls created enclaves where the physical laws of the mists held sway.

A year went by, deceptive strides of peace.

We are now two years from the start of the war.

January came, colder than any ice field, gloomier than a dawn without light. It was so abnormally cold that humans came to suspect the Good Lord was punishing them in one fell swoop for a century's worth of sins, but the elves, well, they knew that the enemy had their own bridge and were torturing humankind with the cruelty of frost. It was during this devilish season that the inaugural event of the disaster occurred, although it appeared quite harmless to begin with: the visit to The Hollows of one of the father's brothers, with all the honors due a decent man who was also, incidentally, an excellent hunter. As was fitting in the land of Burgundy, honors consisted of a succession of "light, *local* fare," which meant they dined on a truffled guinea fowl set amid liver terrine and pot-au-feu en ravigote, garnished with caramelized cardoons, their juice still running down the diners' throats despite the vin de côte. To make it all go down, there'd been talk of a cream tart enhanced with Eugénie's quince jellies—but in fact, it had not only been talk, and it was ever so hard to get up off one's chair when it was time for bed. Then at around two o'clock in the morning there was a terrible stir upstairs: Marcel, who had had more than enough liver terrine, was now at death's door with a colossal liver infection.

They are beautiful indeed, those women who launch a crusade against evil, of that beauty that expresses the essence of their sex: from her mother, Eugénie had inherited a love of flowers, a talent for quince jelly, and the gift of healing. Maria, as it happened, had the power to enhance that gift, and, splendid and dangerous as are all handmaidens to great causes, they formed a league, joined in secret by Clara, who was watching them from her Roman villa. The alliance of the two little magicians' powers was placed at the service of Eugénie's gift, and, against all expectation, Marcel was saved. But while the forces of our worlds may be exchanged, none can be created and, too late, Maria realized that Eugénie must die in order for her godson to live. Is it any surprise to learn that the auntie herself had received the message of this pact between life and death in the form of an iris with petals streaked pale blue, a deep purple heart, an orange-tinted stamen? The red bridge of concord provides the images of truth with strength, and it knows how to signify important moments. It is from the bridge that Petrus, one hundred and thirty years earlier, had received the tea poem, as well as the premonitory vision of Eugénie and her iris, for he knows what has occurred and what will occur at all times and on every level of that strange thing we call reality.

Alas, Maria was convinced she had killed her granny and, in truth, such a young soul could not understand what she had actually given her. Before being told of her imminent death, Eugénie had a vision of the son she had lost in the war, sitting before her at the feast of St. John, at the table decorated with solstice irises. He was just as she remembered him, although he had already fallen in battle along with so many of our young men, and she said to him: *Go my son, and know for all eternity how much we love you.* And then the sorrow of thirty years had been transformed into an explosion of love so intense that Eugénie had thanked the Lord for this final, generous gift to his pious lamb. In the end, she died happier than she had ever been.

But Maria didn't know this, and the first battle was looming. Marcel's miraculous recovery had drawn Aelius's gaze upon the farm, and he unleashed on the low country the controlled anger of a raging storm, a wall of cyclones and floods, masking human mercenaries at the ready. It was the first battle of a notorious war that wouldn't begin until two years later, and it was fought on the marl of the February fields, its officers country bump-kins transformed into strategists, with two twelve-year-old girls for generals, one all the way in Rome communicating mentally with the other. What was even more remarkable—although Maria wanted no more of miracles that would cost the lives of loved ones—was that there would be three more miracles, at least as far as human standards for marvels went.

The first was with the telepathic communication between the two girls: Clara had learned how to compose and play in such a way as to create a bond with Maria that connected them men-tally day and night.

The second miracle resided in the power of the stories and dreams that were catalyzed by the children of November and snow—something neither humans nor ordinary elves could do, for while the former know how to dream, they do not know how to turn their daydreaming into reality, whereas the latter are incapable of fiction, but do know how to influence the forces of nature. Clara and Maria, now united by a shared language and story,[5] opened a breach in the sky through which a troop of elves

---

[5] *all dreams are in you, and you walk on a sky/of snow under the frozen earth of February*
This is the story that Clara forms spontaneously while composing, which comes to her from Maria's heart and from her own poetic powers.

entered the human world and, preserving their powers, fought alongside the bumpkins until they defeated the commando of villains. In the end, a sky of snow ordered by Maria defeated the storm and gave way to a firmament of a blue so pure that all the men sobbed with happiness. In the persons of the little girls, the elves now had a new bridge between magic and poetry at their disposal, and they also revealed a beyond-princely valiance to a handful of yokels—the last alliance was alive.

The third miracle concerned the ancestor Solon had spoken to Petrus about, and who had briefly come back to life when the girls opened the sky to the company of elfin combatants. But we shall not speak of him just yet, for the matter of the elves' ancestors requires an intelligence which, paradoxically, we can only see in the deepest night.

That same day, Sandro, Marcus, and Paulus left Rome and set off for Burgundy. No one could determine how powerful the enemy's pavilion and bridge were, but they suspected that they harbored neither clear vision nor prescience, and that for the moment, the overland route would be safer than trying to cross the red bridge. Besides, Sandro couldn't cross it, because every attempt to do so with a human had ended in failure. When the companions arrived in the devastated village, three days after the battle, Maria and Father François were waiting for them. Sandro immediately took to the peculiar priest, who was loved by his flock because he respected them and valued their hare pâté and indulgence in goose fat. Moreover, the priest had known the sky of dreams Maria and Clara had opened, and he now felt an earthly fervor supplanting the God of his confession within him. He'd always thought that he must accomplish his mission through preaching, but the words that came to him now at funerals and services no longer owed a great deal to the religion of the Churches. He'd devoted his life to the superiority of the mind over the body, and was discovering that he was a man with a deep nature, a messenger of the indivisibility of the world and the unity of the living. He learned Italian because he wanted to understand the girl to whom they'd sent a poem in that language,[6] and he had long been torn between his Christian incredulity that she could be magical and his love of the truth. Now he was resolved to accompany her wherever she went. In addition to his conviction that this was his destiny, he wanted to be at her side, a spokesman for those who could not speak, as he'd been once already on receiving the words of one of the village lads, wounded in the battle, who had confided in him as he was dying. To be more precise, he hadn't received those words directly: Maria was holding the brave man's hand and listening to his dreams while Clara transcribed them into music. Through the bond between the two girls, the priest had been able to hear those dreams and transmit to the courageous man's widow the words the melody had given him. They were fine words, that came from a humble heart and a mind deprived of book-learning, but which spoke of the glory of days standing tall under the sky because one has loved and been loved. And Father François wanted to live like that from now on, in the wake of those little girls who had given life and sparkle to love, and it mattered little to him that this distanced him from his Church and his cozy presbytery.

So many makeshift lodgings in the wanderings to come—we are leaving behind the territory of the story that was told elsewhere[7] to return to our own story for seven long years, six of them years of war. Danger was everywhere, the enemy could

---

[6] *The hare and the wild boar watch over you when you walk beneath the trees/Your fathers cross the bridge to embrace you both when you sleep*
A poem written by Tagore in the margins of a musical score of Teresa's that Clara found in Rome. It was on reading this that the path was opened to Maria's vision. The poem was then sent to Burgundy by Solon.

[7] This is where the story told in *The Life of Elves* comes to an end.

spring out of nowhere. Clara had stayed behind at the Villa Acciavatti, Maria had gone to a region she immediately took to, with its vast plateau swept by raging winds and thick snowflakes.

"It is a magical land," said Alessandro as they crossed the plateau, "a land of solitude and the mind."

There was a farm where they could take refuge for the coming year. Clara would join them there, escorted by Pietro Volpe's men. In his youth, the dealer's hatred for his father had turned him into a hooligan, a young man who fought barefisted in the street. Now he commanded a secret militia of men more loyal and dangerous than Templars.

"What is this place called?" asked Maria.

"The Aubrac," answered Father François.

And, looking all around him:

"It would be a good place to retire."

Clara arrived very early in the morning. On the horizon, the hills of the Aveyron, green and gentle to the gaze, shone intermittently, brushed with dawn; a few shreds of mist drifted by; the world seemed austere and watchful.

A bird sang.

No one understands what happens in the fleeting instant of an encounter—eternity contracts into a divine vertigo, then takes a lifetime to unfold again on a human time scale. The little girls studied one another as if they were meeting for the first time. The tiny dark veins of the first battle throbbed on Maria's face, and Clara raised her hand to touch them gently with her index finger. Then they embraced as sisters but, beyond the enchantment we feel at the sight of fraternity, there was also something else happening in those unfathomable depths which, for lack of a better name, we refer to as the life of the soul. Maria had always been a joyful, mischievous child, quick as a flash and happier than a lark. But she also knew how to feel sorrow and anger, and she wept more tears when Eugénie died than the host of adults on the farm. As for Clara, before she came from Rome, she had not smiled more than twice in ten years, any more than she had learned to feel emotion or to weep. Leonora had begun to soften her neglected heart and Petrus, in turn, had done what he could, in his shambolic way, but the little girl from Italy still lacked that which is received through the grace of a mother and father. In particular, there had been a moment during the battle when the Maestro had said to her: *one day, you will go back to your community*—and she had understood this as meaning, you will go back to the community of women. In a burst of empathy that had reversed the equation of her life, she had had a vision of her mother's face, then of a long line of women singing lullabies in the evening, or screaming with pain on opening the letter from the army. This procession made her understand war, peace, love, and mourning in a way that forged a heart too long deprived of gentleness.

When Maria opened the sky above the fields of Burgundy, the little French girl became every particle of matter and every acre of nature in a sort of internal transformation that terrified her and increased her remorse over Marcel's miraculous recovery. Clara knew all this, and she took her hand in the only way that might calm her. She looked at the little dark veins throbbing beneath Maria's skin, and she promised to prevent anything like this ever happening again in the future. With what steel are deep friendships forged? They require pain and fervor, and perhaps, too, the revelation of lineages; in this way, a fabric with neither desire nor debt can be woven. Her compassion—because she knew the cross Maria had borne since Eugénie's death—rounded out Clara's character and made her a fully-fledged member of her own community, crystallizing the women's message, which in turn opened inside her an awareness of the grandeur and poverty of the female domain.

But while Maria sensed, gratefully, that Clara understood her burden, a strange transfer of personalities occurred, and the mischief and joy of her character passed to the other side of their sisterhood. Now it was often Maria who was seen wearing a face that was stern and inscrutable, while at her side Clara, released from the austerity and solitude of her childhood, was loving and mischievous. It is this light irreverence which, despite the depths of her gaze, will bewitch Alejandro de Yepes eight years hence, and it is this irreverence, too, which everyone will soon be needing, if it is true, as the writer said, that gaiety is the most amiable form of courage.

A few days after Clara's arrival, Tagore and Solon came over the bridge of mists to the farm in the Aubrac. It was a strange feeling—for Maria, who had other parents, and for Clara, who had never had any—to acknowledge these fantastical strangers as their fathers. While the men were strangers to them, they loved the horses, the hare, and the wild boar, with the kind of love only our childhood selves permit. Finally, they walked hesitantly toward them, then Maria ran her hand through the hare's fur, while Clara caressed the boar's spine.

The next time, Tagore and Solon came to the farm in the company of a female elf whose white mare turned first into an ermine. Her gleaming fur enchanted Maria, and then her human features left the girl speechless. Everything was the same: her eyes, her black hair, her golden skin, her oval face, her rather Slavic cheekbones, and her well-defined lips: all the same as her daughter's. Maria studied her in awe; she knew this was her mother she was looking at, but the knowledge poured over her like a rain shower on a roof.

The elf smiled at her through her tears, then changed into an ermine, as the tears vanished.

"I learned a great deal from Rose and Eugénie while watching them bring you up," she said. "I shared their joy as they cherished you and their pride in seeing you grow up, and I'm glad you like violets, and that they taught you the use of simples."

Sandro took a step forward and bowed.

"Maria is the heir to your ermine, is she not?" he asked. "It is through your filiation that she commands the snow."

"If Katsura is covered in snow six months a year, it is because we like to see the flowers bloom in it," she replied.

"I dream of seeing your world," murmured Sandro.

Marcus placed a hand on his shoulder.

"We dream of it with you," he said.

During the trip from Burgundy, and while they were settling on the farm, Father François, Sandro, Paulus, and Marcus had become friends.

"I understand why you get along so well with Petrus," said Marcus the first evening, when Sandro was asking for wine at the inn.

"Don't you drink?" asked Sandro.

"We have tried," said Paulus, "but elves and alcohol don't mix."

"But Petrus drinks," said Sandro.

"I don't know how he does it," sighed Marcus. "We're a complete mess after only two glasses, but after three bottles he's still going even stronger. However, he doesn't feel too well the following day."

"Humans, too, have varying reactions to alcohol," said Sandro.

"Do they have remedies for intoxication?" asked Marcus.

"For intoxication?" said Sandro. "Without intoxication, we could not endure the solitude of reality."

"We elves are never alone," Paulus replied.

A year passed quickly on the plateau in the Aubrac, often uniting the girls, their fathers, and Maria's mother, whose presence unexpectedly comforted the young woman. When she turned into an ermine, she gave off a familiar perfume (different from that of real ermines, for elfin animals may look like their species, but lack certain of their characteristics, such as odor, and manners of expression or even washing), the odor of a village woman who sews sachets of lemon verbena in her petticoats, one of those refinements of peasant women, who could no doubt teach city ladies a thing or two. Maria had the power to communicate with animals; she'd always had a particular penchant for hares, which she found rather similar to ermines; the animals her mother changed into gave her a sense of familiar ease that the woman herself failed to create and, most of the time, the elf stayed at the farm in her winter ermine form. Maria would kneel by her side, breathing in her perfume and burying her face in her soft fur. The rest of the time, they talked, and the elf described the world of mists, its channels, liquid stones, and winter plum trees. Maria never wearied of these descriptions; Clara, at her side, also listened eagerly. Ever since a certain night in Rome, the little Italian girl had possessed the gift of reading the minds of the people she was with: the landscapes the elf described were visible to her and, like her father, she knew how to make them perceptible to others around them. Every day, Maria would hold her close as they listened to the ermine, and the elf knew of nothing more precious than these two girls, their arms around each other, who, now and again, would run their delicate hands through her fur.

Bit by bit, Maria and Clara came to have a picture of the mists, and Tagore, Solon, and Gustavo tried to work out a way to take them there. But every attempt failed, one after the other.

"What do you feel?" Gustavo asked Maria while trying once again to lead her across the bridge, amid multiple doses of strong tea from the mists.

"Nothing," she replied.

Gustavo turned to Clara.

"Can you tell Maria a story by playing something, the way you did during the battle in Burgundy?"

"You want me to give her an instruction manual, but it was really the power of a dream and a story that caused the sky to open," she replied.

Gustavo paused thoughtfully for a moment, and Petrus chuckled.

"She's your daughter, all right," he said to Tagore.

He winked at Clara.

Petrus and Clara had known each other since her first days in Rome, and he and Maria had greeted one another warmly.

"He's never completely sober or completely drunk," Clara had said at the time.

And she'd given Petrus a wink that made him flop onto on his squirrel tail. Then the elf turned into the potbellied red-head that most humans found harmless and jovial. Who could have imagined that this clumsy little man was working day and night to organize what, in wartime, would be a civilian resist-ance so well structured and operational that its mystery would exasperate humans in the highest ranks of army and State? Petrus went back and forth across the red bridge, uniting his future companions at arms, including honest people of both sexes, some of whom, naturally, were winemakers. During the war years they had resisted, and very soon would launch the ultimate operation in support of the League. Alejandro had led the operations with a few of their leaders, ordinary people who had no military experience, but who knew how to say where, what, and how, before returning in silence to their fac-tories or fields. They reminded him of Luis Álvarez, as he'd appeared to him in the vision in the cellar, walking with his comrades in arms through the baking summer heat, and Alejandro knew that that was another sort of resistance, at another time and in another place, but, like this one, it had lived on hawthorns and roses.

Ultimately, Petrus was not only a glutton and a drunk, but also had a temperament cut out for command. In the mists and in the land of humans he'd had to fight more than once, and his composure, his cool head—from inebriation, awkwardness transformed into strokes of genius—all were roundly hailed. With gratitude they watched him stumble, and they liked his amiability crossed with efficiency; although he fought without hatred, he gave no quarter, and that in itself is the model of fighters who win wars.

But now opportunities to fight were plentiful. The enemy had troops stationed in Ryoan, not yet an army, but there was nothing about the ever more frequent skirmishes to suggest the war would be a chivalrous one.

"They behave like orcs," said Solon with disgust, after an enemy commando raid in the outskirts of Katsura, which set off the interelfin war, just before the first battle on the fields of Burgundy.

Aelius's elves had killed irrationally and ruthlessly. Consequently, the defense of the provinces was reinforced, but hearts were heavy at having to reason like the adversary.

"There is no reason for such squeamishness," Petrus protested. "The only purpose of a fight is victory, by any means and any scheme possible. The spirit of chivalry is incompatible with good strategy."

"To what do we owe these exalted military reflections?" asked Solon.

"To the greatest war novel ever written on earth," retorted Petrus.

"Might that be *War and Peace*?" suggested Solon.

He was not a great adept of human fiction, but Petrus suspected Solon had read at least as much as he had.

"*Gone with the Wind*," he replied.

*

The next day, Solon convened a select elfin council to decide how Nanzen would make the main channels impassable to the enemy.

"What does Scarlett think of our plan?" he asked Petrus at the end of the session.

"That Atlanta was lost when the Yankees captured the channels of communication," replied the squirrel.

Tagore burst out laughing.

"In short," said Petrus, "we shall win if we control the channels. I'm not sure the enemy's pavilion and bridge have the power to do so."

"We don't know their strength," said Tagore, "but what worries me more than anything is that we cannot see them. Ryoan appears to us with neither pavilion nor bridge."

Petrus filed his report on the search for the gray notebook. He had gone to Amsterdam, but the archives he collected there revealed little about the son of the former Guardian of the Pavilion. He'd resided there, become a renowned painter, then died in his house on the Keizersgracht in 1516, at the respectable human age of seventy-seven. All that remained of him was the canvas which Roberto Volpe had committed murder to obtain.

A year went by and war broke out.

Petrus, Marcus, Paulus, Sandro, and Father François further reinforced their indestructible faith in the strength of their community. They had to change locations often, for fear of being found by the enemy. Petrus continued to travel and unite the forces of resistance. They tried unsuccessfully to get the two little girls, the painter, and the priest over the bridge, and everyone wondered with little success where that damned gray notebook might be. Battles were fought in succession and all they had in common was the scale of the carnage. Europe was nothing but one gigantic battlefield, and the war spread to other continents. Purges of all sorts were taking place in the countries of the Confederation, more terrible than terror, more despicable than horror: Raffaele Santangelo had succeeded beyond his own expectations in putting to fire and sword countries that desired nothing but peace. The elves of the last alliance remained in the shadows and did not show themselves to the League. As it happened, they had their work cut out for them in the mists, now split into two fratricidal camps.

Sixth year of the war. The last battle is drawing near, and night is falling in the upper chambers in Katsura.

"What will be left of the worlds when it is all over?" Solon asks bitterly.

"Worlds are born because they die," replies Petrus.

Of solitude and the mind
Furious winds and downy snowflakes

Book of Paintings

手帳

NOTEBOOK

Then Petrus found the gray notebook. You see, it just so happened that Roberto Volpe had a little vineyard in Montepulciano that was cultivated on his behalf by devoted tenant farmers. He produced respectable vintages which, in his youth, would have earned him the right to go to Yepes. It was there that, unbeknownst to all, he had taken the gray notebook he had inherited along with the painting.

The guardian thought he was sending Petrus to stand as usual outside the fortress of the castillo, but the elf found himself in the cellar, peering at a bottle of 1918 petrus. Just next to it was the notebook. Twenty years earlier, thanks to the indiscretion of one of the Volpes' clerks, Santangelo had sent a winemaker to Yepes who had copied out the contents.

The gray vellum booklet contained only a few lines: *The gray tea is the key to mutations. It builds bridges and transforms passages. The first bridge is the work of gray tea and a single brushstroke. Ink and gray tea are the pillars of all rebirth.* Above the door in the cellar, carved in stone, was this motto: *Mantendré siempre.* And next to it, an inscription in the hand of the painter from Amsterdam: *I came here first.*

There are eight days remaining until the last battle.

橋

BRIDGE

Alessandro Centi knew the red bridge without ever having set foot on it. Thirty years earlier, he'd painted it without ever having seen it. The canvas displayed only a large splash of ink and three pastel strokes of scarlet. But those who had crossed the bridge were stunned by this miracle, which reconstituted the bridge without representing it realistically.

Similarly, the first canvas that Sandro had shown Pietro upon his arrival in Rome did not represent anything known, but the dealer knew it was the ideogram for mountain used jointly by elves and by populations in the East of the earth.

Sandro was cut out to live on the other side of the bridge, just as Petrus was on human earth, and these permutations of desire are all that can revive the worlds. The first bridge of the mists had once regenerated a world that was stagnating, its mutation by the painter elf had seen to it a second time, and the elves of the last alliance saw that their role was to reinforce the footbridges between the two sides.

The bridge, that icebreaker—as much conquest as metaphor.

RUIN
1938

PREAMBLE

In four days, the elves of the final alliance made a long series of discoveries and deductions.

The gray tea fulfilled the desires expressed in the pavilion.

Twenty millennia earlier, someone—probably the guardian—had infused leaves attained by noble rot, then built a bridge between the two worlds.

Twenty millennia later, through the same process, the guardian's son had succeeded in transforming the bridge and crossed forever into the world of humans.

How had they discovered the power of gray tea? No doubt it was by chance, as are all the great stanzas in the history of the living.

Four more centuries and the traitor, one of Tagore's assistants, offered Aelius the opportunity to come to Nanzen in secret and create a pavilion and a bridge that would be hidden from view, then the power of the fungus in the tea plant was revealed to the members of the last alliance and they were able to see them—golden, arrogant, and deadly—in the absence of Ryoan's mist.

Gray tea was produced by exposing tea plants to constant humidity for twenty-four hours. Prior to this, elves used to burn the leaves decomposed by rainy weather. In Ryoan, they were now being grown in entire fields.

Gray tea enabled humans to cross into the mists and come back out again. Whether through some flippancy or magnanimity on the part of fate, it also made drunkards sober.

Gray tea was dangerous. It left no trace. It figured in no archives. It was careful not to be seen. It edified, then disappeared, so much so that it is easy to understand why Nanzen and Katsura took so long to comprehend the role it played.

One way or another, gray tea had something to do with ink. No one knew the role of the *single brushstroke*, but they were pleased that Sandro was one of them.

Finally, if the gray notebook had fallen into Petrus's hands, perhaps it was because the spirits of Yepes had chosen their camp and an unknown authority in Extremadura had sided with the last alliance—but it is hard to know such things for sure, for despite all their qualities, stories are known to be unpredictable and mischievous, and we never know their conclusion in advance.

ARE WE DEAD ARE WE ALIVE

N anzen, year six of the war. We left the community of the last alliance at the time when the bell was tolling for the tea, and we must now round out the tale with everything that has happened between the intention and its consequences: so many events, so many reversals, so much uncertainty, made forever true by death, in fact, and now that the last battle has been fought, the ruins of what were our worlds, and their legacy, and their tragedies.

How could the elves imagine destroying the foundation of their universe? What despair leads to such a radical path? Katsura was losing the war, and the mists were growing weaker; every time the bond between humans and elves was strengthened, they had regenerated; but the gray tea represented a threat that compelled them to change the configuration of the footbridges. The enemy's bridges and the pavilions would disappear, but Nanzen, which was not built upon tea, would hold.

"We will destroy the tea plantations," said Tagore. "All of them, right down to the last one, at dawn on the coming day."
"But without tea, your world will collapse," said Alejandro.

Tagore shared the vision of the two infants taken in that snowy night and everyone followed the events, great or trivial, of their magical lives, grannies and piano included, up to the first battle of the war. When the vision filled with the fury of

Aelius's storm, Alejandro and Jesús placed their hands upon their hearts. Then their hearts stopped beating when detachments of elfin fighters poured from the sky as it opened above the fields. Before long came the meeting between the two girls, in the courtyard of a farm amid verdant hills before years of fleeing while total war raged. And, in the end, as if through some chemical precipitation of time, some sort of accelerated acquaintance when, ordinarily, one must share years together, the young girls were as familiar to Alejandro and Jesús as if they had grown up with them. Finally, Tagore projected the image of Petrus confronting the former Head of the Council with a book in his hand. Behind them an old plum tree was visible against a background of moss and a wooden veranda.

"What are you reading?" asked Gustavo.

"A prophecy," said Petrus.

And in the calm, late autumn evening he read out loud.

the rebirth of the mist
through two children of snow and November
the rootless, the last alliance

"Maria and Clara are the children of snow and November," Tagore said to Alejandro. "We have consented to the fall of tea because we have faith in the prophecy. Fate did not bring us all together by chance, and ever since we found the gray notebook, we have been trying to picture its role in the last battle. There must be a reason why we have a priest and a painter with us, just as you are here because of the pull of Yepes. That is where the son of the former guardian went for the first time, and where we believe the first bridge of the worlds was built. It is no accident, either, that the heir to the castillo is a member of the high command of the League, nor is the fact that he comes from a harsh, poetic land like all those in this tale."

A new landscape unfolded before their mind's eye. The last

battle was about to begin, and the first phase would be fought on the battlefields of this world. The tea plants of Ryoan and Inari shone gently in the uncertain night. At the edge of the plantations, along lengthy esplanades, leaves were drying, before they would be crushed on long wooden tables. Beyond the esplanades were barns without a facade, and under their roofs of bark, bundles of canvas hung in the air. Slightly to one side of the storage lofts stood the pavilions where the most remarkable vintages of tea were ageing.

The fields at Inari would be burned with no adverse effect, but those in Ryoan were dotted with elves on the lookout, posted in force around the perimeter—for the most part bears and wild boars armed with spears and bows which to humans seemed gigantic. The zone would have to be evacuated before it was set on fire, and in spite of the advantage of surprise, it was not easy to strategize for such an unequal contest. Moreover, they were working against the clock, for there was only one full day left before the empathy of ordinary tea would wear off for most of the elves, and three for the tea the company had drunk in Nanzen. An hour earlier, the Wild Grasses had destroyed their entire stock—it will come as no surprise to you to learn that, of all the authorities in the mists, only the house of Hanase had permission to stockpile dried leaves. The elves collect their daily allotment at their neighborhood lodge, which is supplied every day through the channels or by air— eagle, albatross, and seagull elves. Sometimes, raptors or seabirds would come to offer their services, but elves do not like to take advantage of the labor of other living species. While the dolphins of the mists did work together with the boatman in the Southern Marches, it was more out of friendship than necessity, because the channels allowed for a closeness between them and this relieved their labor of its alienating burden.

"I'm in charge of the tea destruction commando," Petrus told Alejandro and Jesús. "I intend to surprise the enemy with an unusual strategy, and I could use two humans for the task."

Then Tagore offered the hospitality of his dwelling for the rest of the night.

There was an indefinable fragrance in the air of the pavilion. Of solitude and mind, thought Alejandro.

A moment later, they found themselves under an awning on a wooden veranda that looked out onto the forest. The moonlit trees were tall and straight, an orderly row reaching for the sky. At the center of the clearing, the windows of the guardian's residence, which was lower and more spacious than the Pavilion of the Mists, were covered with light veils that floated in the night air. Next to the door, camellias had been placed in a little bamboo vase hanging on the wall. Everyone fell silent and took in the gentle murmur of ancient trees. Clara and Alejandro sat apart in one corner of the veranda, Jesús and Maria did likewise, off to one side. Petrus, Marcus, Paulus, Sandro, and Father François deliberated amongst themselves. Tagore and Solon went inside.

Time rustling, like tissue paper.

"We might be dead tomorrow," Clara said to Alejandro.

She smiled and he understood why he thought she was beautiful. Her brow was too big, her neck was too long, and her eyes were too light, but there was something about her smile that made him feel as if he were embracing the waters of a dream. Not a word was exchanged, but, through their gazes, despite the absence of intimacy to which war condemned them, they concentrated in one hastily-snatched hour all the days of a lifetime of love. It happened in the order everyone is familiar with, and thus they experienced those first gazes where they drowned in the headiness of adoration and temptation; then, after the magic of the early days, they slowly came to reality; after having construed love, they elevated it to its authentic life. After the luxuriant dawns and wild storms, they saw their true faces; he sat at the hearth, tired and worn, and she knew what sort of man he was. When at last they fell asleep, exhausted and happy, they had known their fill of lovemaking, of every parting and every joyful meeting, of every tempest and every wonder ever known to mind and body, through the sharing of tea and the song of ancient trees, and afterwards when they woke, they were a man and a woman enriched by every moment of transport, every transfiguration of love. Just before waking, they shared the dream of a chilly late afternoon on the farm on the plateau in the Aveyron, while clouds of crows whirled and shrieked overhead, gathering under a storm on the horizon. The lovers were hurrying to take shelter when a solitary snowflake appeared, light and fluffy among the birds, that all on its own caused the storm to recede—and though the storm was wild with rage, other fat snowflakes, soft and dumb as feathers, fell tenderly to hide a land of newfound peace.

At the far end of the veranda, Maria was talking to Jesús with the same silent, tea-induced affinity.

She was telling him about the trees in the countryside where she'd grown up, the tall elms and riverbank willows, but also the oaks by the field next to the farm, their quivering branches leaving etchings on the air. She told him about the hill, to the east of the village, that they could reach by a winding trail until it merged into an undergrowth of poplars, where every family was permitted to gather wood and where they would come for their share by first snowfall—and then she described the tow-paths of the six cantons, their lakes of emerald and rushes, Eugénie's vegetable garden, her artemisia, marjoram, and mints. The faces of her grannies, wrinkled like autumn apples, went through their shared vision until there was only the small-est of the four faces, cheerful and stubborn beneath her cap with its ribbons the color of forget-me-nots.

"Eugénie," said Maria.

In the tiny, boundless space that divides loving hearts, Jesús felt her sorrow and mourning as if they were his own. In turn, he told her of his arid land, the dried lake of his childhood, the pain of staying and the wrenching loss of going, but also, some days at dawn, the beauty of the water in a calligraphy of dark mist.

"We were innocent," she said, with a pang of sadness.

He went on telling her about Extremadura, its plains and desolate forts, the onslaught of sunlight, the cruel rocks and his amazement at the way the stones in the mists turned liquid.

Her gaze was full of distress, like that of a wounded child.

"What did Eugénie say to you before she died?" he asked.

She told him how her auntie had lost all desire to live when her son died in the war, how she came to hate violets when the innocent fell in battle, and how she was horrified by the trans-parent skies above the carnage—then one day she recovered from her grief by healing Marcel. In the end, she had come to Maria's little room, to sit on the edge of her bed, and she said, *You have healed me, my love.*

Jesús took her hand. Her palm was like the skin of a lovely peach, her fingers so fine and slender he could have wept.

She shared one last scene where the old granny was speak-ing to her and smiling—a new scene, that was neither a mem-ory nor a premonition, just the effect of the tea and the redemp-tions of a night of love.

"Look," said the auntie, smiling with astonishment and cheer. "Look," she said again, "what I couldn't tell you that night. Oh, he has his ways, the good Lord! Are we dead, are we alive? It doesn't matter, look what you gave me, my love."

She showed them a garden, where two long tables were set and decorated with solstice irises. In the soft evening air, she was smiling at a young man—my son, she thought with amazement, who died in the war, but I was able to tell him how much I loved him. And from this, the gladness of a dialogue between the living and the dead had engulfed the old peasant woman's heart, and she felt such intense happiness that dying no longer mattered to her.

"A dead woman talking about her dead," she said, amused.

Turning one last time to her beloved little girl, she said:

"Don't forget to pick the hawthorn."

Maria drew closer to Jesús and buried her face in his chest.

He put a hand in her hair, savoring the timelessness of hours of love.

Not far from there, looking out onto the trees in the play of light and shadow, Petrus had opened a few bottles he'd appropriated from Alejandro's cellar. Everyone was saying they might all be dead tomorrow, and they all knew the one thing a living being can know about death.

"It always comes too soon," said Father François.

"It always comes too soon," said Petrus.

They could drink the wine from Yepes.

"When I think I might have to give this up," Petrus said.

With a wrenching sigh, he added:

"And women. Woe is me."

Just before dawn the company, along with Solon, Gustavo, and Tagore, gathered in the middle of the veranda, which was bathed in darkness and moonlight.

"Now the time has come for us to say farewell to our culture," said the Head of the Council.

Petrus took one last sip of amarone and opened another bottle. In their glasses, pale gold sparkled faintly in the moonlight.

"A Loire wine—this alliance of modesty and refinement drives me crazy," he said.

"Almost nothing," murmured Alejandro, raising the glass to his nose.

On the palate, the wine had the crystalline texture of soft stone turning to white flowers, with a faintly sweet touch of pear.

"Stones and flowers," said Clara, tenderly.

In front of everyone, she placed her lips briefly on Alejandro's.

Petrus raised his glass and said:

"When I arrived in Katsura for the first time, one hundred and thirty-eight years ago (Marcus and Paulus chuckled over a certain memory of that event—he ignored them), I had no idea of the destiny that lay in store for me there. For a long time, I wondered what was expected of an insignificant squirrel who was constantly out of his mists. Then I realized that it was precisely these qualities that made me the instrument of fate, which uses intelligent men to carry out its plans, but needs an idiot to bring them all together at the appointed time."

"I really wonder what an idiot might be," said Father François.

"An alcoholic who believes in the truth of dreams," answered Paulus.

"What a fantastic gospel," said the priest.

They honored in silence the last of the wine before Paulus gave each of them the sobering flask, and then the strange troop headed back to Nanzen.

The valley of trees rustled with unfamiliar sounds and the moon flooded the path with black stones. Silent and motionless in the hour before dawn, in battle order outside the pavilion, the general staff of the army of mists awaited them.

Are we dead are we alive

Book of Prayers

文体

STYLE

Petrus loved stories and fables for the power they had, like wine, to open the freedom of dreams in waking time, but, in addition to the intoxication from the story, he was just as sensitive to the way they were crafted as he was to the refinement of different varietals. A beautiful story with no style is like a petrus in a trough, he liked to say to Paulus and Marcus (who couldn't give a damn).

What was more, he had a weakness for the French language, its earthy power and courtly *coquetterie*, because roots and elegance are to the text what taste is to wine, with that added grace which comes from a passion for what is unnecessary, and that added significance which, always, is born of beauty.

戦略

STRATEGY

Petrus felt deeply human and, dare I say it, French. While he did value the art, light, and food of Italy, his heart beat resolutely for the slapdash panache of France.

One rainy day in England, in 1910, he went to a match of a curious sport the French were playing against the English. Although at the time he only understood one rule—that the aim was to score a leather ball all the way at the far end of the opposing side—he enjoyed the moves and passes for their demonstration of human talent and ingenuity.

After one play where the French looked like a swarm of ballerinas facing a squadron of sluggish draft horses, the old Englishman who was chewing tobacco in the stands next to him had said: a plague upon those Frenchies, but it's the rugby that everyone wants to see—and this summed up why Petrus ranked France above all else—in addition to wine, women, and pleasant landscapes.

Now, twenty-eight years later, at the hour of the last battle, he had a hunch that the war would be won with a strategy of ballerinas.

N anzen, dawn of the last battle.
There were twenty or more elves from a variety of houses, including a unicorn, a beaver, a zebra, and a black panther. The elves of the central provinces do not often have the opportunity to meet their compatriots from the hotter climes, but Petrus, Marcus, and Paulus were delighted to see their old friends from the Northern Marches again, the zebra and the panther, who were serving as officers in the army and whom they'd already fought alongside. As for the humans, they kept a safe distance from the imposing feline, although they were most astonished by the fact that half the staff consisted of female elves. Although the present-day leaders were all male, in the past there had been memorable female Guardians of the Pavilion and Heads of the Council, to the extent that the increasing absence of women from positions of responsibility now appeared to Solon and Tagore to be yet another obvious sign of decline.

At the center of the elfin detachment, the female unicorn turned into a woman with white hair, black eyes, and very wrinkled skin. She was slender and athletic and, in the end, so stunningly beautiful they couldn't imagine how age could have produced such a vision.

"We are ready," said the female chief of staff to Solon and Tagore.

They went inside the pavilion, where Hostus, Quartus, and ten other assistants were waiting for them. Like the first time, the place, despite its lack of space, seemed perfectly capable of containing the entire company. The members of staff and the guardian's assistants took their seats against the partitions, and the same elves as before formed a circle in the center of the room. The unicorn sat on Solon's right and her first lieutenant, a beaver elf, reported on the army's movements. All the battalions had reached their positions. The troops would intervene at the final signal from Nanzen, and after that, each unit could count only on itself; but all of them had been posted to strategic points and would have the advantage in most of the decisive attacks. In any case, the enemy couldn't imagine someone would ever want to destroy the tea; the elves of the last alliance, on the other hand, were prepared to do so. Naturally, the soldiers had been informed that a return through the channels would be jeopardized; the beaver added that no one had succumbed to regret at this point.

Once the report was finished, Petrus took over and asked Tagore to share a scene showing thirty or more strangely dressed men. Some of them, leaning over the others, formed a confused mass. Others stood to one side, useless and waiting for something to do, on a vast lawn streaked with white lines. There were two teams, one dressed in white, the other in blue, apportioned on either side of the swarming mass, from which one member in blue was trying to remove something. No one was moving, but after a long while, the man in blue succeeded in what he was trying to do and hurled the fruit of his conquest behind him. Everything changed gears and shape. On either side of the melee, the blue and white men began running toward each other, in perfect diagonal lines; the thing that looked like a ball went from front to back along the blue line and, just as the configuration of players met between the two lines, it was transformed and realigned; but the ball was still making its way, bouncing from a forward runner to a back runner in a choreography that drew a whistle of admiration from Father François. Then the man carrying the ball collapsed, tackled in full flight by an opponent and, again, the lads tumbled upon each other while the same player as before struggled to wrest his Holy Grail from the pile. In the rear and in the front, a fluid mechanism wonderfully in tune with the pleasure of watching, the idle players re-formed in diagonal lines and, once again, waited for their time to come. And it came, in the form of a new retrieval very near one end of the terrain that was marked by two gigantic posts. This time, the coveted item was thrown to the right and after a rapid and complicated series of rear diagonal passes, the last blue man on the line flattened himself on the grass, the ball under his belly, and this caused some of the men to raise their arms in victory, and the others to lower them in defeat. Finally, the scene vanished and they all looked at each other cautiously.

"That was rugby, wasn't it?" asked Alejandro. "I went to a village match once, long ago, although it's not a very popular sport in Spain. I didn't understand all the rules, but the sequence of moves was interesting."

"It is rugby," Petrus confirmed, "and strategy, too, as your military eye will have noticed."

"Fixed positions and deployment tactics," said Jesús. "Do we need rugby for that?"

In the center of the circle Hostus placed a round ball made of interwoven maple twigs.

"The maple trees from the Northern Marches are known to catch fire a few minutes after they are placed near a tea leaf," said Petrus.

You will also see plant life becoming fire, Jesús recalled.

"We will have to progress in a linear fashion by leaving the seeds to the fire behind us," continued Petrus, "like in a game with several balls, where the lines move forward and the opponent cannot stop their progress. If we attack from all sides, or concentrate our attack, we cannot set fire to the perimeter without burning ourselves to a cinder at the same time. But if we invite the enemy to a scrum with our rear lines in support, we have a chance of attaining our goal."

"Anyone who takes part in the melee will be sacrificed," Alejandro pointed out.

"It is my hope that the first engagement will incur no losses," said Petrus. "We will be the masters of a game where the enemy doesn't know the rules. They will think we are attacking them, but we will be unarmed, equipped only with our legs for running and our arms for throwing."

"What weapons do they have?" asked Alejandro.

"Bows, swords, spears, and axes," answered the unicorn elf. "And their mastery of the climate."

"They'll chop us to bits if we're unarmed," said Jesús.

"Not necessarily," said Paulus, looking at Petrus, "we've been trained in an art of evasion designed by the only alcoholic elf in the known world."

"Very effective in close combat," added Marcus.

"We can do a great deal of harm by falling," Petrus reassured them.

There was a silence, disturbed only by the sound of the wind in the trees in the valley.

"It could work," said Jesús slowly. "In any case, I'm in."

Alejandro nodded.

They went to the bridge. Dawn was breaking. Far behind the pavilion, beyond the valley, brief flashes of lightning were expiring with the night. Day was coming and the lightning drew fiery streaks upon the sky that faded into the dawn. Then they heard a distant rumbling between pauses in the thunder.

"We're heading toward the storm," said Petrus.

Out of the mist on the middle of the bridge, there came a team of eight elves—three squirrels, two bears, a wild boar, and two otters—and after respectfully saluting Solon and Tagore, they joined Petrus's commando. Alejandro looked at Clara, Jesús looked at Maria, the squadron, now at full strength, bowed to the rest of the assembly and moved forward onto the bridge.

There was a powerful thunderclap.

A few members of staff now entered the mists of the arch. The others went back to the pavilion.

The last battle was beginning.

On the other side of reality, Petrus's commando landed at the edge of the gray tea plantations in Ryoan. On yet another side, the staff materialized around the plantations in Inari. At the far end, or side, or quadrant of the world, Aelius and Santangelo, in the golden pavilion, were beginning to suspect that something was brewing.

And so, the action got underway in Ryoan. The only inter-species rugby team ever was deployed with lightning speed and efficiency, increased tenfold, I must say, by Petrus's gift for encouragement. No sooner was he back on his feet, crouching behind the rows of tea, than he pulled a bottle from his bundle and generously shared out the contents, then stood up straight, like the very devil, brandishing his first ball of maple twigs—at which point the team swarmed onto the plan-tation and almost immediately encountered the opponent. Alejandro and Jesús closed the diagonal on the left, keeping the right distance from the last elf on the line. They saw the first ones, including Petrus, collide head on with a group of bears armed with spears, then deceive them with the art of evasion Paulus had praised—and it was magnificent, because the elves of the alliance fell like drunks between the enemy's paws, then slipped away like eels, leaving their opponents behind them, now busily hitting each other. For a moment Alejandro and Jesús only had to run, but finally, they drew level with the ruck and faced their first adversaries. Ordinarily, higher-ranking officers do not excel in close combat, but Alejandro de Yepes and Jesús Rocamora were the sons of arid lands, where lords and serfs labor under the same yoke and the same rigorous climate. They were as agile as any survivor of hostile conditions, and they knew when to fall to the ground and twist sideways to avoid a blow with an ax, a toss of the spear, or those odd whirlwinds, miniature tornadoes, that whistled like arrows in flight then disintegrated on reaching the ground. After a moment, real arrows began to fly, aiming at random above the rows of tea, and new tornadoes came swooping down in bursts, sometimes coming close to the very enemy they were supposed to protect. But it was all happening very quickly, and it would have taken a clever soldier on Aelius's side to thwart the plans behind such a mysterious attack. The commando spread out by passing, dodging, dropping, passing again, with a diabolical precision that no doubt would enthrall numerous coaches in human lands, and I must say that this match, absurd as it was for being played only by one side, was nevertheless an impeccable incarnation of the essence of rugby. Petrus didn't like chivalry and its moral sentimentality; he thought that, of all the evils, war was the ugliest and vilest; that one must win quickly, brutally, and absolutely; and that spies and assassins were the true artisans of victory. But he hated these requirements of war as much as he hated war itself, and since he knew that the aftermath would be as hideous as the enemy's hatred, he was not sorry that the opening scene was a good performance. The beauty of rugby stems from its organic quality: the team is nothing without its members, who are nothing without the team. When, after lengthy entanglements, endless scrums, and pitiful advances, the line spreads out and covers giant portions of the field, it's not just the fluidity of movement, but also the combined effort of heart and legs that rouse the spirit, because the player who scores is heir to the precision and enthusiasm of all the others. And so, Petrus of the Deep Woods, this meticulous and fiery elf, sly and crafty, but also frank and amiable in the company of friends, and ultimately passionate about *elsewhere*, although he was loyal to his fathers and his mists, had in this war at least one battle which, like French rugby, suited his nature and evinced a refinement and panache that Scotch whisky truly had not spoiled. He knew that a succession of massacres lay ahead, and he was savoring this last engagement, fought without damage or casualties. At the dawn of a tragic time, he put the heart of despair into his work and saw it as a tribute to the courage of the just.

When the two Spaniards broke enemy lines for the first time and, gliding like fish in a river, found themselves on the far side of the battalion of huge hares, they felt such jubilation that the first ball of maple passed to Alejandro really felt like the Holy Grail to him. He carried it one hundred yards or so and put it on the ground between two tea plants. Then he went on running behind a row that was shorter because of the dislocation of the initial lines. Arrows whistled and fell at random, Aelius's side had given up on the tornadoes, and if they hadn't been running with the wind in their ears, they would have heard the sounds of alarm all around the perimeter. Our heroes had already run a league when enemy reinforcements descended on the plantation. Alejandro passed the ball he'd just received from the forward to Jesús, and ran smack into the stomach of a wild boar. The shock dazed him and he had difficulty getting quickly back on his feet. Jesús watched with horror and shouted as the boar raised his ax; Petrus, in front of the line, turned around, and with a classic skip pass, took aim and hit the pig right in the snout. The ax fell an inch from

Alejandro's skull; shouting with relief, he rolled over and got promptly to his feet.

Opposite him, armed with a huge ax, stood a gigantic elf who didn't look like he was in the mood for sipping tea.

"Grizzly!" shouted Paulus from the other side of the field.

The ax was raised. Alejandro plunged between the monster's legs and felt his right shoe fly off into the air. He scrambled frantically forward, but the elf had turned around and Alejandro knew, from considerable experience, that the next strike would split his back open.

Hopelessly crawling, he waited for the blow.

Behind him, Jesús shouted again.

The blow didn't come.

To the south, behind them, the plantation caught fire.

The rows of gray tea went up all at once. There was a huge rushing sound, a wind of flame, and the plantation began to burn. Petrus started shouting too and, tearing himself away from the spectacle, the alliance team continued to advance. The enemy, horrified, froze on the spot. They could hear a bell ringing—a bucket brigade was being formed—but the commando reached the end of the first crops without incident. They'd gone a league and a half, and had a clear path for the two remaining leagues. They distributed their last maple balls, then reached the deserted storage barns. Petrus tossed the last vegetal fireball into the bales of tea hanging in the air, where it stayed calmly swinging and vibrating among the packaged leaves. Before giving the signal for the transfer, Petrus stopped at the edge of the burning tea plantations. The sky now had a wild, tawny hue and, in the shimmering of fire, tongues of flame resembled swaying flowers.

Then they all went back to Nanzen.

At that moment, the unicorn chief of staff of the mists was gazing at Inari's demise. From the vast fields of green tea, a hundred times more expansive than those at Ryoan, billows of smoke were rising, the likes of which they'd never seen in the mists, and she watched them rise skyward as the world of her youth vanished in the dawn. She who had observed the other world from the pavilion, who had visited the Head of the Council on human land, admired the genius of humans, their prodigious art and the hope it gave its people, knew, in the end, of nothing more beautiful than the mists rising over the front at Katsura. In these absolute, gilded dawns, as the community of elves, dusted by the ash of Hanase, whispered among themselves with every drift of mist, the voices of the living and the dead joined in a communion that no humans—and this she was sure of—could ever equal.

Embers from the fire fell at her feet. She took two steps back and felt a tear flow down her cheek.

The first phase of the last battle was over. On the horizon, thick clouds of smoke gathered and sat stagnant over the land. The atmosphere changed subtly, and everyone could hear Solon's final address to his people.

"The plantations at Inari and Ryoan are burning," he said. "Never before have the leaders of the mists had to make such a painful decision, but we hope for times of rebirth like those we have always known after a hard fall. I ask those who have never doubted our wisdom not to fear change. To those who went over to the ranks of the enemy, I will say how saddened I am by this disaster orchestrated by hatred. We are a dream, a magic place of trees and stones, the reverie of a spirit swept with mist, the vapor through which the energy of life circulates. We are a breath of atmosphere, a glittering of dust on the rivers of time that unite things and beings and cause the living and the dead to mingle. We are a harmony traversed by the winds of dreaming, an infinite plain welcoming roses and ashes. But we are also a nation more ancient than all others, old and disenchanted, imprisoned in a modern world where we no longer know how to live. Through the logic of decline, our ancestors entered into lethargy just as our mists were beginning to weaken. Twice, a footbridge built to the shores of human land regenerated the mists. Tragedies have always come of divisions and walls, rebirth from bridges built on unfamiliar shores—thus the fall of the tea must be the gate to new alliances, if it is not to remain vain and tragic forever. Inhabitants of the mists, I know your reservations regarding the human race. Are they not to blame for every negligence in their management of the world, for every display of cruelty toward the living? And for how many massacres and wars? And for such cynical exploitation of other kingdoms, when they have neither mist nor tea to bring about a concord of consciousness? And yet, they do possess one treasure we do not have. They have the faculty of painting that which does not exist, and of telling that which will never happen. As strange as it may seem to our spirit immersed in the flow of the world, that faculty creates a parallel truth that enhances the visible and shapes their civilizations. We must invent the future now, and that visionary gift, allied with our natural harmony, will have the power to save our worlds. At present the tea is burning, and I do not know how much longer we will be connected in consciousness, but I am confident that when words no longer suffice, thought will continue. As for me, I will do what I must: I shall maintain."

He fell silent, and Tagore projected the faces of the humans and the elves of the last alliance into the mist. In return, the community loyal to Nanzen sent the message of their allegiance, mixed as much with worry and sorrow as with their refusal to hate and their trust in the integrity of their leaders. Finally, they voiced their unexpected enchantment with the two little girls born on a night of snow.

Before leaving the pavilion, the chief of staff put her hand on Petrus's shoulder.

"Your little incursion with backward passes was quite clever," she said.

"When this is all over," he replied, "I'll take you to see a real match."

"Who knows what we'll be watching, a joust or a battle?"

"One must be blind to see," said Petrus. "Maybe we are too clear-sighted."

We are headed toward the storm

Book of Battles

TREES

Plant life is existence in the absolute, the integral communion of nature with itself. Plant nature turns everything it touches into life. It transforms the radiance of the sun into a living thing. Far from adapting, it engenders. It creates the atmosphere through which everything comes into being and mixes without melting into one. It fabricates the fluidity without which there can be neither coexistence nor encounter. It gives birth to the matter that makes mountains and seas. It exposes the life of one to the life of all the others. It is the source of the first world, of breath and movement, of *misty regions* and the divine creation of climate. It is the paradigm of the vital immersion and liquid circulation of all things.

We inhabit the air, thought Petrus, after his fall into the mist in the channel in the Southern Marches. A tree, in its solidity, immobility, and power, is simply the most material, most poetic expression of that truth, the boatman of respiration, the native figure of the life of air—in other words, of the life of the spirit.

STONES

S tars wander across the sky, and trees will change them
into life. This is why stones and mist enjoy such close solidarity, and why Clara, given her childhood in the mountains, has conceived of her art as a melody of pebbles in a
stream.

And so, the gardens of liquid stones found long ago in the
mists are what we have just described: the root of life, the mineral nature of the heart, and the path to redemption.

The community loyal to Nanzen swore allegiance to the last alliance; the elves' flow of sympathy toward Alejandro swept away, in a great gust, any last vestiges of his old solitude; for Jesús, the water of a stream bathed the wounds of treachery; but the people of the mists were immeasurably enchanted by the two young women.

The girls were awakening to romantic love and they were in charge of the battle of the era. Those who are loved can bear the rigors of winter; those who love, find the strength to fight: Maria and Clara knew love in every conceivable way, and saw that their turbulent fate was bringing its just reward of caresses and gifts. What was more, their fate had bonded them like two branches of the same bough, and only Clara understood what terrified Maria; she alone knew how to calm her fears, and only Maria, in return, gave Clara the strength that forges boatmen—what I mean is an absolute, blind trust, with neither hesitancy nor doubt; and I believe that this mad bond explains why Maria's impertinence and gaiety spread to Clara, through a sort of transfer where the stronger of the two took care, for a while, of the other's most precious possessions. Despite physical separation, the young women added to the merging of their souls the singular trait of their foreign blood or appearance which, over and above the ineffable alchemy of encounters, made their friendship indestructible—to a degree that ordinary humans, or elves, could not even imagine.

Let us look at them through the eyes of the two Spaniards, who give no thought now to their absence from the League, for they are driven by the certainty that the real battle is being fought alongside the magicians of November. They are beautiful, the way all beloved women are beautiful, but the fairness of one, the golden skin of the other, their sleek, natural elegance are merely the rough outlines of their invisible grace. Fortunately, Alejandro and Jesús, because they were soldiers and came from poetic lands, wanted to die in the sun and see the invisible quality burning their gaze. They wanted to become acquainted with that land which they could just make out at the edge of their perception—that invisible land that has neither soil nor borders, known as the female continent. The fact that two young women born in the snow and the wind could bear that name so proudly will surely come as no surprise to those who have followed the story this far, for snow, wind, and mist are the filters that reveal the secret contours of things, unveiling their constantly changing essence, and offering a vision of it that penetrates the ages.

Who knows what we are looking at? thought Alejandro. All we want is to burn there or die.

In the meantime, the conflict had begun in every part of the world, and Petrus, to whom the question of women did not seem a thorny one, declared at that very moment:

"The enemy has reacted."

"If it was still necessary to prove that Nanzen has gone mad," said Aelius, "the fact that our sacred plantations will soon be reduced to ashes will amply suffice. Our dead, our eras, our ancestors spoke through the tea, and now they have been insulted by a bunch of demented leaders, a false prophecy dug up by a flea-ridden vagabond, with the iniquitous reinforcements of foreign mercenaries. Humans are beasts, a baneful copy of animal nature, the mutation of its

virtues into vices. They spread death, lay waste to the nour-
ishing earth, and threaten their own planet with annihilation.
They are the survivors of ruinous wars that have taught them
neither the vanity of force nor the virtue of peace. To hunger,
they respond with repression; to the poverty of all, with the
wealth of the few; and to the call for justice, with the oppres-
sion of the weakest. Tell me, you madmen who seek to ally
yourselves with those madmen: do they not deserve death?
and if not a single one remains, would it really be a tragedy
for our mists? I remember what Ryoan was like before the
tea's downfall and I weep. Is it conceivable that this splendor
is gone forever? At dawn, the dark mists passed through our
city; the gold of the sky fell upon the silver streams, we would
savor our shared tea in silence; the channels opened and a
world of tranquil souls lived together. But the snows of
Katsura will not return, and we will not hear our deceased
anymore. We will live on our lands instead of living in our
mists, we will forget the air and its lightness, the song of trees
and the connivance of kingdoms, we will err like humans in
indigence and the opacity of the other, because humans are
merely gregarious, whereas we, in essence, are communitar-
ian creatures. Thus, Nanzen's actions force us to resort to tactics good elves find repugnant, until the only ones remaining
on the field of battle will be the brave elves of the winning
side."

Aelius fell silent.

"He's better as an orator for misfortune than he was as a
speechifier in times of peace," said Petrus.

"*To resort to tactics good elves find repugnant,*" Marcus
repeated. "The battle will not be a pretty sight."

"We won't forget that the greatest war of all time was
desired and started by an elf," said Petrus, "who worked to
make humans exterminate one another in the name of the

purity of races, and to ruin the world with camps devoted to total crime. And by the way, let us not forget that he himself destroyed his beloved mist."

"*Humans are beasts,*" quoted Sandro. "Some will believe it."

"I don't care what they believe," said Petrus. "Wars are won with friends."

In successive waves, the elves' tide of appreciation for the young women helped to ease their unquiet souls. Its vibrations swelled then died in a sweet lament and, in the end, one could only remember having heard: *here you are.* All the same, a faraway rumble now covered the threnody of allegiance and sympathy of the Nanzen faithful.

"All the units are engaged in combat," said the chief of staff.

And Tagore shared the vision of an apocalyptic scene.

"Shinnyodo in the province of the Northern Marches, the granary of our mists," he said.

As far as the eye could see, there were blood-splattered fields of wheat and dead elves. Above the slaughter, a sky of lightning snapped like a storm jib. Dull explosions resounded, and the earth steamed and vibrated incessantly. The plains were littered with bows, and with equal numbers of elves, their throats pierced by an arrow or stabbed by a sword. The inhabitants of the mists don't wear armor or carry shields—the energy required to remain in a single essence would distract them from the combat at hand. Obliged to change form, their fatal vulnerability must be offset with dexterity and speed. The others continued the massacre, openly fighting hand-to-hand, forming a melee where the rumbling rose in volleys toward the storm. Eddies of air and water crossed the plain, bringing in their wake all the desolation of a wildfire. When they met, a silent explosion pulverized a considerable area of elves; their blood went on flowing long after the passage of the silent explosion. In the forefront of the battle, those who were crossing swords contended with gaping chasms that opened beneath their feet and engulfed entire cohorts. In places, the earth seemed to be crawling, like some frantic mole, then towered like a mountain to strike the adversary headlong. The speed of arrows and spears was increased by an in-draft that opened a dizzying channel where weapons pierced twenty bodies before ending their flight in one last throat.

At that very moment, in the west, a clamor arose from the enemy camp. Huge clouds of mist drifted up and began to move eastward. Aelius's soldiers went through the mist and raised their arms to the sky, screaming vengefully.

"The very depths of abomination," murmured Tagore.

When the clouds of mist reached their target, they were transformed. For one second, they swirled around, like in more fortunate times, dancers coiling inward, then fanning out with all the grace imaginable on earth, until they formed walls of stunning beauty. Gaining speed, they moved into the ranks of the last alliance, Dantesque blades mowing down the fighters as if they were mere rushes in a stream, and Alejandro, horrified, thought that human weapons cut a sorry figure in comparison with these thunderbolts of depraved nature.

Suddenly the sky exploded with red gashes, oozing their stench into the storm, and waves of mist now went by from east to west, mowing down the enemy elves.

"What about us, what are we waiting for to act?" asked Jesús.

"A sign," answered Solon.

"After waiting for two centuries," said Petrus, "the final hour seems to be lasting a thousand years."

The final hour, good Petrus, is the only one that does not belong to time. The hour for waging the battle, the hour for dying and watching others die: these are the infinity of pain held in an infinitesimal amount of time. Thus, time is transfigured and, in its transfiguration, delivers us to absolute pain.

"An hour in which we will see the worst outrages," said Tagore.

On the western horizon of the battle, a dark stain was spreading like a flood. To the east, the troops had frozen, and then a loud cry arose from all sides. Orcs! Orcs! shouted the soldiers, and in their clamor, surprise could be heard as much as scorn and rage. These orcs were joined together, moving like a giant, wobbly cockroach. Aelius's elves stepped aside to let them through, but their repulsion and shame was evident.

"If you still believed in it, this is the day to contemplate the ruins of elfin chivalry," said Petrus.

The orcs, shorter and broader than the elves, had neither hair nor fur, but an ant's cuticle studded with sticky spots. They walked heavily, almost limping. Oddly, blue wings fluttered intermittently in the background of their repugnant forms.

"Orcs are insects, prisoners of their chrysalis, half-beasts that have never managed to become the animals dormant inside them," said Solon.

"Can you imagine these abject creatures becoming cerulean blue butterflies?" asked Father François.

There was no scorn in his voice.

"In this world, everything is possible," said Petrus, "but at present they don't seem to be in a nymph-like mood."

They could clearly hear a song made up of grunts and panting.

"Or a nightingale mood," said Paulus.

"I cannot imagine how Aelius managed to win them over, nor how many envoys he must've lost during the negotiation," said Solon.

"Where do they live?" asked Jesús.

"In the borderlands," answered Petrus. "It's a hybrid zone that belongs to neither the mists nor the land of humans, and where other similarly aggressive species live."

Father François looked at the wheat. The soldiers' feet had pressed the ears to the ground, but here and there, the rumpled spikes stood up from puddles where soldiers lay dying, pointing their bloody sheaths at the sky; scarlet drops fell like pearls and, one after the other, returned to the earth. Bit by bit, the blood changed; it turned black and hardened, spreading over a large area, reflecting the lightning from the storm as the elves died. Despite the terror of it, there was something magnificent about this explosion of the sky's rage into shooting stars flung against a dark ink. Father François turned to the north, where the plain vanished into the mist, bordered by rows of wheat that were intact, as if exempt from the darkening blood. His gaze embraced the struggle between whiteness and darkness, his heart embraced the battle of the worlds, where the plum tree flowers were being engulfed, his soul embraced the end of the era of great elm trees and mist, and, finally, his entire being embraced the desolation of lands where neither leaves nor petals grow.

He thought of death, which always comes too soon, and of war that never ends, for he had come into the world during the great conflict of the past century, and while still a young man, had lived through the first war of this century. While looking for a guide that might advise him how to survive during times of disaster, he was convinced he had found it in the religion of his brothers. He had believed in an ark of the alliance of souls united by a love of Christ, and he had lived to entrust them to God and shield them from the machinations of the devil. He saw the universe as a battlefield, where the desire for good repulsed evil, where the realms of death retreated from the charging steeds of life. But one day in January, eight years earlier, an old woman had died in the village, and when it came time to recite the last prayer, he had searched his memory in vain for the usual antiphonies. It was a strange moment; in the distance, a new war was coming in the form of a storm sent by the enemy. Now it was up to him, with this coming threat, to proffer the last words for a sister who lost her son on the battlefield; and then he saw things as they really were, draped in darkness and blood, empty and cruel as the sea; and he had known that there is nothing on this earth, nothing in the heavens, nothing in people's hearts save the huge solitude of humankind, where the illusions of the devil and the good Lord have come to stay; nothing but hatred, old age, and illness, to which he no longer wanted to attach the cross of a sin, a crucifixion of a resurrection. For a moment that was deeper than despair, more painful than torture, he faltered, beneath a sky deserted by faith. If he no longer believed in anything, what was left to make him a man? Then he looked around him and saw the cemetery crowded with men and women standing straight in the icy gusts of wind. He looked at each face and each brow and, in a great blaze of light, he wanted to become one of them. Now that eight years had gone by, he remembered the cemetery flooded with peasants come to pay tribute to their departed sister, and he thought: what is greater than one's self is not in heaven, but is standing there before us, in another's gaze, and we must live at their pace. There is nothing on this earth but trees and forests, tall elms and dew-laden mornings, nothing but sorrow and beauty, cruelty and the desire to live—there is nothing but elves, hawthorns, and humans.

The scene vanished, and when another one replaced it, the pavilion gave a violent tremor. Tagore's vision left the battle of Shinnyodo and looked over at another arena of combat. The earth was shaking, a powerful pounding, and the landscape was streaked with a crimson glow, shreds hanging from the ruins of the sky. Batteries of cannons were positioned on the hills above the field. The plain was swarming with soldiers, tanks, and units of both mounted and portable machine guns. Beyond the field, other verdant hills could be seen and, farther still, a blue expanse bordered by light shores and chalky cliffs. The sea: were it not for its presence, you might think you were in the Aubrac. The hills were gleaming with light, a green velvet covered the folds of earth, and the breath of the wind brushed the coves and outcroppings.

"This is the plain of Ireland, its beauty and its fall," said Tagore. "There are many others now that look like this, but I chose this place because it is a land of spirits and fairies, a harsh, enchanted, poetical land of the kind this story seems to favor. It has been home to great poets, one of whom wrote these lines, which, today, seem apt."

It is snowing on the plain of Ireland and the flames are of clay
Snow on the hollows and the blind rivers
Cemeteries raised on the mire of black blood

A louder explosion than the previous ones shook the scene of the fighting. Infantry and gunners were concentrated in the center of the plain behind their cannons and machine guns. Now we could see the men busy at their wretched task, which we call war, or lying dismembered in mounds on the ground ravaged by shells. The men were heavy and feverish, brown with mud and blood. In addition, there was a pouring rain that had nothing to do with the natural rain of Ireland, for the enemy was transforming the rain into spears that froze the moment they reached their targets.

"Caught between frost, mud, and fire," murmured Alejandro. "The only true hell."

The scene grew darker before changing to the estuary of the channel in the Southern Marches. A group of dolphins was circling around the barges moored there. The elves of the Deep Woods would never have imagined there could be so many of them, perhaps thousands. An elf standing firmly on the pier was addressing them.

"The channel is dying," he said, "leave this place and go to the sea."

A cloud of mist around the landing stage parted and let in a bleary light, then another gap formed a few yards further away and the channel swayed suddenly. Through the opening, a strange jumble was visible—whether it was houses, trees, streets, or mountains, no one could say.

The elf on the pier raised his otter forepaws toward the sky.

"The boatman," murmured Petrus, feeling a strong bond with him.

"Farewell," he said, "friendship survives falls."

The dolphins performed a deep arpeggio before diving and disappearing for good. The members of the last alliance looked at the channel and, above it, the city where the ashen flakes were drifting. The decline of the mists was continuing, and from the channels came the sound of a wrenching dirge.

The vision changed, yet again.

"For the last time, before the final painting," said Tagore.

On a patio of roses, Gustavo Acciavatti was holding a woman in his arms and saying *I love you*. Next to him, wrapped in paper and placed against a wall, a rectangular shape was waiting. Farther away, a tall, bent man, of a respectable age, but vigorous appearance, was also waiting. Gustavo embraced him in turn—embraced Pietro Volpe, Leonora's brother, the son of Roberto and heir to the painting that will open the gates to the future.

*

After looking one last time at Leonora, the former Head of the Council, now *direttore* in the land of the humans, set off for Nanzen.

> *It is snowing on the plain of Ireland*
> *And the flames are of clay*

Book of Battles

Tears

There were so many tears in the painting of destiny.

Landscape paintings show the soul of the world in the shimmering that the painter's genius extracts from our ordinary perception, but the tears of a pietà show humans in their invisible nudity.

The soul now liquid, the beauty of fervor visible at last—we must dream of the landscape that contains all landscapes, the tear that encloses all tears, and, finally, the fiction that encompasses all others.

THE FOUR BOOKS

The life of humans can be portrayed through prayers, battles, paintings, and legacies.

Through prayers, so that the world will have meaning.

Through others' wars, where the battle with oneself is fought.

Through paintings—be they gardens or canvases—which, in causing our vision to hesitate, reveal the essence hidden behind what is visible.

And through invisible legacies, which are the only ones that allow us to attain love.

In the Final Hour of Loving

The former Head of the Council appeared on the bridge of mists, the painting of destiny under his arm. When he left the arch of the bridge, he was transformed into a white horse, then into a hare with immaculate fur. When he stepped into the pavilion and became a man once again, he looked at Clara and seemed unsettled.

"I am smiling because I no longer have to play for you," she said mischievously, and the Maestro seemed even more stunned.

When he stood before Maria and handed her the painting, the little veins on the young woman's face darkened.

She gently freed the canvas from its tissue paper.

In the morning light, the painting acquired all its texture. Its splendor was intact, but the Nanzen dawn gave new meaning to the fresh tints and material. It was no longer a scene of lamentation and fervor, but a story, drifting as it waited for its words. And yet it was the same scene reproduced over and over in human art: Mary and Christ's followers, weeping over the body taken down from the Cross; tears like dewdrops, the beauty of the Flemish style, so sharp, crystalline; in spite of this, beyond the story of the image, the members of the last alliance felt something vibrate, something that responded to the wood of the pavilion, the trees in the valley, the stones on the tea path, something beneath the surface of the painting that was struggling to get free. The mist idled in the forest, intact and light. Beyond the last tree-tops, a stormy sky still threatened. A bird sang. Something in the order of reality shifted and the dawn light took on a clarity which reminded Sandro of the landscapes in Flemish painting that he'd once loved. The transparencies of the path flickered and, in the space between two breaths, the trees appeared in sunlight. All along the black stones were hundreds of maple, pine, and plum trees, interwoven above the passage, whose vanished form received the power to transform itself into a vision with an intensity of presence that no living tree could ever attain. The transparencies of the path were turning opaque again and this rebirth from beyond death was the sign that the elves were waiting for. Tearing themselves away from the contemplation of the resurrected trees, they looked again at the canvas.

A transparent wave passed over its surface, altering the scene before them, and mingled with the tears of the faithful. Maria held her hand out to the painting and the wave withdrew, then froze. Tears were flowing down the Virgin's cheek, water in water forming drops that caught a blurred reflection, and what was vibrating below the scene took refuge in these moving pearls.

"The pavilion is revealing the essence of the painting, its internal power of transformation," said Solon.

They all felt their hearts beating as if at the moment of a new birth.

Tagore handed each of them a flask.

"Let us see what the gray tea can do," he said.

When they'd all drunk, Maria and Clara looked at each other.

"First Pietro," said Maria, "then the other battles."

"I would like a piano," said Clara.

A piano appeared in the room.

It was a fine student's piano, smooth as a pebble, although it had traveled far and gone through a great deal. Clara went closer to the object that had come to meet her the summer before her eleventh birthday, and which had initiated her into the profound delight of music, taken her to Rome under Pietro's protection, and led her to the painting which Roberto had acquired by committing murder.

When she ran her fingers over the keys, the notes made an interval that tore the silk of time and revealed a beach swept by mountain winds. You must understand who Clara Centi was, the orphan from the Abruzzo who had learned to play her piano in one hour and was acquainted with the stones of the mountain slopes the way sailors are acquainted with the stars in a black sky. The daughter of Tagore and Teresa knew the path to spaces and souls; through her music she was connected to landscapes and hearts, and this made her a ferrywoman, assembling spirits beyond their regions and their ages and, in the end, giving shape to the dreams that Maria would incarnate in the world.

The music told the story of the father and the son who had hated one another, even though one never knew why and the other would not say why. But Clara played and, through the power of the gray tea, all those present heard Roberto's confession to his son.

Which said: the night before your birth, I killed a man who wanted to sell me the Flemish painting. When he showed it to me, something glittered, but I felt he had been sent by the devil and, on a sudden impulse, I killed him. A murderer has no right to love and I did penance by forbidding you to love me. I have no regrets, because if I hadn't had this determination, the murder would have led to other murders. Farewell. Love your mother and your sister and live honorably.

In the end, moved by one last thought, he added:

May the fathers bear the cross
And the orphans, grace.

The piano fell quiet.

Tagore shared the vision of a great hall filled with paintings and sculptures. The art dealer was on his knees, weeping, the way one weeps in childhood, huge sobs as tears rolled down his cheeks like dewdrops and fell, with a cheerful little bounce, in keeping with the words that came to him in the hour of knowing. As mad as you are, he said, I love you and you will never know it.

Then he disappeared from the mind of the humans and elves in Nanzen.

Against the partition, the painting was changing. Again, water was flowing, erasing the scene of lamentation. The faces trembled before they were washed away by the wave and, before long, all that remained on the canvas were Mary's tears. After a moment, when the tears had swelled to the extreme, there was only one left, a transparent, rounded setting for a new scene, hidden behind the first. Beneath the lamentation, the same elfin hand had painted a verdant, bluish landscape, with hills, cliffs by the sea, and long patches of mist. The Flemish masters are the only ones who have ever attained such perfection in the execution of scenes, which their mastery of light infuses with the glistening of the world, but in this painting, there was an additional sense of soul and beauty, given the fact it had been started in Nanzen then painted over in Amsterdam with the scene of the pietà. It had remained as it was until the conjunction of the pavilion and the gray tea brought it back to light in its dual stratification, offering the visual symbiosis of human and elfin lands and mist.

"It looks like Ireland," said Petrus.

A strong earthquake shook the pavilion, and Tagore shared other visions. The moon lingered in the Irish sky and, despite the heavy downpour submerging the fighting, it shone through the storm clouds. Corpses were piled into dunes of red blood; black blood covered the wheat of Shinnyodo, and the fields here and elsewhere were littered with flesh and mutilated bodies.

And then.

And then Maria entered the battle.

BOOK OF BATTLES

The moon above the plain of Ireland was bloodred, and Clara played a whisper of notes lighter than snowflakes. Everyone heard the story they contained, the story of snow and the soul of the country that met like plum flowers on winter wood and transformed the clay of combat into flames. Then Maria's power brought the melody to life and the clay from the field actually seemed to be germinating and rising up into a tree of fire that did not burn, but warmed the soldiers' bodies and hearts. The cold spell passed, the ground turned solid, and everyone looked at the burning clay covering the fields and stopping the battles. It began to snow.

You must understand who she was, Maria Faure, the little girl from Spain and Burgundy, born of two powerful elves, but brought up by the old grannies in The Hollows. To the totality of art that Clara incarnated, Maria responded with her power to know the totality of nature. Since childhood, she had been in constant contact with flows of matter that took the form of impalpable traces, and this allowed her to see the radiance of things. She recognized no other religion than that of violets, and was stunned that other people could not hear, as she did, the hymns of the sky and the symphonies of the branches, the great organs of clouds and the serenade of rivers. Through this magic, during the first battle on the fields of Burgundy, she had processed and transformed the sketches traced by living things the way one would paint on a canvas of desire. In this way, she had known how to turn the earth and sky upside down in order to open the breach through which the elfin fighters appeared.

It was snowing over the countryside of Ireland and, while the magnificent, idiotic snowflakes were falling, the clay of the massacres became a fire where pain was assuaged.

Clara's music became more tragic in tone.

At the other end of reality, through the power of the young women, the bridge and the pavilion at Ryoan began to burn, and their dull gold rose into the sky in magnificent spirals.

In Nanzen, through the bare openings in the pavilion, they saw the red bridge fade away. It hesitated then vanished like a mirage, while the mist over the arch shot upward in bursts of silver, then hung suspended, uncertain of its death.

In Ryoan, the golden smoke turned to gray, dirty streaks.

Nanzen trembled, and Solon said:

"They have drunk their last tea."

The final message from the enemy passed through the mist.

Mad, insane as you are! What choice have you left us?

History is not written with desire, but with the weapons of despair!

Father François felt an icy shiver down his spine then a furtive presence slipped into his mind.

Give us the words, said Clara's voice.

What words? he asked.

The words of the wordless, answered Clara.

BOOK OF PRAYERS

He pictured himself, after the battle, back on the hill where one of the brave village lads had fallen. He was a country boy, hard-working, more stubborn than a stone, high and mighty in speech, with a rough tenderness, a reveler when feasting, but solemn in friendship, who loved his wife with a love that stood straight as a candle under the stars. As a peasant, he'd been poor, as a man, rich with the only treasure that cannot be owned, and when he died in the fields of Burgundy he gave the priest his confession. It was the dream of a wooden house opening out onto the forest, where everyone would aspire to know love and a peaceful existence; a dream of a land that would belong to itself; of hunting that would be as just as it was beautiful; and of seasons so grand they would make one feel grander. It was a story of desire and hunts, a dream of a woman and her scent of leaves and lemon verbena, the fantasy of a simple heart festooned with mystical lace. This brave fellow's name was Eugène Marcelot, and at the time of his death, he had never learned to read or write. The inner flames rising on the marl of his fields cried out to tell him why he was a prince, but he did not know how he could tell his wife that he'd gone on standing under the sky because he loved her. Maria and Clara's powers had enabled Father François to hear the text from that simple heart, and after closing the valiant man's eyes, to take his message to his widow.

Today, as the tears of lamentation were diluted, it seemed to him that, at last, he understood Eugène Marcelot's mute confession, its significance in the first combat, and its role in the last battle of the war. He'd seen the landscape behind the tears at Eugénie's funeral, in the moment when he was searching inside for Christ's words, and all that came to him was the proof of the grandeur of trees and the incantations of the sky. To our suffering, he thought, death suffices, and to our faith, the fervor of the world. He suddenly remembered another painting that had left him thunderstruck when he was a young man—a German painting from the sixteenth century representing Christ between his Deposition and the Resurrection, lying on a sheet in a tomb—cold, alone, and abandoned to the work of decomposition, and Father François says out loud: if the universe is simply a novel waiting to be written, let us choose a story where salvation does not require torture, where flesh is neither guilty nor suffering, where mind and body are two accidents of a single substance, and where the idiocy of loving life does not have to be paid for with cruel punishment. So it goes, in the lives of humans and elves, alternately scenes of passion and vast plains, battles and prayers, tears and sky. I look at Mary's tears and call out to the love of Eugène Marcelot in the total landscape; I look at the landscape behind the crucifixion and I call out for the harmony in the substance of our tears. Through that harmony, all borders to lands and to the mind will be abolished, an act which, since humans became human, we have called love.

Finally, he looked at Petrus and thought: may the blind bear the cross and the idiots, grace.

As Clara was conveying the message to Maria, playing a

melody that seemed to her the exact transcription of his words, beautiful and lyrical, placated and serene, he felt himself falter. The world had changed its appearance. He saw its substance and energy spread out before him in an undulating fan that rippled and snapped like a ship's mainsail. A force leapt through the world with the energy of a will-o'-the-wisp, riding currents and gliding over the foam of magnetic lines above abysses of indistinct vibrations—just as everything vanished, he seemed to discern a luminous painting and he thought: earth and art have the same frequency. When the tempest abated and he came to in the world as he knew it, he thought: this is how Maria perceives the universe, in the form of waves and currents that order the mutation of each thing; and he thought again: such power should have consumed her, but she has only a few marks on her face.

Several new shapes materialized on the landscape of the canvas. What is there to say about this miracle where roses, irises, and hawthorns appear, along with humans, elves, and houses opening out onto the forest? Before their eyes, the painting was transformed into a synthesis of the two worlds, where there were vineyards and tea plantations, houses of wood and stone at the edge of silent forests, cities beside rivers where barges without sails slid by. They could sense Eugène Marcelot's dream everywhere, they could sense the harmony of the mists everywhere; before long, on the surface of the painting there was a spray of sparks where a blurred figure appeared, taking form as it erased men and elves.

It covered the entire landscape.

"Are you the one who is doing all this?" Sandro asked Maria. She nodded.

"But it's Clara's music that gives me the image and the meaning," she said.

On the floor of the pavilion, Solon placed a little sphere covered in fur that looked like the blurry form on the painting.

"An ancestor," murmured Petrus.

The downy sphere began to spin and a first essence emerged from it, that of an otter, followed by a hare, a boar, a bear, and so on until a multitude of species were represented and were turning with all the others in the space of the pavilion, now infinitely expanded. The last essence to appear, a tawny squirrel, ended the dance and stood there quivering with its fellows, in a perfect representation of the entire animal kingdom.

"Is this what we are going to become?" asked Jesús, looking at the resurrected ancestor.

The painting changed again, the ancestor disappeared, and two figures appeared: a jovial peasant and a little potbellied ginger man, Eugène Marcelot and Petrus of the Deep Woods. Then the landscape began to melt, the outlines of creatures and things faded under a new flow of water that formed little eddies on the canvas, the impact of invisible tears falling from a sky of black ink. The landscape was engulfed, then vanished completely, again revealing the scene of lamentation.

It was transfigured.

There was nothing more marvelous than seeing the delicate touches Maria gave to the scene, because through the power of the gray tea, her mind had become the bristle of the brush modifying the story of life. The music Clara composed, echoing Father François's words, ended in a wrenching ode, a murmured farewell—the last gaze—the last battle. The nails of the crucifixion faded first, then the stigmata, the crown of thorns, and the blood on Christ's brow, and all that remained was a dead man surrounded by the affliction of his loved ones, while superimposed upon the faces, the landscape of trees and hills reappeared, carpeted in hawthorns and roses.

So it goes, in the lives of humans and elves, alternately scenes of passion and vast plains, battles and prayers, tears and sky, thought Father François. Why add suffering to suffering? There is only one war, and it is enough for our sorrow as living creatures. And he thought again: so be it, may the idiot triumph over the madmen.

The piano fell silent.

BOOK OF PAINTINGS

Hostus placed a sable brush before Sandro, along with black ink, and I must tell you that this black ink was not there by chance, either. It came from a quarry at the edge of the mists, by steep slopes where lampblack was mined, and through it, Sandro's life was endlessly reflected to him. The first painting he'd shown Pietro on arriving in Rome featured four lines of India ink, made in a single gesture, a single breath. In the language of elves, this was the sign for mountain, and Pietro, who knew how to read it, was astounded that Sandro could have imagined the sign without ever learning it. After that, Sandro only painted works he found trivial, although in Rome they called him a genius, until Pietro showed him the Flemish painting and its incandescence burned his eyes with a beauty he didn't know how to survive. But before leaving Rome and heading for his retreat in L'Aquila, he produced a final canvas of flat tints of black ink with neither figures nor outlines, simply enhanced by three strokes of carmine pastel. And everyone who had ever seen the bridge of mists immediately recognized it.

After that, he gave up painting for good.

On the floor of the pavilion, the silver dust froze, then escaped in flurries of tiny stars. We are adrift, thought Sandro, looking at Petrus, we are vagabonds blindly searching for a kingdom, because *they* know that they are *from elsewhere* even though they are from *here*. We are adrift from being in two worlds at once: the one that gave birth to us and the one we desire. Petrus was born in a sublime universe, and all he thinks about is drinking and telling stories; I come from an imperfect life where I drank more than I painted, although I aspire to the silent, absolute nature of visions. We who know the price of land and the message of the wind, the taste of roots and the headiness of uprooting, can be pioneers who build the unknown footbridges.

Tagore handed him a last flask of gray tea.

"Plums from the garden," he murmured after drinking.

He dipped the brush into the ink.

There was a strange quivering in the air—or was it in the earth, the sky, the universe? They blinked.

The world had become black and white, except for the creatures of flesh, and the ancestor, who was vibrating through his multiple avatars.

Reader, do not think that the authentic line is born on the canvas, it occurs before that, in the intake of breath through which the painter absorbs the totality of the visible, in the exhalation with which he prepares to restore it to the tip of his bristles. When they touched the floor, the pavilion trembled slightly. How long did the gesture last? It was fleeting and infinite, concentrated and widespread, unique and multiple, but Sandro had been nurturing it for sixty years, and the line was traced with a flowing ease that made the members of the last alliance rub their eyes, because on the wood of the pavilion there was only one line.

———▲

a single naked line
that contained all the others
a single black line where
all the colors and all the shapes
could be seen
a single line starting on the floor of the pavilion
and extending to the surface of the Flemish painting
absorbing its figures and its stories

Petrus had already seen a similar line in Katsura, drawn by the Head of the Council who, it was said, had witnessed the birth of the bridge. His curving calligraphy looked like a single line which, in turn, represented every possible curve, just as today they could see only a single brushstroke and yet they perceived everything that was visible. What illusion of vision enabled it to bring with it the consistency and prolixity of the world? While this world was regaining its colors and Maria was focusing her mind on Sandro's line, Petrus thought again: it is the visionary who gives his flesh to the story, but he must have the power of these little girls to write the text.

On the floor, the ink dried, and gradually the line grew larger until it passed through the wooden partitions of the pavilion, which had become transparent. Outside, the line changed into a colossal structure that expanded to create a bridge sparkling with darkness, with neither arch nor pillars, a simple black streak leading far away to the outer reaches of one's gaze.

"The new bridge," said Maria.

The mist that had once engulfed the arch coiled in on itself in one last graceful sigh of languor, then pulled apart, before melting slowly into the arch. Mist from all the provinces appeared on the horizon and, unrolling over the valley, they too headed toward the new bridge between the two worlds.

When there was no more mist they looked at the bridge and saw that it ended in the void. Its pure line flowed into *nothing,* where one could discern neither mist, nor trees, nor clouds. Below it, a dark lake had appeared.

"I have lived for no other reason than to see this vision," said Sandro.

In the room, the ancestor in his multiple incarnations began to spin and, with each spin a species was absorbed into him, while it went through the partitions of the pavilion and melted into the lacquer of the bridge. And so, Clara played a hymn—a strange hymn, as free as the clouds, as dangerous as fervor—and on the painting, which had become a simple spot of black ink, there were inscriptions in the language of elves that humans could now understand—the drifting story they'd foreseen in the beginning, the one that simply wanted to be written and was waiting for someone who was willing to continue the work of the painter from Amsterdam—the story that told of the tears of love and the landscapes of fervor.

In the final hour of loving
Everything shall be empty and full of wonder

How does one capture the passing sparkle? All that is required—something elves know how to do—is to reduce life to its most basic framework and inscribe it on a final landscape in its essential nudity; then in the end, turn the landscape—something humans know how to do—into the setting of the last story—the novel of novels, the fiction of fictions.

In the final hour of loving
Everything shall be empty and full of wonder

The inscriptions, on leaving the surface of the painting, passed through the partitions of the pavilion and melted into the bridge of ink. The mist had lived and now was making room for the void where creatures and things move about. Just like the miraculous mist that rendered the world never completely visible—sometimes opting to cover all the universe except for a single bare branch, then contracting to allow the greatest possible proportion of things to be seen—the void restored the balance of invisible wholeness.

You must understand what it is, this void we are talking about, because we people in the West are accustomed to thinking it is simply nothingness, absence, or lack of matter and life, whereas the void that the new novel of the world wished for was an authentic substance. It was the valley in which things bathe, the inhabited breath of life which takes them into the cycle of their mutations, the invisibility of the visible, the inner image of living essences, the nakedness of the currents where the winds of dreams are engulfed; it was the energy that makes the world turn on its invisible hub, the palpable impalpability of the mystery of being there, the ineffable become presence; and it passed over the wonder of the hawthorns and the roses in a painting that preserved the precedents, although it never stopped abolishing itself—I would like for you to touch this beauty that exists only thanks to the victory of the void over fullness, the recomposition of the world's paintings in keeping with waves of effacement where what kills and encumbers us is drowned—that beauty which sends its roots into the earth and sky and is not born of the continuity of things, but of the destitution that reveals the heart. New landscapes from the story passed over the painting, taking shape, then vanishing in successive volleys of rivers and verdant hills, of valleys of white trees or branches drowning in the invisibility of clouds. The void encircled them with breathing like an ermine stole, made them shine in their brilliant nakedness, then gently dissolved them before giving birth to a new configuration of nature, a new victory of the wonder of visions.

Here, anything is possible, thought Petrus.

"We have heard the gospel of the idiot," said Maria to Father François.

"Empty and full of wonder. The old song from Extremadura that Luis reminded you about, yesterday, in the cellar," said Jesús.

———▸

"Yesterday," murmured Alejandro. "An eternity has gone by since then."

In the final hour of loving
Everything shall be empty and full of wonder

Book of Fathers

ONE

One must know the language of the elves and the peoples of the East of the planet in order to bring about the union of nature and the spirit, but one must also have the imagination of humans to tell the story that commands all the others.

The single brushstroke is the unit through which multiplicity comes about, the bridge between species and worlds, the mold of all novels, the unveiling of the passing sparkle, the feast of wonder, the freedom of the void, and the enchantment of the world.

And what is more, a single brushstroke is proof that reality is always generated by a vision transformed into fiction. The vision offered by the gathering at Nanzen was clear: wonder is born from the void which, in turn, generates the simplicity of beauty.

And, in its wake, the complexity of fervor.

父親

FATHERS

The fourth Book is the Book of Fathers.

One's understanding of *fathers* must not be any different from one's understanding of the other great Books. The female continent fully subscribes to the mandate through which we learn to live. We say fathers the way we could write mothers, brothers, sisters, or friends. But men and elves, beyond gender, beyond culture, inscribe the reality of invisible transmissions upon paternity, the proof that the living are responsible for the dead, and the dead are responsible for the living—thus, the Book of Fathers is the depositary of territories, lineages, and legacies that cannot be detected by the naked eye.

Real prisons and real legacies are always invisible, transmitted by the wind of dreams and the breathing of trees.

The fathers came to the rescue of the last alliance.

There are no sons without fathers, there is no life without a mandate, no freedom without legacy. Alejandro had watched in silence as the red arch was transmuted into a black footbridge, and the dead trees appeared above the transparencies of the path. Their vibration was similar in nature to that of the cemetery in Yepes, and there he also found the sparkling of bygone days. The dead of each kingdom speak to one another, he thought, and he wanted to share this thought with his beloved. Looking at Clara, he saw she was gloomy, her gaze distant and dark.

"What's the matter?" he asked in a low voice.

"Something's not right," she said quietly, "but I don't know what it is."

Tagore showed them the battlefields of the two worlds, where the fire was subsiding. The clay of fire had consumed weapons and bodies: the surviving soldiers from Ireland and elsewhere were wandering, sobbing, through the snow. Alejandro looked at the wheat of Shinnyodo, imprisoned in its black blood, the field where orcs, bows, swords, and dead bodies had vanished into the flaming earth, and he thought he could hear a new sound. The guardian handed him a flask of near-black tea, which had a familiar taste, and he murmured: sherry. The sound rising from the fields of Shinnyodo grew louder, and the gray tea revealed its source.

Do you know what it means to inhabit the province of life and death? It is a strange country, but only those who speak its language are human. They are called on to address the living and the dead as if they were only one being, and Alejandro was familiar with that idiom. As a child, no matter which path he took, he was irresistibly drawn back to the walls of the cemetery at Yepes. There, among the stones and crosses, he felt he was among his loved ones. He did not know how to speak to them, but the peacefulness of the place rustled with words for him. What's more, even when it meant nothing, the music of the dead reached him in a place in his chest that understood, with no need of words. In these moments of great fulfillment, he could discern an intense sparkling at the edge of his vision, and he knew he was seeing the light from some form of unknown, powerful spirit. Now, in Nanzen, it was taking on a new form and he understood the power the gray tea could give him.

He looked at Maria, and she nodded to him. Clara, drawing on their silent dialogue, played a psalm in tune with the legacies conveyed by the heavens.

BOOK OF FATHERS

The dead of Shinnyodo were the first to be reborn. It was a fabulous sight, not only because Alejandro's desire resurrected the dead, accompanied by Clara's music and catalyzed by Maria's power, but also because the world became atmospheric and they all felt themselves drifting in the reality of the great mixture, where the living and the dead are united. We live in the atmosphere, thought Petrus—in the newly liquid world, where the present, past, and future came together on the infinite span of an instant, and the dead of all eras stood up and joined the soldiers on the side of the last alliance.

Men, women, and elves of eras long buried appeared, not in the form in which death had taken them, but as they had been in that moment in their life when they had been happiest. And so, dressed and prepared according to the customs of their century, they came into sight, incarnate and tangible, with none of the singularities that common faith grants to phantoms.

One could see this crowd, or rather, this army of the dead on every field, and the survivors fell to their knees in shock. It was an army that carried no weapons and did not want to fight, wandering through the snow of battles and sowing the flowers of plum trees, speaking of invisible legacies and bringing shame upon the folly of war. One could also sense, in the heart of this crowd, a puff of air in the form of a rose or, perhaps, a snowflake, and one could hear, flowing through every consciousness like a river, the women's singular message. They murmured: *we are with you*, and everyone could feel the power of the lineage, its liquid force and the grace of a wild continent. Then Clara's piano fell silent.

Two men came into the pavilion and Alejandro embraced Luis Álvarez and Miguel Ybáñez, restored in the final hours by the great mixture. I have given the mercy of poetry to my prayers, Alejandro thought, and I have accepted the mandate. As a reward for this devotion, I see the life of my dead—and, indeed, he saw them returned from death, while the past reasons for their fate were revealed to him. He saw Miguel's murderer, an assassin of the same sort as the Yepes killers, all recruited by the traitor, then sent into the void from which no one returns: it had destined them for the mists in the same way one might be destined for Nanzen or Rome, and the unfortunate souls had disappeared forever. This is what had enabled the enemy to kill the general who could defeat the Confederation, without leaving a trace, along with the witnesses, in Yepes, of the quest for the gray notebook.

Outside, the new bridge vibrated with the totality of life. Below it, the new lake of time was filling. Its shores were submerged by water that flowed away into the void and, on the other side of this void, rejoined the land of humans. Water lapped against the walls of the castillo in Yepes and flowed onto the plain of Extremadura in a scene of great beauty because the lake, in covering the landscape, also changed its configuration. Was it that the black waters offered one's gaze a form so simple they created wonder, or was it that one sensed the world was less *full* in its plain liquid nature? Or was it that the waters told a story without a Church, a fable to greet the wishes of every heart?

The battle was coming to an end.

"We have to go, and we don't know whether murder or poetry will carry the day," said Luis.

"What began with one murder ends with another," said Miguel.

"What came about through treason engenders treason," added Luis.

"Something's not right," Clara murmured again.

"Something's not right," said Solon.

Sandro Centi stood up.

As shared by Tagore, the scene at Yepes was changing.

The lake was burning.

Tall, raging flames rose above the water and as they spread, roaring, the world was filling up—yes, the world was becoming *fuller* and denser, until all these crowded panoramas became suffocating, with their cities, houses, factories, and throngs of people moving indifferently through their surroundings.

Luis and Miguel vanished. Sandro staggered.

He collapsed on the floor of the pavilion.

They ran over to him, and Maria and Clara, kneeling by him, took his hands.

He was burning with fever.

"He's dying," said Clara.

Gustavo, Solon, and Tagore had leapt up and were peering out at the world—casting all the power of their great minds into the struggle as they searched through the universe with the force of the tea, going over every acre and every pathway, trying to find the seed of betrayal, every breach of strength and every tremor in the dream.

It is the visionary who dies, in the first exchange of gunfire, and when he falls in the snow, and knows he is dying, he recalls the hunts of his childhood, when his grandfather taught him to respect the deer.

Who told me that? thought Petrus.

Then he remembered.

"It was the writer," he said.

He knelt down next to the painter.

"Give him snow," he said, to Maria.

She looked at him, not understanding.

"He is dying," said Petrus. "Give him the comfort of snow."

"He cannot die," she said.

Sandro opened his eyes.

"My little one, for ten years you have been there, whenever I've been reborn and whenever I have died," he whispered. "How many more times will this happen?"

With an effort, he added:

"I have lived only for this peace."

It began to snow in the Pavilion of the Mists, and there came a breath of air, which filled their thoughts with the image of a deer at the edge of a snowy forest, then of a cascade of transparent plums in a summer orchard.

The air stopped moving.

"He is dead," said Father François.

The snow was falling gently.

Minute gilded cracks slithered like lizards across the new bridge.

"We've been blind," said Tagore, "the enemy has been playing us from the beginning."

"*History is not written with desire, but with the weapons of despair*," said Petrus. "The gray tea is deadly."

Must one be clear-sighted or blind to thwart the machinations of destiny? Of them all, Petrus was the one who foresaw how that which touches our hearts is always that which we come to understand last—alas, at first we see only the inessential, and our hope is always caught up in its net, and we pass by the garden of our soul without seeing it. The gray tea was deadly. By agreeing to let it rule their vision, Katsura and Nanzen had sealed their own ruin. Had Aelius activated its toxicity only toward the end, or had he made use of it right from the start? It was too late to go solving riddles. The enemy preferred its own destruction over a victory of the alliance. All those who had drunk the tea would die there today, enemies and allies alike, in a final tragedy.

Some are born to assume responsibility for other creatures. That is our realm, and our mandate, the ministry that gives life to the powers of death, to their territory and legacy. This eternity and this responsibility are henceforth incumbent upon you, because you have drunk today from the thousand-year-old tea.

"Who said that?" wondered Petrus.

Then he understood.

Those who had drunk the thousand-year-old tea would survive the poison, because they would be traveling forever in the company of their dead. Since the boatman from the Southern Marches had presented the three elves with the tea upon their arrival from the Deep Woods, Petrus, Paulus, and Marcus would go on living.

Those who had not would die.

"We've failed," said Solon.

"There are no prophecies," said Petrus, "only hopes and dreams."

"Those who drank the thousand-year-old tea will live," said Tagore. "And perhaps our daughters, who are from both worlds at the same time."

On the fields of the two worlds, the resurrected had disappeared, and the fighters from each side were burning with an invisible fire. Cries of suffering could be heard; Tagore maintained their clamor for a moment, until the terror of the sight gave way to the lake in Extremadura. The fire had gone out and a brown mire, a plague that had infiltrated the black water, was overflowing onto the shores of the lake. It spread across the world, over the ground, and through the air, beneath the crust of the earth and into the strata of the sky, poisoning fields and clouds for more years than one could count. The trees were weeping, and they could hear a wrenching requiem rising from the transparencies of the path. Finally, the dead foliage faded away until it disappeared from view altogether.

"Our presence was revealed to humans," said Solon.

"How will the war end?" asked Alejandro.

"Fighting will resume on earth," said Maria.

"The tea has had its day," said Solon, "we no longer have any purchase on the tide of History."

"Other camps will be built," said Tagore.

"The pavilion is still there," said Father François.

"Amputated of its mists, its dead, and its bridge," replied the guardian.

*

When death is drawing near, there is only one lake that can distract us from it. We all have one in our heart that stems from the favors and pain of childhood. It remains in our breasts and become granite, until the enchantment of the encounter makes it liquid again.

The images of the dried lake came back to Jesús, the place where his father and the long dynasty of poor fishermen had suffered; the taste of betrayal and the redemptive relief of burdens came back; the wars he'd fought as son and soldier, their insanity and afflictions came back; he looked at Maria and once again he saw the stones that the mist turned to liquid. In the end, everything is empty and full of wonder, he thought; so must we die to understand nakedness without suffering? And with a heart that was now unburdened of regret, he looked forward to going to join the dead souls of his fathers—the great Eugène Marcelot, who loved his wife the way one lights a candle in a church, and all those who, before him, had known the peace of encounter.

To Alejandro, the image of Luis's calm, dark lake came back, a lake where men pray when they want to live and love. I have spent my entire life pleading that my dead might be saved, he thought, and they are the ones who are saving me in the hour of my death. He saw again the bowl where one could contemplate a life of effacement and of the land, he remembered the presence of the elves in the mists, he looked at the woman who'd elevated him to love, and heard the last message from those who had come before him. Empty and full of wonder, he murmured. Ideas always triumph over weapons and, whatever Luis might think, poetry triumphs over murder.

Every major tale is the story of a being who leaves the

desolation of the self to embrace the vertigo of the other and, from this freely given absence of self, finally embraces the wonder of existence. Jesús Rocamora and Alejandro de Yepes had laid down their burdens. They looked at the women they loved.

In that hour when dreams were crumbling, and they did not know whether they would live or die, they were transfigured. The transfer that had come with the war, making Clara joyful and mischievous, was reversed once again; there was an ultimate migration of hearts, and Maria was the child she had been, lighthearted and full of cheer like a clear stream, spreading the charm of her impertinence all around her. But she looked at Clara and plumbed the wild soul the little Italian girl had regained through this reversal: that soul once bereft of laughter and tears had reconnected with her former gravity, but now she was unable to shed the traces of gaiety that had been entrusted to her for a time, and thus she forfeited the darkness and solitude of her newly recovered childhood. In this way, Maria Faure and Clara Centi, finding themselves equally balanced as sisters, stepped together onto the female continent and, comforted by the compassion of the lineage, prepared to live or die in the company of their loved ones. Everyone felt the presence of that guild, its seal of exalted solidarity. Everyone felt Maria's burden of grief and power vanish like a dream upon waking, and Clara's gravity acquired a sheen of stippled silver as she was grazed with happiness.

Paulus, Marcus, Hostus, and Quartus wrapped Sandro in a light-colored cloth and the group left the pavilion.

"The dead never leave us," said Petrus, walking side by side with Alejandro. "The second sanctuary was the heart of this world. I wish I had understood it earlier."

"Would it have changed anything?" asked Alejandro.

"You would have drunk the thousand-year-old tea," he replied.

"If you drank the thousand-year-old tea, it was because you deserved to," said Alejandro.

"Fate is unacquainted with dignity," said Petrus, "but it has earned me the right to be in charge of the rest of the story, like all those who stay behind to contemplate the fall of their worlds and the deaths of their friends."

"Of the lot of us, you're the aristocrat," said Alejandro.

They reached the shores of the lake. The brown mire muddying the waters on the other side of the bridge troubled the surface here with ripples that resembled hostile writing. The black bridge began to break in a strange way: the little fissures became cracks that disappeared in on themselves and created nothingness where previously the mist had lived. Then it seemed that this nothingness produced a new substance, thick and clogged, where vast metropolises and buildings could be seen through the fog—a yellow, viscous fog that stuck to creatures and things while the sky opened and let in harmful rays.

"Nothingness is not emptiness," said Solon. "From the void come dreams, fullness proceeds from nothingness, stifling and killing us."

"How could we have lost this war?" asked Tagore.

"The first murder is never the first," said Father François.

"The world was not ready for the fiction of fictions," said Petrus.

"It was a beautiful dream, though," said Father François. "A tale without a chapel, a story without a Church."

"Who wants to chart their own destiny when others can choose it for them?" asked Petrus.

And all at once, the time had come to say goodbye, the way

it always comes, too soon, and there is no way to be prepared for it, because it is difficult to live well, but even harder to die well. It is autumn, November, the most beautiful month, because everything is decaying with beauty and dying with grace—and this loss, which means that everything perishes, leaving in its wake the fervor of an ephemeral sparkling, is the very thing that we call love. And so it is that in these hours, when everything is declining, the last Book makes itself known, the most precious of all, the only one that matters to the living and the dead. I cannot describe to you precisely what was in the heart of those who were about to die, but you must know that on the face of the little French girl, who was also a little Spanish girl, there were once dark little veins, and now there was not a trace of them, and Petrus pointed this out, mumbling something only Father François could hear: *in the final hour of loving.*

The elf took a dusty bottle from his bundle.

"This one picked me," he said.

On the label, decayed with moisture, one could read:

1918 – Petrus – Grand Vin

Need I tell you that the moment they all drank from the crystal glasses—miraculously preserved in the idiot's bundle—the last wine of this last day, strange figures appeared on the surface of the evil waters?

Wild grasses upon the lake.

END OF THE FOUR BOOKS
OF THE PRESENT TIME

景観

LANDSCAPES

There have been two major landscapes in this story—the cellar at Yepes, on the one hand; the harsh, poetic lands of Burgundy, the Abruzzo, the Aubrac, Ireland, and Extremadura, on the other.

If the cellar attracted pilgrims among winemakers and caused ghosts to appear, it is because the vine and the dead both participate in the great story of the world—and what better metaphor is there for this than that of voyagers carrying the elixir of fables into the laboratory of the novel?

Finally, if all the protagonists of this story grew up in lands of solitude and the mind, it was because everything is born of the earth and the sky, and everything decomposes when that native poetry is forgotten—as Alejandro de Yepes and Luis Álvarez had once found out.

I shall always maintain was the motto of the mists and of the castillo at Yepes. What is there to do in this life other than maintain the magic of a story of phantoms and roses?

小説

NOVEL

Q uand il n'est pas songe, le roman est mensonge—*When it is not a dream, the novel is a lie*, said a writer whom Petrus may meet someday.

The spirits of the world are no different from those of the novel—consequently, the writer who holds the pen holds, in the ink, the totality of what was and of what will be. If the first elf to have crossed the bridge of mists went to Yepes, it was because he wanted to reach the limits of reality, the heart of the strange stronghold where the borders between lands and the mind are abolished. And if the first elf to have opted for a human life also went to the poetic land of Extremadura, it was because my pen had decided so, and my dream, and the totality of the world to which my kind give their voice.

Ultimately, I also included phantoms and wine, because everyone is heir to a story that they must make their own, something which, as we know, would be most compatible with the magnanimity of a good reserve vintage.

暗い森

The idiot, given his blindness, can see far into the future; given his heart, he knows space and time; given his mind, the layers and alluvia of reality; it is because of him that all have gathered here, because he is the servant of stories and I decided it would be so.

Petrus knew the power of hope and the inexorability of the fall, the grandeur of resistance and the eternity of war, the power of dreams and the perpetuity of battles—in short, he knew that life is only what happens in the interstices between disasters. There are no better friends than those who despair, no more valiant soldiers than the adepts of dreams, no more brave knights of wonder than unbelievers and drinkers, when faced with the apocalypse.

Proof of this is the words he said at the end, when everyone was standing by the black water, and the humans and elves who had not drunk the thousand-year-old tea were dying in the arms of those they loved.

We have lost the battle, but time does not stop with this defeat—thus, I am destined to continue the novel of this strange country of war and dreams which we call the life of humans and of elves.

Chronology

4,000,000 B.C.
Birth of the Pavilion of the Mists.

100,000 B.C.
First decline of the mists.

20,000 B.C.
Birth of the first bridge in Nanzen.
First regeneration of the mists.

1400
Beginning of the second decline of the mists.

1501
First definitive passage of an elf into the world of humans.
Beginning of two centuries of regeneration of the mists.

1710
A hare elf from Katsura (Gustavo Acciavatti to humans) is elected councilor to the upper chamber.

1750
Beginning of the third decline of the mists.

1770
A hare elf from Ryoan (the future Aelius) becomes head of the gardeners of the Council.

1800
Petrus arrives in Katsura.
Gustavo is elected Head of the Council, a boar elf from
Katsura (Tagore to humans) is appointed Guardian of the
Pavilion.

1865–1867
Franco-German war.

1870
Aelius's nephew finds the painting and the gray notebook in
Amsterdam.
Roberto Volpe kills him.
Birth of Pietro Volpe.
Petrus finds the prophecy: birth of the idea of an alliance.
He becomes the Council's envoy to the human world.

1880
Birth of Leonora Volpe.

1900
Death of Roberto Volpe.
Gustavo marries Leonora.
A hare elf from Inari (Solon to humans) is elected Head of the
Council, Tagore remains Guardian of the Pavilion.

1908
Birth of Alejandro de Yepes and Jesús Rocamora.
A boar elf from Ryoan (Raffaele Santangelo to humans) enters
the service of the head of the garden.

1910–1913
First World War in the human world.

1918
Birth of Maria and Clara (beginning of *The Life of Elves*).
Aelius discovers the contents of the gray notebook.

1922
Aelius builds the pavilion and the bridge in Ryoan.

1926
Raffaele Santangelo becomes governor of Rome.

1928
Clara arrives in Rome.

1931
First battle on the fields of Burgundy (end of *The Life of Elves*).
Beginning of the inter-elfin war.

1932
First year of the Second World War among the humans.

1938
Sixth year of the war.
Petrus finds the gray notebook.
Last battle of the era of the mists.

ACKNOWLEDGMENTS

My thanks and gratitude to Jean-Baptiste Del Amo and Édith Ousset.
Many thanks, too, to Shigenori Shibata.

In the memory of Meziane Yaici and Sayoko Tsutsumi.

ABOUT THE AUTHOR

Muriel Barbery is the author of the *New York Times* bestseller, *The Elegance of the Hedgehog* (Europa, 2008), *Gourmet Rhapsody* (Europa, 2009), and *The Life of Elves* (Europa, 2016). She has lived in Kyoto, Amsterdam, and Paris, and now lives in the French countryside.